# Kingdom of Make-Believe

# Kingdom
# of
# Make-Believe

A Novel of Thailand

by

## Dean Barrett

**VILLAGE EAST BOOKS**
NEW YORK

Published in the United States by
Village East Books, 129 E. 10th Street, New York, NY 10003

E-mail: Village-East@mindspring.com

Web site: http://www.bookzone.com/asia

Publisher's Cataloging-in-Publication
*(Provided by Quality Books, Inc.)*

Barrett, Dean
    Kingdom of make-believe : a novel of Thailand
/ by Dean Barrett — 1st ed.
    p. cm.
    LCCN: 98-87830
    ISBN: 0-9661899-0-6

    1. Thailand – History – 1945 – Fiction  I.
    Title

    PS3552.A7337K56 1999          813'.54
                                  QB198-12271

                    Printed in USA

Cover Design – Mayapriya Long

For my sister, Jackie Jr., with love, and for all those in the Thailand, Laos, Cambodia Brotherhood (TLCB).

It seemed to me that by a long journey to some far distant country I might renew myself . . . I journeyed to the Far East. I went looking for adventure and romance, and so I found them . . . but I found also something I had never expected. I found a new self.

–W. SOMERSET MAUGHAM

# 1

*Vietnam 1968*

THEY WERE COMING—and so were the memories. It seemed as if, in the few remaining minutes of his life, the spectral mist of the Vietnamese mountains was transforming into the drifting fog of California's Monterey Peninsula, and he was once again a small child peering at his grandmother sitting alone in the early morning darkness.

A cup of clear, unsweetened tea held unsteadily in white, wrinkled hands with enormous blue veins at 5 a.m. A pair of ancient eyes partly clouded by cataracts silently penetrating a rectangle of six small kitchen window panes and beyond to stare at the grey-black stillness of an early California morning—his widowed grandmother's morning ritual which Paul Mason had never understood.

It was only now when he fully realized they were coming and that there was no escape that he knew. Even as a streak of light began to dispel the darkness and moving shapes grew larger on the ridge, in his mind he could see his grandmother sitting alone watching the sunrise. It was only a great many years after her death that he understood how good it was to see a place before it began its activity. It was like saying, "Here, you see, I have seen you when you were deserted and alone, without your makeup. I have seen you naked before you were clothed with human usefulness and significance."

Paul always felt a tremendous confidence during those days which he had seen being born. Late-risers never knew the day intimately as he did and the day would always belong more to him than to them. This hidden secret and its accompanying confidence was always with him.

And now, as he realized they were coming, he also understood that his grandmother's early morning cup of tea had meant much more. It was a ritual; a way of meeting death every day so that there could be no surprise when, for her, the streets became dark and deserted forever. It was a way of momentarily suspending all human values and of being at peace with the universe. It was a way of preparing.

Paul let his damaged rifle fall to the ground. A lone bird flew quietly against the waning moon and sped on to its destination. Paul had never noticed how clear the Asian sky was. How vast. How beautiful. But, above all, how clear.

Several flashes suddenly appeared from the moving shapes. Paul wondered if they had no flash suppressors on their rifles—why else could he see the flashes so clearly? And then, with just the briefest hint of pain, the flashes merged into one great overwhelming white light and dissolved into the black of an eternal morning.

# 2

## *New York - 1988*

BRIAN MASON stood in the theater's crowded lobby listening to his business partner explain his point of view with the exasperated tones of a patient adult trying to make himself understood to an obtuse child. "I am simply trying to tell you that if we give the other board members a bit of what *they* want then they'll most likely be in a mood to give us more of what *we* want. That's right, isn't it?" John Adelman began to light a Kent as he stared at Brian.

An annoyed usher's voice came from somewhere behind them. "Please go downstairs or outside if you wish to smoke, sir."

His partner blew out his match and again resumed his explanation. "You've wanted to publish a fiction series by Asian writers for years, right? So don't blow it simply because some of your partners' personalities irritate you. This board meeting could determine the direction of Barron Books for years. It's crucial. Am I right or am I right?"

Brian leaned to the side to throw his empty coffee cup into the bin. "You're right, John." He looked at the blow-up of newspaper reviews of the play behind his partner's head. "The board meeting is important. It will be the smash hit of the season. Uncommon fun! Emotionally exhilarating! A stunning performance not to be missed!"

His partner turned to see what Brian was reading and looked at Brian with a mixture of resignation and pity. "Look, I'm going downstairs to light up. You coming?"

"I think I'll get some air before the second act. I'll catch you inside, OK?"

"OK. We'll talk later."

Brian pushed his way through the crowd to the doors. He felt refreshed as soon as he stepped into the cool September air.

On the sidewalk surrounded by about a dozen well-dressed the-ater-goers and passersby, young male violinists had just finished one selection while coins were tossed into an open violin case placed on the sidewalk before them.

The black-clad driver of a black horse carriage stared across the brightly lit street at the various theaters and restaurants. His solemn expression and stiff posture seemed to suggest disap-proval of or at least dissociation with what he saw. He looked toward the violinists and to Brian it seemed he then gazed di-rectly at him. The driver's lips widened in an ironic grin. He pulled his top hat forward and down so that its white plume now pointed straight up, and urged his horse forward.

Brian slowly crossed the street, passed between a Cadillac and a Lincoln and entered Sardi's downstairs bar. He ordered a Scotch on the rocks and sat beneath framed caricatures of show business people. As he stared into his Scotch, the woman's laugh came back to his mind.

A woman's laugh: It seemed the older he got the more power audience reaction had to spoil a play for him. She had been seated several rows behind him and across the aisle; he never did see which woman it was. But her laugh—recurrent, unexacting, shrill and immoderate—irritated him enough to take his mind from the actors and, by the end of the first act, he found himself actually waiting for it. He disliked the woman for being so easily moved and then himself as well for being so easily annoyed.

He seemed to have lost all grace and patience when it came to tolerating the normal and inescapable annoyances of society. Is this what passage through one's 40's meant? Irascible, churl-ish and testy responses to unthinking, insensitive and insensate stimuli? He wondered if his moodiness was due to the fact that he hadn't yet come to terms with his being in his 40's or if he simply needed a change. To a certain extent, he seemed to have lost his ability to feel: Mozart's music no longer excited him de-spite its exquisite beauty, and the alarms of parked cars no longer angered him despite their maddening intensity.

His eyes scanned the posters along the opposite wall, from the mask of *The Phantom of the Opera* to the dark, mysterious figure of yet another revival of *Amadeus*. Then he noticed the photograph on the wall above him. It was of the actor Jose Ferrer dressed as Cyrano de Bergerac. The famous nose was so long that the frame had been specially constructed to accommodate it.

The uncompromising spirit of Cyrano, portrayed by Edmund Rostand as the romantic poet-swordsman of 17th century France, had been Brian's early hero. Except for his childhood veneration of his older brother, Paul, it was the only time in his life that he had allowed himself a hero. He wondered if the spirit of Cyrano would 'thrust home' with his sword through the hypocrisy known as compromise at the board meeting the next morning. Or if the carriage driver's near sneer had already given him the answer.

# 3

**B**RIAN sat at his cluttered desk collating his notes and, for the last time, mentally marshaling his arguments in favor of his proposal. With less than ten minutes to go before the start of the board meeting, he reached for his morning mail.

He left the large brown envelopes, no doubt containing manuscripts from hopeful writers, to one side. He shuffled through the bills, letters and advertisements until the stamps on one letter caught his eye. The right side of the square blue envelope was nearly covered by commemorative stamps with scenes of Thai temples and, above those, several small stamps each depicting the king of Thailand in royal regalia.

Brian could feel his heart quicken as he turned the envelope over. The return address was written in both Thai and English: "Mrs. Paul Mason, 24/3 Ayudhya Road (near Mahathat Temple), Ayudhya, Thailand."

Brian stared at the address for several moments without moving. He held the envelope closer to him as memories of Thailand in the 60's flooded upon him. He carefully tore along the top edge of the envelope with his finger and pulled out the letter. It was written on thin, unlined, off-white paper and dated September 12th.

*Dear Brian,*

*Please forgive me for writing to you after all this time. I would not want to reawaken pain in you if I could avoid doing so. But I have some trouble now that I cannot solve. I need someone's help desperately and I think you can help me. I need you here. Please, if this letter reaches you, let me know if there is any possibility that you could come to Thailand. Please forgive this strange letter and sudden request but I think you know I would not ask if there was any other way.*

*Please let me know if you can come.*

*Love,*

*Suntharee*

As he stared transfixed at the elaborate curlicues and precisely drawn rounded letters in front of him, emotions from another time and another place began engulfing him. He felt almost physically immobilized by the stream of images unleashed by the emotions: Thailand two decades before, and his brother, Paul, and himself—both in love with the same woman.

Brian heard his name called in a way that made him aware he had been addressed more than once. He looked up to see John Adelman staring down at him from the doorway. "At the risk of sounding like a Jewish mother, what the hell happened to you last night?"

Brian placed the letter with his notes inside the folder. "My mood changed, so I decided to opt for Johnny Walker over another Neil Simon. Sorry."

"I thought so, but I was hoping you had gone home to prepare your arguments for this meeting. I know damn well David spent hours preparing his. I only hope you did."

"We'll know shortly."

"David's got our finance people and our computer printouts both showing that the least risk is with computer-related books. I hope you—"

"John, I'm so old I can even remember when *editors* made editorial decisions."

John Adelman sighed and shook his head. "There's an old Yiddish saying, Brian: 'We live and learn, and in the end we die stupid.' But I hate to see you *live* stupid."

Brian shrugged. "Chalk it up to mid-life crisis. Anyway, you go on ahead. I'll be there in a minute."

The secretary had left him a copy of the minutes of the last meeting and an agenda for the one about to begin. Brian glanced over the sterile minutes, amazed at how the proper brief entries could so effectively conceal the sharp difference of opinions and heated arguments. Then he studied the agenda for the present meeting: Discussions of loan repayment dates, new mini-computer systems and final preparations for the Frankfurt Book Fair all preceded what everyone knew was the main issue of the meeting: the new line of books that Barron Books should be publishing in the future. Brian tried to concentrate even as the sights, sounds and smells of Thailand Past grew more vivid. He suddenly realized his doodling on the agenda formed the outline of a Thai temple.

At the sound of someone clearing his throat, Brian looked up. Richard Collins, the chairman of Barron Books, was standing in the doorway. The man was nearly sixty, and had been in publishing longer than anyone in the company. His blue eyes and full head of white, wavy hair were complemented by his elegant 'business blue' suit and perfectly pointed, hand-rolled white linen handkerchief in his breast pocket. His patrician, old-world manners, as well as his naturally refined voice, always set the tone of the boardroom meetings and, while others might resort to cynicism or flair up in anger, he would remain unruffled and expertly interrupt, contain or defuse arguments about to get out of hand.

"I wonder if I could have a word with you, Brian?"

Brian stood up and gestured toward a chair. "Of course, Richard. Please. Sit."

Richard Collins closed the door behind him. Both men sat down. Collins folded his hands on his lap and smiled. "I know this is somewhat unusual but I think we are both aware of the fact that David Martin has three solid votes for his proposed line of computer books, and you, on the other hand, have three equally solid votes for your proposed line of novels by Asian novelists. That means I shall shortly be placed in the thankless position of casting the tie-breaking vote."

Brian smiled and nodded. "That's how I see it, too."

"Well, then, allow me to take just a minute to see if I understand your proposal correctly. You do agree that our fiction line and our guidebook series will continue with new titles added as scheduled. But whereas David believes the market for computer books is booming you would be inclined toward a line—a new imprint—of good quality fiction held together by the fact that all fiction material would be set in Asia."

"With particular emphasis on Asian writers," Brian added.

"Yes, I understand. So you don't agree that computers are the wave of the future?"

"Computers, yes. But general books on computers certainly

aren't anything this house should be getting involved with. There are already too many on the market and the best writers on computers are already locked in with houses that can do a lot more for their kind of writing than we can. Several companies—far larger than ours I might add, Richard—are now trying to get *out* of the computer book business, not *in*."

A ray of morning light evaded the skyscraper opposite and streamed through the room's only window, basking the side of Richard Collin's face and neck in a golden glow. "I see your point. But what Barron Books is known for is its reliable, well-researched, up-to-the-minute guidebook series; and to a much lesser extent our fledgling line of quality fiction. So far we've managed to hold our own on the fiction titles, but not much more. What makes you so certain that your suggested line of fiction is the proper direction for us to take?"

"Because I believe there are a great many talented writers in Asia who can interpret their part of the world in a way that reflects the fascination of the Orient. We can begin by choosing the best six or seven Southeast Asian writers to work with, publish their best work in a new imprint, and assign introductions by well-known Western writers such as Theroux or Clavell—big name writers who have an interest in that part of the world."

"So you're saying that, out of that, we'll eventually get our best-selling books and have the inside track with tomorrow's major writers from Asia."

Brian's enthusiastic gesturing almost spilled his coffee. "Exactly. And we can also include Asian writers living in this country or anywhere in the world as well as expatriates writing on Asia as long as in some way their work reflects an Asian theme. We need to lock in tomorrow's Maxine Hong Kingston and Han Su-yin *today*. Computer books aren't the wave of the future, Richard. Asia is the wave of the future. We can't compete with the specialists in computer books and I think it would be a disastrous mistake to try."

Richard gave him a slight smile and even slighter nod. "Allow me one last query. You've mentioned before the possibility of printing in Asia. Is that your intention for your new line?"

"Yes. If you'll allow me to fly to Hong Kong and check printing quality and prices, I could then fly on to Bangkok and meet with the best writers from Southeast Asia. I've lived in Thailand before and I've visited Hong Kong as well. Let me put this together."

Richard Collins leaned forward and spoke with a tinge of skepticism. "May I ask how you plan on meeting Southeast Asia's best writers in Bangkok?"

"Because the annual SEA Write awards are presented in October at the Oriental Hotel. And the winner from each ASEAN country will be there to receive his or her award. I can meet with each of them as well as investigate the work of other Thai writers and possibly expatriate writers as well."

Collins allowed himself a slight chuckle while he stared at Brian. "So you *have* done your homework." He glanced about at the rows of shelves crammed with books and at Brian's Ayudhya-style 'walking' Buddha placed at the top shelf, its bronze submerged in a layer of rusty green patina. "Well, to tell you the truth, Brian, I'm not as certain as you are that your venture will show a profit...." Brian started to interrupt but Richard held up his hand. "But I do feel that because of your previous successes and long years with us, you deserve an opportunity to pursue something you believe in so strongly. And our balance sheet tells me that Barron Books will still be in good shape even if you fail."

He leaned back in his chair and smiled inwardly before continuing. "I guess the truth is I'm still old-fashioned enough to like a good read. I don't know if any of your future Asian writers will give me any, but I do know computer books are not something I like reading in bed after a nice hot bath. So I wouldn't be at all surprised if I vote that we send you off to Asia as soon as possible to get started."

He stood up and stretched out his arms. Light glinted from his three-time-zone Rolex. "If I do so, that would mean, Brian, that we are delivering the outcome of this project into your hands. You in turn had better deliver also. Fine writing and good quality printing at low cost."

Brian stood up. "I'll do my best, Richard. You know that."

In the conference room, Brian took a seat facing David Martin. Martin was a rotund man in his late forties with a fleshy, sanguine face and a receding hairline inadequately concealed with hair brushed forward in an unnatural direction. He gave Brian a look just short of a glare. Brian had decided long ago that David was a Type A personality and was always a bit puzzled that his expected heart attack had never materialized.

Martin addressed Brian under his breath. "I think if your proposal is accepted it's going to be the road to ruin for Barron Books."

Brian smiled at John Adelman beside him. "Well, David, there's an old Yiddish saying. 'We live and learn and in the end we die stupid.' I'm about to live and learn, but the votes aren't in yet on how I'm going to die."

# 4

THE cold in Brian's chest intensified. He had managed to keep up with his son for two full laps around Washington Square Park but he knew now, as they jogged past the handsome Greek revival houses of red brick, white columns and tiny gardens, that he couldn't complete a third lap. He slowed to a walk. "Let's slow down a bit, Kevin. You may be running on 16-year-old legs but I'm not."

His son slowed to a fast walk and grinned back at him. "That's fine with me, dad. We're not on any schedule."

Brian caught up with him. There was something in his son's British pronunciation of the word "schedule" that irritated him; a reminder of his ex-wife's victory in gaining custody of his son and taking him to England. "Schedule, goddamnit, *sche*dule! In Greenwich, England, they speak English, in Greenwich Village, we speak American."

"Sorry, dad."

"It's all right, son. You're not a bad fellow for a half-lymie, half-Yank."

Brian looked over the park's early morning activities. Joggers wearing earphones gave wide berth to Village residents walking energetic dogs straining at their leashes. Homeless men with pint bottles of cheap liquor inside brown bags lay on park benches under the watchful eye of two policemen in a blue-and-white Plymouth parked inside the square.

"How long will your mother be in New York?"

"We leave next Friday, dad. You didn't call her yet?"

"Oh, I will. Thing is I've got to leave for Asia in a few days. I was thinking it would be nice to have a traveling companion."

His son shot him a sly glance. "I know you wouldn't even ask mom to ride the tube with you; so you must mean me."

"Subway, Kevin, *subway. Never* tube. Tubes are what tooth-paste comes out of."

They watched squirrels chase one another on the lawn around a dogwood tree. Pigeons flocked to an eccentric old woman standing beneath a statue of George Washington. She admonished them for their greed even as she fed them. Kevin smiled. "Sorry, dad."

Brian glanced at the intelligent, handsome young face beside him and immediately felt ashamed of himself. He sighed. "I'm sorry, too. Sorry that I'm taking my bitterness toward your mother out on you. I've become a dyed-in-the-wool Anglophobe, haven't I?"

Brian leaned against the rail and began scraping bits of the fan-shaped leaves of the Ginkgo tree from his shoes. He felt a pang of regret at not seeing his son more often.

"So, son, what do you say? Interested in seeing Hong Kong and Thailand?"

"God, I'd love to. But I'll be late for school in London as it is. Mom would never let me go. But maybe if you talk to her."

I could never talk to her, Brian thought. "No, you're right. I forgot you're due back in class. Book-learning first, then travel. You've got plenty of time. It was a bad idea."

"But we will do Asia one day, right, dad?"

"You bet, son. We'll do Asia one day."

A woman immersed in several layers of shabby but colorful clothing sat on a bench arguing loudly with herself and glaring at passersby.

"Why are you going back to Asia, dad? Business?"

Brian had tried to answer that question honestly since Suntharee's letter arrived. His affection for her, his love of Thailand, poignancy of the past, restlessness at mid-life, a simple business trip. It had proved impossible for him to answer even for himself. But something he had not felt for years was stirring in him.

"You remember I once told you about your Uncle Paul's wife, Suntharee?"

"Sure."

"She needs some help. I don't know what yet but I think it's past time I visited her, anyway."

"You never saw her after Uncle Paul died?"

"Oh, sure. But not long after Paul's cremation I was discharged from the army. Then I became a monk for three months. Suntharee visited the temple a few times. After I left Thailand, we wrote to each other a bit. Until we both sensed it was too painful."

"So you stopped writing?"

"So we stopped writing."

His son glanced at several girls his own age running beneath the Arch then gave him a puzzled look. "God, I just can't get over you being a monk, dad."

"It's no big deal in Thailand, Kevin. Just about every man becomes a monk for a short period. It's a way of gaining Buddhist merit."

"But you must have really been into things there, dad. To become a monk, I mean."

"When your mother was angry at me, she used to say I should have stayed a monk."

"Jesus, dad, where would I be if you had?"

"Exactly."

They watched a red balloon rise slowly and lodge in the branches of a nearby tree. Brian paused to read a leaflet stuck to a newspaper vending machine: 'Roommate wanted. East Village. Someone who doesn't wear sunglasses after dark.'

"Will you see the monk? I mean the head of the temple where you were a monk?"

"The abbot? Yes, that's something I must do. As far as I know he's still alive, but he must be pretty old now. And I especially want to see one of the monks who helped me while I was at the temple. The swarms of mosquitoes were so bad I couldn't meditate, so he told me to light a bundle of incense and wave it around my room just before meditating. It worked."

Kevin dodged a large rubber ball and began jogging again. "Wow, that's neat! Are you still meditating, dad?"

Brian reluctantly jogged after him. Again he felt the cold in his chest. "Infrequently. New York lifestyle doesn't lend itself to meditation. Nirvana doesn't come easily in a brownstone."

"You going to reach Nirvana?"

"Probably not this time around."

# 5

*Hong Kong*

**B**RIAN watched the junk slowly, inexorably collapse. Its once proud battened sails and high poop were fast disappearing. It was only one of several ice carvings spaced out around the crowded room, but it was the only one which dripped water into the trays of hor d'oeuvres. And, by now, several tiny, black soggy Beluga caviar eggs were running out onto the Persian carpet only to be inadvertently crushed under the heels of both foreign and Chinese guests. The exquisite, hand-woven carpet's liquid gold, royal blue, medium brown and wine red were now joined by tiny dots of Sturgeon egg black.

Brian raised his glass and returned the smile of the Chinese printer across the room who was hosting the party partly in honor of their recent 'agreement' and partly in honor of visiting printers from China. As Brian had neither promised nor signed anything, he decided the man must simply be hungry for publicity and wondered what, if anything, his mainland Chinese guests thought of Hong Kong's opulence. In another decade it would all be theirs.

Brian crushed his cigarette into an ashtray already full with the butts of various nations and returned his drink to the table. He wondered how much cocktail party gossip a person could hear without going mad. He edged his way toward the large balcony window and the lights of Hong Kong's harbor below.

The humid September day was damp and windy and the lowery sky's blue-black darkness continued to threaten the colony with rain. Mist was quickly settling over the ships in the harbor as well as over the shore's huge neon advertisements, merging even bright colors into a dull grey.

A reflection of a young woman's face appeared above the distorted reflections of a model of a junk and several colored glass bottles along a nearby shelf. The light rain on the glass gave her face a tear-streaked impression. She stood quietly at the other end of the window looking out, remaining to one side as if she feared blocking someone's view.

She could have been English or American. Her shoulder-length red hair framed an attractive oval face. The hair parted in the middle and fell forward well below the eyebrows before curving suddenly off to the sides of the face and down. Her face was as shrouded in thought as the harbor was in mist. Suddenly, he saw the girl's intelligent green eyes notice his reflection in the window.

Brian spoke to her reflection. "Hello."

The woman looked at his reflection without turning. "Hello, Brian."

The woman saw his puzzled expression and turned to face him. A playful expression lit her light green eyes and suffused her face. She was dressed in a stylish blue satin jacket and matching satin skirt with a white blouse. With its double-breasted front and padded shoulders, the outfit was perhaps a bit too sophisticated for a Hong Kong cocktail party but set off as it was by her flaming red hair and lipstick, she was both stunning and captivating.

Brian stared hard at the woman as an enigmatic smile played across her thin lips. "Oh, my God."

She held out her hand. "You win the prize."

Brian leaned forward and held her while kissing her cheek. She moved her lips to his. It was Brian who broke the embrace. "Karen, I'm sorry. It's just that . . . your hair is completely different and—"

"And I'm 20 years older and ten pounds heavier since our Geary Street days."

"What are you doing here? In Hong Kong?"

"I live here. I'm a local reporter. A *journalist* of all things. That's how I knew you were in town—your picture in the paper shaking hands with a local printer. So I used my journalism techniques—not to mention fading womanly charms—to find out your movements. And here I am."

"Well, this calls for a drink." Brian signaled a passing waiter who brought over a tray with champagne glasses. Karen smiled. "It looks great but I'll have a gin-and-tonic if you don't mind."

"I'll have a whiskey-and-coke."

Karen grew thoughtful. "Whiskey-and-coke. Isn't that—"
"A waste of good whiskey and a waste of good coke? Yes, I know." Brian leaned closer and continued in a conspiratorial tone. "At the wrong party in Hong Kong, with veddy-veddy British colonial types, it might even get me thrown out."
"No. I meant isn't that what you were drinking in San Francisco? It seems to me I remember that strange brew of yours."
Brian sighed. "San Francisco State. 1968. Riots and strikes."
Karen responded. "Grass and narcs."
"Police and hippies."
"Students for Democratic Action."
"Committee for an Academic Environment."
A tall Englishman in his mid-thirties approached them and stood beside Karen. "Karen, you didn't tell me you knew anyone at this party."
Karen turned to him and pointed her finger at him. "Pigs off campus; power to the people!" While still looking at the nonplused newcomer she pointed to Brian for a response.
"On strike, shut it down! Hayakawa's an Uncle Tam!"
As both laughed, Karen affectionately touched the man's shoulder. "I'm sorry, Jonathan. Brian's an old friend from way back and we were just reliving our college days. Brian's a publisher from New York. Jonathan is night manager at the Mandarin Hotel. Brian Mason—Jonathan Hunt-Smythe."
Jonathan Hunt-Smythe's politeness was of the perfunctory kind just barely concealing the contempt he felt for anyone below his station. His thin, blank face was dominated by his long nose, along which his gaze went forth to analyze and report back to his over-developed ego as to whether the situation called for a degree of arrogance or politeness or, less likely, a facade of humility. The chemistry between the two men insured immediate dislike.
"Oh, yes. That would have been San Francisco, I believe Karen said. It must be very interesting there. I've never really been, you know."
"It is an interesting place. Kind of like a small town in many ways."
"Yeess. Well, I do prefer a *city*. Hong Kong seems to have excitement in the air."
Brian smiled. "Well, it's exciting for tourists who want to shop

and for businessmen who want to make money but I'm afraid I never found much in the way of lifestyle here."

"No lifestyle? That's bloody nonsense! We go out on our boat every Sunday—and there's always a party at someone's flat."

"Well, I was thinking more of real bookstores, uncensored films, cafes that let you sit all afternoon drinking one cappuccino, parks larger than postage stamps. And theaters and jazz clubs and street fairs and museums and galleries and—"

"All very interesting, but I dare say Americans might learn more than a bit from Hong Kong on how to improve their abysmal balance of payments."

"Oh, I don't deny Hong Kong is an amazing economic success. I'm simply saying a convenient place to work isn't necessarily a pleasant or exciting place to live."

"Yes, well, I suppose you—"

Karen gave both a squeeze on their arms. "O.K., boys, fight's over; it's a draw. Jonathan, be a dear and get me some sherry, will you?"

"Certainly." Jonathan made a brisk about-face which suggested Sandhurst training and disappeared into the crowd.

Karen frowned at Brian for several seconds and then burst into laughter. "You mustn't be nasty to the locals, Brian. I'm ashamed of you."

Brian imitated Jonathan's accent and demeanor. "Yeess, well, my dear, I dare say underneath that stiff upper lip he *is* a sterling chap."

"You do that well."

"Sorry. I hate snobbery. And your friend is obviously the type of Englishman who was little more than a clerk in London and out here he's still little more than a clerk; but he's been given all the perquisites including a house on the Peak, maid, the use of a company boat on weekends, and other allowances. As his allowances grew, so did his ego. I know the type."

"You're not an Anglophile any longer, I see."

"In England they're different than they are here. And there are even a few nice ones here. It's just that Hong Kong seems to attract the worst of any nationality. Oh, God, I'm sorry. My big mouth. I didn't mean you."

After a brief pretense of being offended, Karen smiled. "It's all right; I know you didn't. But I think I enjoy seeing you ill-at-ease.

I can't think why."

For a few moments they stared at each other. "This isn't Mr. Right, is it, Karen?"

"No. He's very nice really and he's been very helpful in some ways; he knows everybody in Hong Kong."

"You mean all the colonial types?"

"Precisely. And you? Is Janet still sweet and totally devoted?"

"Janet and I split up long ago. . . . Look, I'm on my way to Bangkok. I'd like to see you again before I leave Hong Kong."

"Only if you promise to make improper advances."

"Didn't I always?" Brian handed her a pen and a pack of matches.

Karen wrote her phone number and handed it back to him. "You've got it. If you lose the matches just call me at the *South China Morning Post.*"

Brian pocketed the matches. "I won't lose them. Ask dear old Jonathan to give you up for a night."

"I don't have to; I'm liberated, remember?"

From the corner of his eye, Brian saw Jonathan approaching. He continued to look directly at Karen and spoke in a loud voice. "Yes, I understand, but why do you say British men are better lovers?"

Karen's perplexed expression was replaced by a grin as Jonathan handed her the drink. "Really, Brian, you must stop doing that."

"Yes, I must." Brian put his glass on a nearby table. "If you'll excuse me I'll be off. My company in New York has plans to print books here in Hong Kong and I'm trying to find the right printers for us. Although, God knows, I don't even have any writers lined up yet."

"All you had to do was ask. I know a few writers and I've been fighting with printers here for years. Give me a call at the paper and I might be able to give you some leads."

"That sounds great, Karen. I will. And it was great seeing you again. Goodnight, Jonathan."

Jonathan smiled slightly and nodded while placing his arm around Karen.

Karen smiled after Brian. "Goodnight, Brian. Great seeing you too."

Karen spoke after watching Brian quickly thank his host and

leave. "Well, Jonathan, tell me the truth."

"The truth? What about?"

"Was that display of antagonism genuine jealousy or just your natural animosity toward Americans?"

"I thought the man uncivil and gratuitously flippant."

Karen kissed him on the cheek. "Flattery will get you nowhere with Brian, I'm afraid."

# 6

WITH Karen's Help, Brian met with three writers and two more printers in three rain-filled days He met the first of the writers on the high, flat and slippery stern of a traditional Chinese junk moored at Hong Kong's Aberdeen Island. She was of Hoklo descent and had achieved local fame for her knowledgeable and sympathetic newspaper articles on the fisherfolks' lives aboard their junks as they sailed the South China Sea. Her short novel on the plight of the boat people during the Cultural Revolution impressed Brian. Only her plotting would require work.

Brian's second contact was an impoverished Chinese ex-policeman whose "novel" was little more than a diatribe against his unfair dismissal from the Hong Kong police force many years before. During his career, he made several large seizures of opium. When he was informed that the largest of these had been analyzed as "soap powder," he vigorously protested. He was then told he could share in the "squeeze," and be given a post with the largest bribes—a post known as an "oasis," or he could refuse to participate and be given a post with very few opportunities for bribes—a "desert." The man played along until he could no longer reconcile his life with his youthful dream of being a policeman. Finally, he had been declared "unsuitable for the force" and dismissed. The injustice and the end of his police career had destroyed the man. Brian had returned the manuscript, apologized and left the man's dingy Kowloon apartment.

The third manuscript was a short outline for a still unwritten spy thriller set in Macau, clever but shallow, by a British property development company's P.R. man. The man had first insisted that Brian come to his office and then had reluctantly agreed to meet with him in the Mandarin lobby. After arriving

25 minutes late, the man immediately displayed the manner of a long-suffering schoolmaster having to deal with an unruly student. When he became indignant and insulting over Brian's announcement that his company did not pay four-figure advances against four-page outlines by unknown authors, Brian abruptly left the bar.

He spent two afternoons touring printing plants finally settling on two Chinese printers whose work, according to samples and satisfied customers, was both professional and reasonable.

He spent his evening with Karen talking, walking and reminiscing. As long as their conversation was confined to reports of how former classmates had fared or to memories of student days at San Francisco State, there seemed to be no hint of awkwardness between them; it was as if they had simply been on a long vacation between semesters and were now catching up on the news before the next semester or rather before the next series of school protests began. On his fifth day in Hong Kong, Brian accepted Karen's invitation to check out of his hotel and to move into her apartment.

# 7

KAREN lay with her head on Brian's stomach, her hair flowing across and over the bed. The last light of the day filtered into the room through the curtain's backing and painted the bed in a warm golden glow. Only Karen's hair resisted the late afternoon's immersion of colors and its shade of red seemed to grow richer and deeper as the surrounding light softened. She spoke in a tone of mock regret. "Did you know they've changed the name of the Colonial Cemetery to just plain old 'Hong Kong Cemetery?'"

"So is that good news or bad news for people buried there?"

"Very funny. I just mean it's typical of the changes taking place as the Brits get ready to turn Hong Kong over to Beijing." She put her ear to his stomach. "Hey, I can hear your stomach. It's making all kinds of noises."

Brian stroked her head. "Sure. I've been to the Lincoln Center so much I sound like it. What you're listening to now is a concert for gastric juices and enzymes being performed in Alice Tully Hall."

Karen lay on her side and began stroking him.

"Lower."

She moved her hand lower.

"Slower."

Brian looked at his growing erection and at her. He moved closer and began touching her but Karen remained motionless. Brian sat up. "What's the matter now?"

"If you weren't such a chauvinist you'd know what's the matter. Did it ever occur to you to ask me if I was in the mood for making love?"

Brian sighed audibly, stood beside the bed, and leaned against the table. He picked up the clock and looked at the gaudy painting of a Chinese junk in a sunset. Brian replaced the clock, reached for a Salem and lit up. For a moment they stared at each other.

"Did it ever occur to you that when a man reaches his forties it isn't always possible for him to get a firm, faithful and fully packed erection every time he wants it? I wasn't suggesting love-making because I'm a chauvinist but because I have one of the best erections I've had for a long time and I knew I could please you."

Karen reached for a cigarette. Brian threw the pack to her. She lit up and looked at Brian. "Had."

"What?"

"'Had' not 'have'. You *had* a great erection, now it's gone."

"All right. Had."

It was several seconds before Brian spoke. "We never could stop fighting."

Karen finished her cigarette and covered up with the sheet before speaking. "I'm sorry."

"Forget it."

"I mean you are a male chauvinist but this time I was being self-centered. I hadn't thought that you might. . . ."

"Not be able to get it up?"

"I didn't say that!"

Brian pulled on a robe decorated with Han Dynasty clay pots, walked to the desk and sat down. He opened his notes on Aberdeen. He glanced back at her and they stared at each other for several seconds. "Don't worry; their's still lead in my pencil, all right. But let's not rush it. We still seem to have a lot of anger between us."

"I know. I hadn't realized it was still there." She yawned and felt her forehead. "Why am I so sleepy?"

"Because you've had three martinis-on-the-rocks, and we ran out of Vermouth with the first one. Remember? Take a nap. Maybe I'll take advantage of you while you're sleeping."

"Why not now?"

"Not yet. First, I want to think of something interesting to do to you."

Karen turned on her side facing away from him and closed her eyes. "I suppose you're going to tie me up while I'm asleep. And then, while I'm completely helpless, you'll. . . . You men!"

Brian opened a desk drawer and took out the novel on Hong

Kong's boat people. "I think you're coming 'unglued'—as we used to say in the sixties. Pleasant dreams."

Nearly an hour later, Brian closed the manuscript and finished his coffee. The woman's writing seemed to improve each time he read it. He made another note regarding plotting and characterization, stood up and stretched. He walked to the window of Karen's Happy Valley apartment and watched the storm blow through the streets below. The window itself gave forth small grunts of protest in response to the force of the wind.

It was the third day that the colony was feeling the brunt of the typhoon as it lazily and erratically moved west-northwest toward Hong Kong and the South China coast. Yet, for the people of Hong Kong, even a typhoon described as 'raging' was nothing particularly new or exciting, and as rivulets of water rose, crossed streets, and joined together to form shallow rivers, many shops turned on their lights and remained open.

Across the road from his building, hawkers, partly protected by straw hats and large squares of canvas used as cloaks, pushed their covered wares along flooded sidewalks beneath wildly swinging signs already damaged from previous typhoons. The contents from fallen purple-and-yellow litter bins briefly joined whirlwinds of leaves swirling about the street, became watersoaked, and joined the floating debris. Pedestrians huddled forward, and held their umbrellas like shields against the wind. Closer toward the harbor, at a construction site, bamboo poles blown loose from scaffolding fell onto an abandoned crane now covered with a coating of mud and debris.

The explosive sound of Chinese cymbals and drums rose from an almost deserted street as a small truck with young lion dance performers sped on up the hill.

"Are you always so thoughtful during storms?"

Brian turned to look at Karen lying on the bed. The subdued light from the hall outlined her figure under the sheet. He began walking toward her. "Not always. Sounds of Chinese music wake you up?"

"Uh, uh. A dream. The two of us running across the campus of San Francisco State. The police after us. I've had that same nightmare over and over. Since it happened. How many years has it been?"

Brian sat on the bed and pulled the sheet down to her waist.

He ran his hand slowly and affectionately over her face, neck and breasts and began stroking her stomach. He placed his hand gently on her stomach as he had done twenty years before.

*She lay supine on the soggy, debris-strewn lawn near the college's cafeteria holding the right side of her stomach where the police baton had struck her. Each time she inhaled her face contorted in pain. Tears streamed over her ears and onto the torn placard beneath her. Her long red hair, full of grass and twigs, spilled out onto the lawn. She groaned softly with each breath. "The bastards! Oh, Brian, the bastards!"*

*Around them students fled from the police charges and frightened, snarling dogs barked wildly. Muddied leaflets protesting the war in Vietnam lay scattered about the lawn like litter from an abandoned picnic.*

*Suddenly one of several rocks thrown from somewhere in the center of the students hit a policeman. He fell to the ground and lay still. The frenzied police charged the crowd, chasing some up the library steps and others in Brian's direction. Brian ripped off Karen's red armband and shoved it under the placard, then lay over her body covering her with his own as hundreds of fleeing protesters and pursuing police ran by.*

*Above them, through powerful loudspeakers on the roof of the administration building, the words of the college president droned on: "Your rally is illegal. I order you to disperse immediately in the name of the people of the state of California!"*

Karen read Brian's thoughts and raised her arms. Brian threw off his robe and lay on top of her. He kissed and caressed her and as both felt their passion rise, he entered her. Karen moaned as Brian thrust deeper, her raised legs nearly touching her breasts. After a short while, they climaxed together. It was an intimate, urgent act of passion and a desperate but doomed attempt to resurrect and preserve a receding past through a satisfying sexual union. Brian rolled off her onto his back and lay beside her. "You still have smooth skin, firm breasts and a great passion for sex."

"You mean I'm hired?"

"I mean you haven't changed. You're still a 'great chick,' as I must have said in the Sixties."

"Then why didn't you 'hire' me in the Sixties?"

Brian remained silent.

Karen sighed. "Sorry."

"It's all right. I'm the one who should say that. I thought I knew what I wanted then. And along came a beautiful British girl with a British accent who 'turned me on'."

"As we used to say in the sixties."

"Right. So, unscrupulous cad that I was—"

"Bastard."

"Right. Unscrupulous bastard that I was, I dropped you and, as we used to say in the sixties, got it on with her."

"Marriage. No children."

"Broken marriage. One child. A son, now 16 and living as an Englishman in London."

"And Janet?"

"She's back in England. Public Relations executive."

Brian stood up and walked to the window. Through a window in a building opposite he could make out the figures of four Chinese around a table playing mahjongg. He reflected that the world wouldn't go out with a whimper, but with the bang of a mahjongg tile. He sat on the bed again while Karen disappeared into the bathroom. When she returned she lit a cigarette and handed it to him. "Where will you stay in Bangkok, do you know?"

"The Oriental, probably. It's the only one on the river."

"Wow! You must have been away for a long time. When's the last time you were in Thailand?"

"Nineteen-sixty-eight."

"Well, there have been a few changes. Three more hotels are on the river now."

"How do you know so much about it?"

"I was assigned to do a series of articles on Asian nightlife. Of course, I couldn't afford the Oriental."

No sooner had they again stretched out back to back on the bed when Brian felt himself drifting off to sleep. He felt Karen nudge him again. "Hey."

"What?"

"You really have to go to Bangkok?"

"Yeah. An old friend has some problems. I don't know what they are yet but maybe I can help."

"Just a friend?"

"Paul's widow."

"Oh."

Brian rolled over to face her and took her chin in his hand. "Hey. I don't know when I'll be through here again, so let's enjoy each other's company for now, O.K.?"

She turned to look at him over her shoulder then again looked away. "Thanks for telling it like it is."

For a few minutes both listened to the rain hitting the windows and to the howling of the wind.

"Do you still love her?"

"Who?"

"Paul's widow."

"What makes you think I ever did?"

"You told me."

"I *did*? When?"

"In my Geary Street apartment when we were high on grass watching the first men land on the moon. One of them was bouncing up and down and we couldn't stop laughing. Then you started both laughing and crying. You said you and your brother both loved her but she married Paul. I don't remember her name. Then something about his having been sent to Vietnam where he was killed."

Brian said nothing for several seconds. "Suntharee."

"What?"

"Suntharee. Her name was Suntharee. Paul and I were Thai linguists with the American Army Security Agency. We were cleared top secret, cryptographic. When Paul married a foreign national, he lost his security clearance and was sent to Vietnam. He worked with hilltribes in the Highlands. Somehow he got cut off from his unit during an attack, and the Vietcong shot him. . . . And I did love her."

"I'm sorry."

"Yeah." Brian adopted an air of nonchalance. "Well, when a man loses the woman he loves to his brother and then his brother as well, it does tend to make a body think."

The sound of the wind-driven rain hitting the windows began to merge with the hum of the air-conditioner. From somewhere on the floor above, he heard the sounds of meat being chopped, kids crying, and the ivory tiles of a boisterous, interminable mahjongg game being loudly shuffled and banged on a table. The thought of yelling for silence flickered only briefly through his mind—maybe in New York but not in Hong Kong.

Such sounds were centuries old and would be heard in Hong Kong after the last *kweilo*, or foreign devil, had been kicked out. Brian began laughing softly.

"Something funny?"

"I was just remembering when you got angry about something and threw the Beatles' album at me—*Sgt. Pepper's Lonely Heart's Club Band.*"

"It was *Country Joe and the Fish.*"

"Oh."

"If you want to be nostalgic, be accurate." Karen sighed. "For a moment there, I thought you wanted to be romantic."

Brian placed his arm under her neck. "Being nostalgic with you is romantic."

Karen shot him an exasperated glance, then smiled and shook her head. "You're the only one."

"The only one what?"

"You're the only man I ever met who could both charm and disappoint a girl at the same time."

# 8

*Somewhere In The Golden Triangle*

THE sun's rays began to penetrate the mist-covered hills of the Golden Triangle where the borders of Burma, Laos and Thailand meet, or rather, disappear into vast areas controlled by bandits and local warlords. In the light rain, the H'mong women spread their poppy seeds on the neatly hoed fields among the maize stalks.

The mule caravan, which had been moving toward them almost imperceptively from the mountains to the north, now passed within a hundred yards of the poppy field. The leader of the caravan, Aung Gyi, waved to the women who returned his greeting.

The caravan continued to make its way slowly along winding paths leading downhill into the valley. The familiar figure of Aung Gyi, the stocky Burmese leader of the caravan, was recognized by several villagers. Finally, the mules halted. While riders adjusted packs and rifles, the leader entered a small shop, built partly of wood and partly of thatch.

Several of the men of the caravan sat on boulders or on mounds of earth lighting up their long pipes or sucking on fermented tea leaves. Young boys stretched the rubber bands of crudely carved slingshots to shoot stones at nearby birds and pigs.

The activity was suddenly interrupted by Aung Gyi as he stormed angrily out of the shop and turned to shout at the shopowner. The man in the doorway was elderly and wrinkled and from his simple dress he could have been one of several hill tribes or even a northern Thai villager. He and Aung Gyi spoke in Yunnan-accented Mandarin, the Tai-yai dialect of Chinese living in the mountains of the Golden Triangle.

Aung Gyi reached his mule and began shouting again. "Your offer is an insult. I will never sell to you at such a ridiculous price. Never!"

The elderly man spat a red stream of beetle nut juice onto the dirt by the door. "U Aung Gyi, it is the best I can give you; I cannot sell such vast quantities of fruit and vegetable. How—"

Aung Gyi motioned for the caravan to move out. His deep-set black eyes glared at the storekeeper's face. "You offer so little because you know the fruit and vegetables will spoil if we do not sell to you. "The hell with you and your offer!"

The man in the doorway remained silent for several moments with head bowed as if searching for a solution in the dirt. "Perhaps General Li—"

Aung Gyi headed the silent caravan away from the village onto a slippery and narrow mule path bordered by stumps of trees—trees long before cut and carted off for firewood. He spoke without turning. "The hell with you! And the hell with General Li!"

# 9

*Bangkok*

BRIAN entered his commodious, teak-paneled room in the Oriental, tipped and thanked the bellboy, and lowered the air-conditioning. He moved a chair upholstered in rich Thai silk nearer the window, slouched into it and put his feet up on a footstool. He reached into a basket of Thai fruit and twisted open the leathery shell of a reddish-green rambutan. The rambutan had been his favorite Thai fruit, and as he bit into the inner soft white pulp, he realized it had been twenty years since he had one. For a brief moment, the red and green colors of the shell's whiskers as well as the translucent white berry reminded him of Karen. He reached for another fruit and moved to the window.

To his right, in fading light, was a magnificent view of the murky, flat, wide Chao Phya River. Large patches of apple green water hyacinth sluggishly floated on the Bangkok side of the river and through it sped *hang yao*, sleek, narrow boats with long-tailed motors, endless lines of heavily laden rice and sand barges pulled by tugs and crowded ferries crisscrossing the river's wind-blown wavelets between the banks of Bangkok and Thonburi. Smaller boats tied onto the rear of the barge processions hitchhiked rides upriver toward Ayudhya or downriver toward Paknam, the mouth of the river. An abandoned rice silo rose upriver on the Thonburi shore, its faded, yellow tower resembling a prison. Directly below him, tourists ignored dark, ominous clouds, strong gusts of wind, rustling tree branches and a rumble of thunder and swam in the leaf-littered blue water of the hotel's pool.

Brian washed up and changed into slacks and a short-sleeve shirt and rode the elevator down. He walked across the spacious lobby and passed through the corridor into the old wing of the hotel.

The thin, middle-aged woman behind the travel agent's desk gave him a list of train schedules to Ayudhya. "I hope it won't rain too much and flood the tracks like last year," she said. "You might be better off hiring a car. It's about two and a half hours by train but maybe not even an hour by car."

Brian didn't tell the woman that he had first traveled to Ayudhya with his brother by train; that they had first met Suntharee on that journey and that he wanted to travel the same way two decades later out of nostalgia; that by traveling the same route in the same way somehow everything could be the same; or at least poignantly recalled.

He thanked the woman and entered the Edwardian atmosphere of the Author's Lounge with its cases of books written by those who had stayed at the hotel over the years, its elegant white walls covered with black-and-white pictures of Thai nobility long dead, tall palms shading white cane tables and chairs under yellow-and-white parasols—all bathed in perpetual golden summer light filtering through the translucent fiberglass ceiling.

Once outside, he followed the path to the riverside terrace. Upriver he could see the hotel's cruise ship coming back from its daily trip to Ayudhya, dwarfing and scattering all riverine craft nearby. In the growing darkness, green starboard lights and red port lights moved slowly up and downriver. Even Thonburi seemed less forbidding in the soft light.

Near the shore a man and a boy sat inside a constantly rocking boat eating from small bowls. The man looked at Brian and shouted with a mouth full of rice. "Boat! Boat! You want boat?"

Brian smiled, waved and shook his head.

He walked along the river beside the swimming pool, its water a sterilized light blue, dotted with clean white bodies of white-haired European tourists, their paunches overhanging their brightly colored bathing trunks like exotic and overripe fruit. The staccato sounds of boat engines rose and fell like the water's swells. More white bodies dove into the pool and erupted onto the surface of the light blue water like freckles caused by the heat of the tropical sun.

Brian glanced up at the billowing white clouds growing steadily blacker and drifting lazily but stealthily over the river toward the hotel, unnoticed by frolicking tourists; and the afternoon's inevitable brief but forceful shower caught them immersed in their aquatic amusements. In great haste, as if a part of a film screened at twice its proper speed, they abandoned their riverside tables, poolside chairs and half empty glasses to the rainy season's sudden display of temper, as the crumbling temples of ancient Asian kingdoms were once surrendered to and reclaimed by luxuriant jungle growth.

Within seconds, Brian's surroundings were drained of their bright colors and recast into a dark grey uniform drabness illuminated only by brief flashes of lightning. Only the river's coarse brown turbidity was strong enough to retain its own speed, its own color, its own identity. Brian stood alone in the early October downpour accepting the raindrops soaking his skin and the heavy peals of thunder as his official welcome home.

# 10

INSIDE Bangkok's central Hualumpong station, Brian entered the train and sat by a window. Sweat quickly formed on his arms and legs. Around him passengers sat quietly using fans and newspapers as fans to cool themselves in the oppressive heat. Across from him a soldier in jungle fatigues nodded fitfully.

After a short wait, the train made a few tentative lurches and then began slowly moving out of the station. As it increased its speed the wheels moved from a dull, heavy roar of having just woken up to an excited click-clack, eliciting waves from children playing on the muddied ground surrounding wooden slum houses near the track.

The train moved slowly and steadily beneath a light blue sky punctuated with fluffy white clouds, past boys swimming in a picturesque canal covered with lotus, past the airport and into flat open land.

At each stop, a conductor in khaki uniform would emerge to hold up a green flag and the train would continue on its journey. Despite the breeze through the window the heat and glare began to make Brian drowsy and sights began to blur: birds nesting on the backs of water buffalo; huge logs piled beside a dilapidated temple; papaya trees and areca palms bordering fields of deep green rice; a barefoot girl in a bright blue-and-red sarong standing beside her bicycle patiently waiting for the train to pass.

The train rounded a curve and slowed beside a house on stilts set beside a picturesque canal. Just between the house and a row of banana trees a middle-aged woman wrapped in a sarong dipped a plastic red bowl into an earthenware *klong* jar full of water and threw the water over the head and shoulders of a small, naked child. In the sunlight, the water's iridescence sparkled like a many-faceted gem. As the child giggled loudly and waited expectantly for the next splash of water, she closed her eyes tightly and held her hands, tiny palms pressed together, in front of her. Her mother teased her by pouring only a few drops of water on the girl's tiny outstretched hands.

*Brian watched the lustral water pour from the conch shell onto Suntharee's hands and pass below into the decorated silver bowls set on pedestals filled with elaborate arrangements of flowers and flower pedals: the lotus, the love flower, and the 'flower whose petals will never fall off,' symbolizing the strength of the marriage.*

*"May you have a long and happy life." The woman before him in line finished pouring the water and handed the conch shell to the elderly Thai neighbor who served as Master of Ceremonies for Paul's wedding. Brian moved forward to take her place in line directly in front of Suntharee and Paul kneeling below, arms outstretched over a decorated table and hands together as if in prayer. Loops of sacred white cotton circled the tops of their heads and these were connected to each other by a strand of white yarn. Both wore necklaces of floral leis.*

*The Master of Ceremonies handed Brian the conch shell. Both Paul, in his best suit, and Suntharee, in her elegant outfit of Thai silk and gold brocade, remained perfectly still, eyes straight ahead. Brian began pouring water on Paul's hands. "I wish you great happiness and all the luck in the world." Paul lowered his head in the customary nod.*

*Brian took one step and stood before Suntharee. He held tightly to the conch shell. Several seconds passed. He saw her hands shake and as she moved her head slightly to the left the sacred cord joining her with Paul tightened. Finally, Brian began pouring, felt the conch shell slipping from his grasp, and recovered it, splashing some water on Suntharee's sleeve. Several drops landed above her eyes where three white dots of perfumed powder blessed by monks anointed her forehead.*

*She looked up and for one brief but eternal moment their eyes met. Brian mastered his emotions and continued pouring water over her outstretched hands.*

*"I wish. . . . I wish you the greatest happiness that life can offer. Now and forever." Brian quickly handed the conch shell back to the Master of Ceremonies and left the room.*

Waking from his reverie, he saw several shades of green merging into still deeper shades of green and, far in the distance, rising majestically above the flat, rich Central Plain, the ancient spire of a ruined temple of Ayudhya.

# 11

A S Ayudhya came into view, passengers who had withdrawn into themselves or had managed to fall asleep on
the hard wooden seats now became animated and made
hurried, almost frantic preparations for leaving the train—boxes,
bags and baskets of fruit were taken from racks and seats and
placed on the floor beside the seats nearly barring the conductor as he made his way down the aisle.

The train slowed, stopped, moved ahead slightly and stopped
again. Brian immediately felt the heat and humidity return. He
looked across neatly trimmed hedges with yellow and blue flowers onto a platform of vendors, children and dogs and long concrete benches where adults sat or sprawled deep in sleep.

Brian picked up his one piece of luggage—a black airline
'Captain's bag'—and followed an elderly man with a lined, brown
face and the hands of a farmer to his small, motorized samlor.
He felt a surge of joyful anticipation at everything he saw and
he concentrated on trying to remember if houses and roads and
gardens had been there when he had last been to Ayudhya.
Temple spires and grass-covered brick ruins were everywhere.
Surrounding patches of ricefields ranged from dark reddish
brown to light green as if Brian, like a tiny Gulliver, had been
dropped inside a woman's makeup case. Puffy cotton-ball clouds
crossed unhurriedly under a cerulean sky.

Finally, they were on the narrow road which led to the house.
It was surrounded by fields of vivid green rice waving in the
wind. Birds completely ignored scarecrows made of white plastic sheets flapping in the breeze. Barking dogs and excited chick-
ens scuttled to the edges of the dirt road as the samlor wound
its way through the ricefields.

The fields abruptly ended and the road wound around a
small hill to higher ground. In the clearing Brian could see the

main house: a traditional Thai-style wooden structure raised on poles with high-pitched, inward-sloping roofs decorated with stylized serpents. The house had been assembled and reconstructed from several old Thai houses which they had found in the countryside. Brian could tell at a glance that it had been expanded still more, and instead of the one wooden classroom Brian remembered, he could make out three distinct small buildings, also with Thai roofs and upper floors of wood but with ground floors of brick.

Brian asked the driver to stop a bit before the dirt driveway. He paid and tipped the driver and grabbed his case. He skirted mud puddles and walked alongside the white rattan fence before opening the gate. He walked on the colorfully painted stepping stones of a flower-lined path.

On the lawn, children pushed one another on swings and slid down a make-shift slide. Brightly painted oxcarts stood on each side of the path. Riding toys were parked beside one of the school buildings sheltered by the roof overhang and several banana trees. Two dark-skinned gardeners were transplanting trees while another moved sacks of cement on a wheelbarrow.

A young chinless man dressed in brown khaki left a classroom and approached Brian. He adjusted his glasses, smiled and bowed slightly and spoke in English. "May I help you?" Brian could see children in the room behind him leaning over their desks to look at him. "Yes, I'm looking for Khun Suntharee."

"She is in the next building. Upstairs." The man raised his arm in the direction of the building, yet not to the extent of pointing which for Thais would be impolite. "Would you like me to take you to her or tell her you are here?"

Brian gave the man a reassuring smile. "No, thank you. I'll find her. I'm an old friend of the family." Brian felt the man's curious eyes on him as he approached the wooden staircase of the next building. Dozens of tiny shoes and sandals lined both sides of the lower steps. Just above them was an adult's pair of brown sandals. Brian set his case down, took off his shoes and climbed the stairs.

As he stood in the doorway of the classroom, several of the children stopped repeating their lesson to stare at him. Suntharee had risen from her desk and had just started walking around it. By the time she turned toward him, the class was quiet. She saw

Brian and stopped suddenly as if struck by an invisible force. It was a face of unusual proportions, poised somewhere between handsome and beautiful, yet one which reflected strength of character and natural charm without conforming to the expected norms and confining symmetry of visual appeal.

Her long black hair was parted in the center and drawn back into a bun, highlighted by the afternoon sun. Vertical strands of hair in front of each ear framed her face, the same intelligent face Brian had last seen 20 years before; still beautiful, but now with the fullness of middle age.

Her face was rounder, less angular, but the strong chin, wide jaw, shapely lips, almond-shaped eyes and light olive skin had not changed. She wore a short-sleeve white blouse with white lace and blue skirt, ears pierced with tiny round blue earrings.

Her expression of shock suddenly gave way to one of joy. Lines formed by her wide smile framed her lips in a diamond-shaped enclosure and her eyes filled with tears. "Brian!"

"Hello, teacher. Sorry I'm late for class. Got room for one more pupil?"

She turned to the students and spoke to them quickly in Thai. Then she picked up her books on the table and walked to the door. "I've told them—"

"That you have to leave for a while and will get another teacher. I haven't forgotten *all* my Thai, you know."

Brian let her pass by him and followed her down the stairs. They put their shoes on and Suntharee went into a classroom to find another teacher. Brian could see into the room but it was only when he'd walked a few steps closer that he could see the children. They were taking their naps, lying on individual floor mats the entire length of the room. Boys and girls in every sleeper's position imaginable, a few clutching toys or dolls. A girl with the face of an angel looked up at Brian and smiled.

Suntharee came out and together they walked on the colored stone path toward the house. They walked quickly in silence, only their exchanged glances suggesting the emotional turmoil inside them.

At the house they again removed their shoes and walked upstairs. They crossed a verandah lined with potted plants and shaded by a huge breadfruit tree to the central building and entered a living room. Brian sat on the couch. Suntharee called for the maid. "Brian, what can I get you?"

"A cup of tea and a glimpse of your famous winsome smile."
Suntharee blushed and spoke to the dark complexioned maid
who turned and went off.

She sat in a chair facing him. "Have you had your lunch?"
Without waiting for a reply she continued. "Brian, I'm so happy
to see you. You don't know. . . ."

Brian leaned forward and held her hands. "'Suntharee'. It
means, 'One who is beautiful,' doesn't it? You were so well named."

"Brian, please. My emotions are all . . . at sea."

Brian released her hands. "Sorry. It's just that you've become
even more beautiful. But tell me about yourself."

"You can't imagine what your coming means to me. When
did you arrive?"

"Yesterday afternoon. From Hong Kong. I wanted to get out
of New York for a while, anyway. Tell me about yourself, teacher."

"Well, you can see how much we've added on since you and
. . . you and Paul were helping me. We've expanded the house
and now we've got three brick-and-wood classroom buildings,
not just the open-air—"

As Brian's grin widened, Suntharee stopped abruptly. "I'm
sorry. I'm nervous. I don't usually talk so much."

"You're doing fine. but who is this 'we' you keep mentioning?"

"Oh! I just mean the teachers and the . . . the gardeners and
carpenters. And, of course, the children."

The maid returned with tea and a plate of fruit covered with
wire mesh. She bowed slightly again and spoke to Suntharee.
"I'm sorry, Brian, one of the parents is outside. Please be comfortable; I'll be right back. And, for goodness' sake, take the fruit
cover off—there are no flies in here."

Brian took his teacup and walked around the room. He and
Paul and two Thai carpenters had installed glass windows instead of all-teakwood panels so that the room was brighter than
those of most traditional Thai houses. The windows and doors
were screened. The house was built completely in teakwood except for the poles and floors. The well-shined floors were of thick,
long planks of wild mango wood, and the intricately carved wall
panels were held together by dowels rather than by nails. The
roof overhangs kept out the heat, rain and glare of the Thai sun.

At the opposite wall Brian stopped before a corner stand with three shelves. On the wall above was a framed teaching certificate, and several small pictures of Suntharee with children and other teachers. The pictures had been taken over a period of several years and both she and the compound changed from picture to picture. Vases of orchids and a collection of betel nut boxes partly hid the photographs behind them. In the first, Bob Donnelly, an American Army friend, had lifted up Nalinpilai, Suntharee's daughter by her first marriage, and together they posed in front of the house with Paul and Brian. The three men were in their green Army fatigues and each had a different tool in his hand. In the second, Paul and Suntharee stood among the foliage and trees at the back of the house, their figures framed perfectly by the exotic traveler's palm behind them. Brian had taken the picture just before the wedding, long after he had known that Suntharee had chosen Paul. They gazed at each other with eyes full of love.

The third picture was of Brian alone with shaved head and eyebrows and wearing a monk's robe. His face bore the appropriately somber expression of one in the monkhood, but not far behind him a giggling Nalinpilai was covering her mouth with both hands in a failed attempt to remain serious and silent. The last picture was of Paul lying in a hammock he had fixed between two palm trees in the back yard. Nalinpilai stood near him trying to wake him while Paul pretended to be asleep.

Brian had knelt to take the shot and the slightly out-of-focus print conjured up the image of Paul's funeral, his body inside the elaborate casket on a high, decorated catafalque; the large photograph of Paul in uniform; Suntharee's friends and American Army officers sitting quietly; monks' chants, burning joss-sticks and beautiful wreaths.

Later at the cremation inside the temple compound, his eyes had brimmed with tears and Nalinpilai had hugged him and kissed his cheek. "Uncle Brian, you mustn't cry. Mother says when someone we love dies, if we cry for him, his spirit has to swim through our tears. My daddy has no more suffering now."

Suntharee returned with her make-up freshened. Brian joined her again on the couch. "So. Brian. Can you stay? How did you get here? My God, I'm forgetting to ask everything I should be asking."

# 12

**B**RIAN washed and changed his clothes and walked out to the verandah. He sat on a low wooden bench beneath the shade of the breadfruit tree. Beside the hanging plants and sprays of orchids, birds in small bamboo cages bustled about nervously and threw questioning chirps in his direction. His position gave him a panoramic view of most of the school area and the ricefields beyond. It was as if an idealized painting of the Thai countryside had come to life: Red brick and brown wooden buildings against a green horizon; children in uniforms exercising to music like exotic blue-and-white butterflies.

Suntharee came out from the kitchen area with a plate of pineapple and oranges and sat next to Brian on the bench. She slipped a toothpick inside a slice of pineapple, dipped it into a tiny dish of salt, held it to his mouth and smiled. Brian felt again how deeply he had once loved her.

"Why is there no mosquito net over my bed?"

"But we have screens now, Brian; mosquitoes won't get in."

"It doesn't matter. It's not romantic without a mosquito net. I'm not going to let progress steal romance out of my life. I'd like a mosquito net."

Suntharee smiled and gave the order in Thai to one of the servants passing on the lawn below. "If you're too hot we can go inside."

"No, I'm fine. I just can't believe how much you've done with this place since I last saw it."

"It's been very hard work but I do love it here. There is always something to do. If the water isn't out, the electricity is weak. Yesterday the phones went dead."

Brian's mind tried to concentrate on her words but his emotions kept pounding like an overheated engine drowning her voice in the tumultuous whir and unrestrained convulsions of its ruptured mechanism. Her voice was as he remembered, and her posture, her grace, her laugh. But even in her flustered demeanor caused by his sudden arrival, he could feel that years of independence had given her a self-assurance and a confidence she had lacked as the young bride of his brother. He had loved her once. He had lost her. Now she was before him. His brother's widow.

As they walked down the steps into the yard, Brian stopped to watch gardeners struggle to keep several trees on a wheelbarrow. They seemed unhappy with their chore.

Suntharee sighed. "I caught my gardeners planting pomegranate trees in front of the house. Everyone knows pomegranate trees may have malicious tree spirits in them. They should always be planted at the back of the house. You would think gardeners would know that."

Brian laughed. "That's one of the many things I always loved about you. You are such an incredible mixture of a modern westernized woman and a very traditional Thai. I never know which one I'm dealing with."

As they approached the school area, Suntharee introduced Brian to a man with a cherubic brown face and a slight bulge under his shirt. The man's demeanor immediately changed from one extreme to another as only Thai demeanor can. From the essence of an ominous, threatening presence, his face lit up, he *waied* Suntharee with a slight bow and spoke to her as an inferior might address a superior.

As they walked on, Suntharee whispered to Brian that the man was a gangster.

Brian wiped his brow. "What a relief; I thought he might be a farmer."

Suntharee laughed and held his arm. "I mean, one of our students has rich parents and there is a rumor of a kidnapping; so the family hired some of the most notorious gangsters in Central Thailand to pledge their lives to the child. And there is one near the boy at all times on an eight-hour shift."

"Things the tourist brochures forgot to mention."

Brian followed Suntharee through classrooms, up and down stairs and around the grounds of the school. They walked back toward the house and then to the border of the compound, midway between the house and ricefields. Suntharee led Brian around a partly enclosed one-story wooden building. "In here we have a library of children's books and music equipment. Here, in back, we have an area we call our 'Kingdom of Make-Believe.' This is where the children can create their own story. The child that tells the most creative and original tale is allowed to act it out with his friends in this area."

They rounded the corner of the building and Brian looked over the school's Kingdom of Make-Believe. It was a diamond-shaped area loosely set off from the compound and nearby fields by banana, coconut and palm trees and several mounds of earth. Inside the area were well-tended trees and vegetation of all description: Indian coral trees, with green-and-yellow leaves; shoulder-high hibiscus with white flowers and clusters of long, rubbery leaves; fragrant flowers of the frangipani, and the majestic, fan-shaped leaves of the traveler's palm. In the center of all this profusion of color and exotica was a small pond with fish and enormous circular floating leaves of royal water lilies.

At the back of the house they crossed the clearing where Paul had once happily reclined in his hammock. The hammock was gone but the long, elegant leaves of traveler's palms still partly shaded the area from the heat and glare of the sun. Brian stopped where the hammock had been and stared at the open ground. He spoke without looking at her. "It's been 20 years. Why did you never remarry?"

"I never wanted to. I loved Paul very much. Why should. . . ."

Brian turned to see her eyes flood with tears. He walked to her and held her. "I'm sorry. I shouldn't have asked. Maybe I shouldn't have come. The past is too painful."

She looked up and smiled. "Of course you should have come, Brian. I love . . . I mean, I love having you here. You don't know what it means to me." Brian kissed her forehead and released her.

At seven in the evening, after a dinner of specially prepared Thai delicacies, they moved to the small screened verandah at the back of the house for fruit, tea and coffee. Outside the screen a string of lightbulbs surrounded by bugs lit up the fronds of palms and the large, broad leaves of tropical trees. Shadows of the only tree with long, narrow leaves quivered and danced in front of the nearest bulb like a frustrated spider.

Suntharee had changed into a blue blouse and blue-and-red

sarong. Her hair had been released and fell well below her shoulders. She felt his stare and turned toward him. Brian smiled at her. "Do you know, I was preparing for a board meeting when your letter arrived. It unleashed all my buried memories of Thailand and of you and Paul and Nalinpilai. Two decades were washed away in one letter."

Brian noticed Suntharee stiffen. Her voice rose. "My letter?"

"The one you sent. I just got it about ten days ago."

"Where?"

"Where? Where you sent it. New York. Your timing was perfect. I was- What's wrong? Have you seen a ghost?"

"Brian . . . I didn't send you any letter."

Brian stared at her for several seconds then abruptly left the room. He returned, handed her the letter and sat down. "This isn't your letter?"

Suntharee read it carefully and placed it in her lap. After a long silence, she spoke softly. "This is Nalin's writing."

"Nalin? Why would she write me pretending to be you?"

Her eyes studied his face carefully as if in search of an answer. "Nalin studied Thai music and dance in the School of Fine Arts. Then she began studying Western theater in Thammasat University's Faculty of Drama. She was staying in a dormitory during the week and here on weekends." Suntharee put her fist to her mouth and bit her lip on the verge of tears. She attempted to conceal her turmoil with a cough. "Excuse me."

"Suntharee, what's wrong? Where is Nalin now?"

Suntharee straightened up and placed her hands in her lap. She spoke while keeping her eyes on the letter. "Nalin left school and is working in a bar on Patpong Road as a go-go dancer."

Brian listened to the sounds of the wind among the leaves for what seemed like a long time. "So you mean you think she fell in with a bad crowd and left school to work in a bar?"

Suntharee folded the letter carefully and handed it to Brian. "Do you remember Bob Donnelly?"

"Bob? Of course. He stayed on in Asia, I remember."

"Yes. He's a businessman now. A very successful one. I believe he owns the Horny Tiger bar on Patpong. He called me one day about three months ago and told me Nalin had gone to him for a job in the bar. He offered her an office job but she wouldn't take it. He tried to persuade her to go back to school and to patch up her differences with me but she wouldn't listen." Suntharee waved the approaching maid away. "Finally, he gave her the job and called me."

"So you and Nalin had an argument and that's why she left?"

"Nalin was always very hot-blooded. She never knew how to keep a cool heart, as we say. She may have misinterpreted something I wrote in an old letter to Paul. Or, rather, in his letter to me. The maid had cleaned out some drawers and mistakenly thought they were some papers Nalin had misplaced and she sent them to her in Bangkok. They were my personal letters. Nalin came to see me about them. We argued. She packed and left."

"And something in those letters caused her to leave home and school and become a go-go dancer?"

Suntharee leaned forward, drank tea and stared into the cup. Brian noticed lines and shadows on her face as if the subject of her daughter had visibly aged her. As she spoke her voice seemed almost disembodied; the weary voice of someone reconciled to inevitable sorrow. "Something she must have misunderstood. I won't pretend that Nalin and I were always on the best terms. She was always so independent."

Brian moved closer to her and took her hand. "Maybe if her father hadn't died in the car accident just after she was born, it might have been easier for both of you. You've lost two husbands and now this. Whatever it is, I'm glad she sent for me. I'll talk to her and-"

Suntharee looked out at the trees. "Brian, I'm very tired. I'm going to bed now. But, first, would you hold me?"

Brian put his arms around her and did as she asked. They sat like that for a long while. From the verandah Brian could just see into the Kingdom of Make-Believe. Bamboo stalks had been placed along the edge of the fish pond and at the top of each was a bamboo bowl filled with coconut oil and a wick. The flames of the bamboo and the dimly lit trees and plants gave the area a romantic air of untamed luxuriance and a slight breeze constantly rustled among the mysterious exotic shapes. A magnificent white royal water lily rose above the huge, circular floating leaf and its sweet fragrance drifted over to Brian. Brian knew in the morning it would turn pink and die. He listened to the sounds of unseen insects and frogs. It wasn't until Suntharee shivered that he felt the romance and nostalgia of his homecoming in danger of shattering. Finally, the outside lights went out. Suntharee sat up straight and stood up. "Goodnight, Brian, and thank you for coming. Maybe you *can* help."

# 13

A S Brian dove still deeper under the water, Paul's face loomed up before him. He was dressed exactly as he had been for his wedding but his eyes stared into Brian's in terror.

Brian opened his mouth to speak. Water rushed in and his lungs tightened in pain. He struggled upwards. He surfaced to find himself entangled in the bed's mosquito net. Outside, the shouts of workmen and the complaining engines of ancient pick-up trucks were interspersed with the lilting, repetitive calls of birds.

He parted the mosquito net curtains and walked through the back door to a small, partly covered, screened-in-verandah. Sunlight coursed through swaying tree leaves and palm fronds, dappling the golden brown earthenware water jar's glazed dragons, red plastic scoop and low wooden shelves.

Bathed and shaved, he re-entered the room. He opened the bedroom door, crossed the open porch and paused to enjoy the cool of the morning. In the distance, their saffron robes contrasting with the emerald green of the ricefields, a single file of Buddhist monks walked unhurriedly in the direction of the house.

Brian recognized one of the elderly monks as the one who, years before, had offered Nalin an orange only to be rebuffed by the child as she insisted on sweets. The monk had taken the incident in good spirits but Suntharee had scolded her. In a fit of petulance, Nalin had run into the nearby field, been frightened by a snake, and, in her panic, had fallen on a pile of rotting wood and nails. One of the nails had left a small "L" shaped scar on her right leg.

As Brian walked to the kitchen, he noticed the door to the small room known as the Buddha Room was ajar. He stood

beside it and silently pushed it open.
Early morning light bathed the room in warmth and lent it a delicate reddish hue. Along the far wall, specially made shelves held Buddha images, lifelike statues of elderly monks, flowers, peacock feathers and a tiny golden tiered umbrella. On the top shelf a Buddha looked out through half-closed eyes beneath arched eyebrows.

Below the Buddha was a framed print of Paul, his face lit up in a mischievous smile. Beside the picture was a small house in which his spirit might rest and also some of the belongings he had owned in life. Next to the picture, on a separate shelf, was a bronze urn with his ashes. Beneath rounded lids the Buddha gazed down upon the kneeling form of Suntharee, positioned Thai-style with her legs stretched behind her. Her eyes were closed and her hands were pressed tightly together holding a lighted incense stick.

Brian closed the door quietly and walked to the kitchen. When Suntharee entered, the uncertainties and embarrassment of the night before seemed to have dissolved in the warmth of her smile.

"Good morning, Brian. Sleep well?"

"Perfectly. I can see *you* did."

She glanced at herself in the imperfect reflection of a window. "I overslept. I must look a sight. I never put on makeup until after I pray."

"You look fantastic."

"I see you still have your golden tongue. Come. They're almost here."

Brian walked with Suntharee and stood just outside the gate. They placed their hands together in a Thai *wai*. Suntharee spoke softly in Pali: "*Nimon kha* (please stop.")

The monks neither returned the wai nor looked up from their bowls. As each monk moved forward, Brian and Suntharee placed food in the bowl and thanked him for allowing them to gain Buddhist merit by offering him food.

# 14

FOR two days, by boat and by pickup truck, they toured Ayudhya, its temple ruins, old fortress walls, quiet museums and elephant kraal. At a riverside restaurant, the proprietors were pleased to personally serve the teacher of their children. In an antiques shop, despite Suntharee's demurrals, Brian bought her an antique silver bracelet and felt an inexplicable surge of joy in her genuine delight in wearing it.

Most of the places they visited Brian had first seen long ago with Paul. It was when he and his brother were exploring Ayudhya's ruins together that they first met Suntharee. Nalin had peeked at Brian from behind a brick foundation pillar of Wat Mahathat and Brian had played with her. Even on the first day, Brian remembered, Nalin seemed to favor him, while Suntharee had been attracted to Paul.

As if by unspoken agreement, they had left the exploration of Wat Mahathat's sprawling ruins for last, and they now walked side by side avoiding muddy ground and stepping carefully on abandoned bricks. Finally, they sat on a brick wall facing a Buddha's head imprisoned in the enormous roots of a mammoth banyan tree and watched the moods of the Buddha's face change with the colors of the sky, now emblazoned with delicate and equal shades of pink and azure.

In the fleeting moments of twilight they sat mesmerized with the crumbling remains of the abandoned temple and glimpsed the still-living soul of the kingdom. A soul whose poignant ruins spoke of god-kings and magic rituals, gilt spires, gabled pavilions, sacred scriptures and throne halls. And, then, within its still glittering facade, the kingdom's defenses crumbled before the surrounding Burmese armies. And the starving survivors of a nation's golden age searched the fields for wild roots and bamboo sprouts.

They sat completely still, as if even the slightest movement or word would be inappropriate—irreverent—before the totally silent mounds of earth surrounded by broken walls, the uneven rows of headless Buddhas with kites fluttering overhead, the ravaged spires encrusted with decayed vegetation surrounded by grazing water buffalo and frolicsome children, and the moss-encrusted brick stairs leading to nowhere.

Brian looked at Suntharee and slowly put his arms around her and leaned forward to kiss her neck. He gently turned her face toward his and kissed her lips. She accepted the kiss without response then pulled away and stared at him. Slowly, diffidently, she moved her lips closer and in her kiss—timorous at first and then passionate—she gave him an unambiguous answer.

She squeezed him tightly, and, still holding him with all her might, broke off the kiss and rested her head on his shoulder. Brian felt her tremble and listened silently to her quiet sobs. He rocked her gently back and forth and stared into the serenity of the Buddha's smile.

Suddenly, she released him and stared at his arm. He followed her gaze to his shirt and saw the red ants scurrying about on his sleeve. She brushed the ants away but continued to rub his arm, as if determined to brush the outside world away. Brian wiped tears from her eyes and cheeks. She sobbed even more. "You see? There is always something to spoil . . . something . . . some. . . ."

Brian reached out and held her wrists. He reached around her arms, pulled her to him and kissed her hair. He spoke softly while looking at the Buddha. "Shhh. Nothing is going to spoil this. Do you understand? Nothing." He held her until the sobbing stopped, and when she sat up, they rose and walked slowly, arm in arm, to the pickup.

That night they made love. Tenderly. Passionately. Wordlessly. Beneath a mosquito net, accompanied at first by the shrill sounds of insects and agitated croaks of frogs and then by thunder and lightning as monsoon winds and torrents of rain swept across the house and trees and ricefields and schoolyard and flooded the pond in the Kingdom of Make Believe.

The rainstorm began, tentatively, diffidently, with the soft, steady, soporific sounds of fat sizzling in a frying pan and then, once assured of no resistance, roared unabated, pounding the roof, shaking the walls, snapping branches, slapping leaves and turning earth to mud and paths to rivulets. Frenzied flurries of wind blew under the house and rose up to protest against shuttered windows, the despairing moans of a grieving royal ghost still unable to accept the fate of his once glorious city.

# 15

FLUORESCENT lights flickered uncertainly into a deepening twilight bathing the people and platform of Ayudhya's station in a soft pink ethereal glow. A large white shrine stood at the edge of the ricefields, its orange roof drained of color in the gathering darkness.

The double clang of a bell sounded and a train—in no apparent hurry—pulled into the station and slowed laboriously to a stop. Many of the Thais gathered their possessions and walked quickly to board the train. The thin, sallow-faced station master, his Khaki uniform too large for him, walked by the train ready to hold up his ancient lantern with its green light. Suntharee briefly grasped Brian's hand. "You'd better go."

Brian stared at her. "I've never wanted to kiss someone goodbye more in my life."

Suntharee smiled and shook her head slightly. "You know better than that. Thai customs allow almost everything but only in private."

Suddenly, loudspeakers crackled and all movements ceased. A woman's voice emanated from the speakers and began singing the Thai king's anthem in a high-pitched tone imbued with patriotism. In contrast to the piercing soprano voice, the tempo was slow, somber and lugubrious. The sky had progressed from magenta to mauve to azure and in the gloaming nothing moved, and there were no sounds but the stately almost funereal solemnity of the music and the incessant hissing of the train.

Seconds before the music ended, people began moving, and children's voices again shouted out their wares. As Brian and Suntharee walked side by side to the steps of the train, she surreptitiously squeezed his hand. "Please talk to her, Brian. And help her if you can."

"And then?"

"And then come back."

He quickly kissed her hair and boarded the train. At the window he faced her and smiled. He peeled a rambutan and held it out to her. She reached up for it. As she took it, Brian's other hand held hers tightly then let go.

As the train moved away, he watched her stationary, evanescent figure recede into the landscape, then sat back and tried to quiet the growing hope and rekindled emotions that welled within him.

# 16

*Somwhere in the Golden Triangle*

FROM the open bamboo square which served as the basha hut's window, the men at the table could look out on withered coconut palms surrounding a fence of sharpened bamboo leaves partly concealed by lush banana trees. Beyond a deeply rutted cart track were several other frugally furnished huts raised on stilts with roofs thatched with rice straw, palm and banana leaves, and walls of woven bamboo. Jungle growth—thick and green—covered nearby hillocks and disappeared into the mist of distant mountains. Underneath the huts, along with the water buffalo and the bullock carts, soldiers from various warlord armies waited patiently while maintaining a loose watch on the trails leading to the huts.

Women in Burmese sarongs and blouses ensured that food continued to be served even as the men spoke. The walls of their kitchen visible to General Li had been streaked black with smoke from a large charcoal-fed fire. Sunlight streamed in the window and warmed the battered wooden table and banana-leaf place mats covered with Thai beer, Burmese coffee, rice whiskey, tea, food and, in several chipped saucers, chili sauce. A woman knelt beside General Li's boot to place a table leg in a coffee can half full of water to discourage ants and other insects. On the wall above his head were the symbols of their dual loyalty—photographs of the Thai king and queen, and, nearby, photographs of Sun Yat-sen and Chiang Kai-shek.

Most of the men were middle-aged or older. Some had aged through opium. Their clothing ranged from hilltribe dress to army fatigues, their ethnic features from light-skinned Chinese to dark-complexioned hilltribesmen. Their conversation—conducted in a mixture of mandarin and Burmese, and the Tai-yai dialect—was punctuated by the crowing of roosters and other barnyard sounds.

Even as General Li and his son smiled, Yuen Sheung Fuk could feel the hostility of the two men facing him. Unlike himself, they were not men of the world of banking and finance, and Yuen was fully aware how much in contempt they held his profession and himself even if he did provide ready cash for the opium crops which they guarded. The direct stares and crude eating habits of sturdy brown hilltribesmen he could tolerate. They were merely barbarians; pure and simple. It was his own countrymen—father and son—sitting ramrod stiff at the other end of the battered wooden table who most vexed him.

Even now, the grating voice of 'General' Li T'ieh-sheng had the tone of an officer addressing subordinates found wavering in their loyalty or courage. His thin, hawk-like face with its penetrating eyes seemed to Yuen to lack both intelligence and humor. And, although a southerner, Yuen had long ago learned to conceal his distaste for 'out-of-province people.'

The animosity of the men for one another was always well camouflaged in deference to their symbiotic relationship—Li, the protector of opium caravans and jungle-shrouded heroin refineries, and Yuen, provider of ready cash for opium crops.

Many years before, Yuen had left Kwangtung province and taken up residence in Hong Kong. The British colony was tailored to Yuen's personality in many ways. As a gourmand, he found that the city was one of the few places in the world where he could still enjoy 12-course meals of exotic Chinese cuisine with the specially prepared anatomical parts of endangered species—cuisine—according to custom—certain to contain aphrodisiac qualities. As a sexagenarian bachelor, those very qualities were tested by his sybaritic appetite for young and beautiful women of several races, especially by Western women working the bar and nightclub circuit through Asia. And, above all, as a genius in money matters, Yuen exploited the city's convenience as a financial center to bankroll Southeast Asia's drug trafficking.

His concern with state finances and careful avoidance of all political matters had steered him successfully through the various shifts of allegiance he deftly underwent in each of the periods of modern Chinese history. He was well aware of Peking's suspicion that he had fallen prey to a life of luxury in the materialistic British Crown Colony. But it was not any capitalist vice which had ensnared him; rather, he, no less than General Li and his son, existed in his chosen lifestyle thanks to the annual harvest of hilltribe opium and the worldwide demand for heroin. And if the New China disdained his opium connection, it steadily embraced his capitalist skills. But for General Li, the opium trade represented a great deal more. In 1913, in a small and filthy room in northern Shantung province, Li T'ieh-sheng was born into a poor, working-class family. After snatches of formal education, at the age of 20, he joined an ignorant assortment of young men who were fighting for one or another warlord. After a promising beginning, the warlord armies were defeated and Li learned quickly about defeat, poverty, theft and survival. Like most Chinese, Li was disgusted with a weak, divided China. He could still remember the intense expression on the face of the young woman from the city who visited his village and spoke of Mao Tse-tung and other men dedicated to the people and who were fighting to build a strong China.

She would sit for hours, talking to illiterate soldiers and uninterested and often hostile shopkeepers, patiently implanting the Communist ideals: "Poor men do not fight poor men." Her straight hair framed her long, sensitive face and her thin lips seemed always to be lengthening into a slightly embarrassed smile. Even as she shared the foul-smelling rice of the soldiers, she would speak of the new China such men and such beliefs would create. "Poor men do not fight poor men." Again and again, she explained such words and, at last, he understood the hope they were bringing to China's millions.

At some point during their walks and talks together, they became lovers; and the two months they spent together had been the happiest time of General Li's life. But by the end of the second month, his avarice and lust for power had alienated her from him. She loved him but she could not overcome her disillusion with him. And she was not willing to change her own beliefs to accommodate his ambition. When it became clear there was no future in their relationship, she had left him and transferred to the south of China and he had never heard from her again.

In the fall of 1934, at the beginning of the Communist retreat later to become famous as the Long March, Li was one of Hsiang Ying's guerrilla troops who remained behind to cover the retreat. Three times he looked into the faces of Nationalist soldiers of Chiang Kai-shek in hand-to-hand combat; each time he emerged the victor. But a wound from a bullet which pushed through his thigh and down into his leg remained untreated long enough to insure that his pronounced limp would remain for the rest of his life.

Although he had not been in command, General Li, then a captain, bore much of the criticism in Yenan for the annihilation of the Communist Army. He was finally sent to command troops in southern China but his part in past military failures would insure that his rank in the Peoples' Liberation Army would never rise higher.

His decision in 1949 to flee China and to ally his troops with remnants of Nationalist China's armies in Northern Burma marked the beginning of his personal success. Repudiating the Communists just at the moment of their victory, he was, at last, a successful military leader—a warlord of the Golden Triangle. It was opium that had presented him with that opportunity: As long as the opium trade generated such enormous profits for all concerned, there would be fighting, treachery and the need for protection. General Li and his men were skilled at all three. As shrewd a businessman in his own way as Yuen was in his, General Li had learned to specialize. He neither grew nor processed opium. He simply provided protection for both—and reaped the rewards.

Li recognized the irony of at last becoming a successful Chinese warlord leader—*outside* of China; and aided by Communist funds laundered through Hong Kong. And the threat to his continued success was also ironic; as it came not from ethnic armies, bandit gangs or any of the various hilltribe militia with which he had fought. It came from the government of Thailand's periodic determination to teach hilltribes to grow crops other than opium. Substitute crops rather than indigenous warlord armies was the threat he now faced. No one would ever need his army's protection for crops of beans, tobacco and strawberries.

After women had cleared the table, the man known as Aung Gyi held out his palm to an elderly man called Kuan Yo. Everyone stared in silence at the bright red peppers in his leathery hand. Aung Gyi threw the peppers to the dirt floor of the hut and cursed. "Last week the merchants again offered practically nothing for our crops. They know if we refuse to sell to them, the crops spoil and we lose everything. I would rather starve and watch the harvest rot than see them grow fat on our sweat."

Kuan Yo stared with his one good eye first at the beans and then at Aung Gyi. "The peppers—"

"The peppers, the carrots, the apricots, the tea, the strawberries, the coffee—all worthless. There is only one crop that is worth growing."

For several moments the men sat in silence as Kuan Yo inhaled deeply on a Camel cigarette and closed his eyes in thought. "U Aung Gyi, I have given my word to the Thai government that we will cultivate alternative crops to opium."

An elderly H'mong leader, his eyes watery and his breathing labored, cleared his throat. "With opium, the buyers come to us. With these alternative crops we must transport them to the villages. Who will help us farm these new crops on the steep slopes?"

General Li's son spoke up. "And, Kuan Yo, who will ensure that the merchants give you a fair price? If you cannot sell what you grow, you cannot eat. What happened to U Aung Gyi will sooner or later happen to all of you."

General Li allowed himself a quick glance at his son, the last of three. He immediately felt a swell of fatherly pride as his eyes took in the intelligent dark face, sharp profile and close-cropped hair. And he thought of his other sons; their strength and courage—and the way they had died.

His first was lost somewhere inside China in the days after the Communist victory. At that time, he and his men abandoned their former ideology forever and joined with remnants of the nationalist armies which were aiding the American Central Intelligence Agency in various activities of intelligence gathering and harassment in southern China. His son had entered China on one such mission and had never been heard from again. Shortly after the death of his first son his wife had died.

As the missions grew fewer and the support of the Americans waned, the Golden Triangle warlords placated the Thai government and encouraged their non-involvement in the affairs of the far north by contributing hundreds of men as a para-military volunteer force. General Li was especially generous in aiding the Thai army in routing well-entrenched indigenous communists in various areas of northern Thailand. He had lost hundreds of his men in those battles—including his second son.

Kuan Yo spoke with little hope in his voice of being able to dissuade anyone of their intentions. "Coffee can bring us in nearly four times what opium brings us."

"Yes, but growing coffee is not as simple as growing opium, and think of the distances involved in getting it to market."

Yuen now spoke up. "I can advance you money to grow poppies as before. I will pay for the seed and the fertilizer. And when it is time to harvest my men will pay you in cash for your raw opium. Opium does not rot. If merchants try to cheat you, you can wait for a better price. But with the vegetables and fruits, you have no choice. Rotten cabbage buys few rifles and rounds of ammunition. We offer you cash in advance for planting opium. Now."

Kuan Yo looked carefully at each man assembled around the table. He stood up slowly and all rose. "U Aung Gyi, you will not starve. And your crops will not rot. General Li, let your men know. From now on, as before, we grow only opium. We will again be needing protection for our convoys."

Although inwardly pleased, General Li nodded solemnly as the hilltribe members rose and left the hut. Opium would remain in demand and with it the need for protection of caravans. He sipped his tea, surprisingly as bitter as he liked it, and reflected that it was the Americans who were prodding Thai government officials to substitute other crops for opium. An idealistic, impractical idea for all concerned. And one which, if it succeeded, would be particularly disastrous for him.

Several years earlier, an American congressman was even proposing that the American government simply buy up all the opium in the Golden Triangle in order to keep it from reaching American streets in the form of heroin. Again, idealistic and impractical. But one had to give the Americans credit for providing warlord politics and infighting with a bit of color and humor. Not to mention the incredible boldness of such a suggestion. And their unshakable belief that enough money could solve anything.

He reflected for several moments on the old days, during the Vietnam War, when everything was so simple, yet lucrative, thanks mainly to human greed. The Laotians and Vietnamese at all levels had been corrupted easily, but it had been more difficult to enlist a small group of American officers and enlisted men working with the Montagnards in the Central Highlands of Vietnam.

That part of his opium-smuggling operations had lasted only about a year and, with hindsight, he realized how small in scope and lacking in ambition that particular project had been, but it had given his army the funds to buy the weapons they needed to challenge both the Shan armies and the dwindling private armies of Chinese Nationalist generals in the Golden Triangle.

General Li's men would send mule caravans full of opium from northern Burma into Pakse, Laos. Then, with the highly paid assistance of the Vietnamese Air Force, they would airdrop tons of opium into the hills north of Pleiku. From the drop zone, under protection of Americans, the opium was then shipped to Saigon where Chinese syndicates organized and controlled by Yuen Sheung Fuk and his Chiu Chau partners would refine the opium into heroin and place it on board freighters bound for Hong Kong.

General Li drank his tea and reflected on the enormous amount of money he had made. Until one of the Americans had threatened to expose the drug trafficking; a decision which had caused his own death but not fast enough or discreetly enough to avoid ruining the operation. It seemed Americans were determined to somehow spoil the success he had worked for his entire life. And he was far too old now to allow that to happen. In the few years he had left to him, he was determined to enjoy the fruits of his labor—Americans or no Americans.

# 17

*Bangkok*

MIDWAY down a Patpong Road inundated by recent rains, Brian spotted the red, blue and green neon letters of the Horny Tiger Bar. The large sign also accommodated a picture of a bikini-clad dancer lying back seductively inside a champagne glass. Beside her, poised to leap into the glass, a green and yellow tiger stood on all fours roaring in her direction.

The samlor sloshed slowly to a halt in front of the bar and Brian leapt to the puddle-strewn sidewalk.

A young hostess in blouse and tight shorts opened the bar door with a flourish. "Inside please, suuhhh!" Her suggestive yet pleasant smile combined with her pronunciation of 'sir'—antebellum Scarlet O'Hara accent with steadily rising inflection—colored her invitation with lascivious overtones.

From inside the bar, two bikini-clad dancers standing near the door joined in. "This best bar in whole Thailand!"

"Best bar in whole world you bet your ass!"

Brian looked at the girl who invited him to 'bet his ass.' Over her pageboy hairstyle, she wore a seven-pointed, slightly oversized, green styrofoam Statue of Liberty crown. Its black lettering spelled out: "1886 Liberty 1986." The girls laughed and chatted to each other in Thai as Brian entered the bar.

He was expertly led through the semi-darkness of the room by the flashlight of another hostess. He sat on a bar stool, near a bell and cord hanging from the ceiling. The hostess put her hand on his arm. "What you like drink?"

"Singha beer."

She left him long enough to give his order and wipe some spilled beer off the counter. "Beer Sing!" she shouted above the music.

A sign behind the bar near a long, rectangular fish tank

informed customers as to the purpose of the overhead bell.

HE WHO RING THE BELL BUY THE BAR A ROUND
ONE RING: CUSTOMERS ONLY
TWO RINGS: CUSTOMERS AND GIRLS
GIRLS ONLY: SEE CASHIER

Brian opened a pack of Salem and lit up. The hostess brought his beer to him, carelessly throwing a 'Kloster bier—Happiness you can Drink' coaster on the counter and then carefully placing the beer mug precisely on top. Brian anticipated that she would stay to chat him up and cadge a lady's drink but more customers entered the bar and she scampered off to greet them.

In his mind Brian conjured up the most recent photograph of Nalin that Suntharee had showed him. As he turned and looked about the bar, he felt a vague sense of guilt, as if by arriving unannounced, he was betraying her right to privacy in a world she had chosen. He wondered if she would regard his presence as less a demonstration of his concern for her welfare and more as an act of voyeurism and interference.

The darkness of the room was unevenly dispersed by an assortment of lights attached to the room's ceiling. Red ceiling lights prowled the disc-jockey's tiny semi-enclosed alcove then swept across the room to light a large fish tank and the area behind the counter, intermittently illuminating the female cashier's activities and the various equipment at her station behind the bar. Lights fixed behind slowly rotating gelatin filters shot out colored streaks across the customers and dancers, and constantly revolving multi-faceted globes—as well as several diamond-shaped wall mirrors—reflected the colors in all directions.

In the center of all this, an ornate chandelier—unmoving and incongruously elegant—both absorbed and reflected the lights surrounding it. As Brian's eyes grew more accustomed to the bar's interior, he saw several of the girls posing together in their bikinis for a Thai photographer. Some smiled while others made faces at the camera, ranging from grimaces to lascivious smirks. Brian stared briefly at each of the girls but none bore a close resemblance to his image of Nalin.

In the large wall mirror behind them Brian could see reflections of several dancers across the room. Three were dressed in skimpy bikinis and two in one-piece bathing suits with tiger skin patterns, tawny colored with black stripes. Each danced precariously on her own tiny stage and gyrated wildly and inexpertly to the loud music.

Near Brian's stool was another large stage on which three girls danced together. As they danced, their stage shook slightly and sent vibrations along the counter, adding a tactile experience to the already overwhelming visual and auditory sensations. Brian again wondered what occurrence could have driven Nalin to work in such an atmosphere.

"Hi. This first time you come this bar?"

Brian reached out and shook the small pudgy hand that was proffered him. The girl was the one Brian had seen in the doorway with her Statue of Liberty crown. Her straight black hair framed her round face, ending in front in bangs just above her eyes and at the side just below her ears. Her large eyes were surrounded by thick blue streaks of eyeshadow which flared out an inch toward her ears then disappeared beneath her hair.

The excessive amount of blush highlighting her cheekbones and the inexpertly drawn eyeliner pencil lines masking the width of her almost negroid nose gave her face an unintended comical effect. The personality that shone through was of equal parts of sincerity, enthusiasm and mischievousness, dominated by an overwhelming desire to laugh.

"Yes, first time. In fact, my first time on Patpong since, let's see, 1968."

The girl's shocked reaction sent her green-and-yellow parrot-earrings into a spin. "Oh! You no look so old."

"Ah, but I am. They didn't have go-go dancing on Patpong Road then."

The girl tilted her head and raised her eyebrows in surprise. "No have go-go dancing. What they do?"

"Just what we're doing. We talked." Brian reflected briefly on the days when Patpong bargirls were fully clothed and when it was best to be introduced to one by a friend and how only after a few meetings would there be any talk of leaving the bar together.

The girl leaned close to his open shirt, briefly *waiied* his permission, gently lifted up the front of his neck chain, and then gingerly held the small silver case with its enclosed Buddha amulet between her thumb and forefinger. "Very nice. Who give you?"

"A monk in a temple in Ayudhya gave me that a long time ago. I think it's very old."

She examined it closely. "Yes. Very old. Very nice." She again *waiied*—Brian wasn't sure if the gesture was to him or to the amulet—and then carefully placed the locket in its former position. "You never take off?"

"The Buddha, yes. You know, it can be taken off from the chain. But I haven't taken the chain off for 20 years. I'd need a special pair of pliers to do it."

"You are *satsana phut?*"

"Yes, I'm Buddhist."

She let out a shriek of joy and slapped his arm. "Very good! I think you know Thailand well!"

"I think nobody knows Thailand well."

She laughed again, revealing a mouth full of uneven white teeth. "You bet your ass."

"I like your hat."

The dancer reached up and straightened it. "My clown. I go America one time before. I see Statue of Liberty. You ever have seen her?"

"Many times."

"Lady Liberty is beauti*foon!* You want to try my clown on?"

"No, I'm sure your crown looks better on you."

Brian offered the girl a cigarette. She took it. "My name Oy."

"I'm Brian."

"You do business in Bangkok, Blian? You marry?"

"Yes, business. No. Not married. You?"

"No. Before have one husband. Him no good. I no like marry. If marry, husban' fool aloun', or maybe Oy fool aloun' and then have big fight every night. Talk, talk, talk. No good you bet your ass!" Without pausing for breath, she put on a stern face in imitation of Brian. "You too much ser-i-ous, Blian!"

Brian stared for a moment at the fish tank and then spoke quietly to the girl. "Actually, Oy, I'm looking for a friend of a friend. Her name is Nalinpilai."

"Nalinpilai?"

"She probably came here about three months ago. She might be using a nickname. She'd be older than you, about 23."

Her brief frown was quickly replaced by a smile of recognition. "Oh, I think you mean Lek. She my best friend. She go to dance now." The girl pointed behind Brian but placed her other hand on his leg near his crotch as if to prevent his attention from straying too far. Brian felt slightly embarrassed as he gently moved her hand to his knee. He turned toward the far stage. The girl on the stage was leaning back against the rear wall with her hands on her hips.

Brian found himself staring at one of the most beautiful women he had ever seen. She had inherited her mother's almond-shaped eyes but they were even more impossibly exotic, made narrow by eyelid folds which swept outward and ended in an upward curve. The high cheekbones and delicately chiselled chin epitomized the beauty of her Oriental features. Long black hair cascaded nearly to her waist. There was an intelligence and self-confidence in the face and, as she returned his stare, a hint of several facets to her personality, like the different colored lights striking her face and curvaceous bikini-clad body.

Large crescent-shaped silver earrings matched her silver bracelet. A silver chain, with a large Buddha image attached, sparkled around her neck. Like all of the girls in the bar, whether dancer, waitress or cashier, she wore a small round red badge with a number in white letters.

Both her face and posture more than hinted at the sensuality of the girl. Despite her attire as a go-go dancer, she seemed removed from her surroundings, neither laughing nor joking with the other girls, nor jumping about while waiting for the music to begin. When it did she became the center of customer attention.

As the song began the female vocalist's voice bellowed out of Bose speakers on each side of the back stage and from yet another pair near the front of the bar. Red, green and blue sound level indicator lights jumped inside the disc jockey area in response to the song's dynamics. With few exceptions, the lesser attractive girls would dance for the customers, attempting to keep eye contact with them and smile at them, but most of the girls simply cavorted about and aimlessly danced their way through each number.

Nalin kept mostly to herself at the far end of the bar on a small stage and stared either into space or at herself in the mirror. Her movements were languorous, provocative and feline, but she seemed withdrawn inside herself, wrapped in her own mood. Whatever the music, she would begin by ignoring the rhythm, and sway sensually all the while narcissistically moving her hands slowly over her legs, hips and breasts, arms and shoulders. As her arms finally shot into the air, she would at last join into the rhythm, allowing her body to match the tempo of the music. She seldom laughed or smiled while dancing and never attempted to maintain eye contact. In fact, customers and their frequent shouts of approval were completely ignored. A fine, thin sheen of sweat glistened on her back. As she gyrated to the loud sounds and the incessant rhythm, the Buddhist amulet on her gold neck chain bounced from one well-formed breast to the other like a mountain climber trapped in a hurricane.

Above her head revolving globes shot sudden streaks of light and pavonine patterns of color across the room, green against a table of inebriated German tourists with bikini-clad dancers on their laps, red across the crowded bar lined with bottles of Thai beer and ashtrays, orange across the tank of exotic fish and blue across the Buddhist wall shrine shrouded in incense. To Brian, the change of colors and patterns seemed to come not from the lights, but to emanate from within Nalin, as a mood ring changes colors.

As the sound grew even more insistent, Nalin jumped from her own stage onto the one next to it and leapt nearly two feet into the air onto the vertical pole running from the ceiling to the center of the stage. The dancer on the stage had made little use of the device and simply retreated back to the wall, resignedly, almost forlornly, allowing Nalin to do as she pleased.

Nalin gripped the pole with her right hand and hugged it between her thighs, stretched her left leg outward, and threw back her head and left arm. With her eyes closed she pivoted upside-down on the pole a full circle allowing her long hair to slowly sweep the stage. Then she remained completely still, opened her eyes and stared directly at Brian.

*"How does the world look upside-down, Little Tadpole?"*

The concentric green circles emanated from Nalin's face and spread in a wavelike pattern, beyond the stage, across the wall, across the years, and dissolved to reappear at Ayudhya twenty years before.

*"How does the world look upside-down, Little Tadpole? Any better than rightside up?"*

*The three-year-old girl giggled and without answering Brian's question, gripped the young palm tree and tried to bend backwards even farther. But her eyes never left his. Her pink dress blew up in the slight breeze, and she moved her head slowly, allowing her pigtails to drag along the ground. Brian got up from the porch steps and walked to Nalin. He took her out-stretched hands. "I think it's time this young lady had another swing, don't you, Paul?"*

*Brian glanced toward the house just before their expressions changed. He had caught them looking into each other's eyes and in that second, he knew. Suntharee had chosen Paul. With a sudden painful realization, he knew that he was to be the 'best man' and 'Uncle' to the little girl he held, never 'father'; 'brother-in-law' to the woman he loved, never 'husband.'*

*Paul quickly jumped up and walked over. He grabbed Nalin's tiny shoes in his large, crablike hands and lifted her feet off the ground. She giggled now almost uncontrollably. "I sure do. She's way overdue for a swing. Ready? One, two, three!" Nalin's shrieks of joy grew still louder and, as they swung her, Brian looked toward Suntharee. She looked away from his stare toward the ricefields in the distance.*

"You don't feel so good?"

*The ricefields waved mockingly in the breeze and their vivid yellow-green beauty blurred and intensified inside Brian's tears, and the day turned all shades of green. He looked toward Nalin but could see her face only through a kaleidoscopic maze of wet green.*

"You sad, I think, you bet your ass. But nobody allow to be sad in Horny Tiger bar. This best bar on Patpong and nobody can be sad you bet your ass!"

Brian tried an embarrassed smile and wiped the tears away with the back of his wrist. He smiled at Oy. "I'm not sad; it's the lights in here. They bother my eyes."

He looked toward the stage and saw that Nalin had disappeared and an overweight girl with large-framed glasses was listlessly going through the motions of dancing to music. Brian's eyes searched the bar and finally found Nalin sitting alone on a stool set back in the darkness of the bar where none of the lights directly reached. He could see the glow of a cigarette near her face, and the lights reflecting off her earrings and necklace. She sat erect, with legs crossed, one elbow on the counter holding the cigarette, the other arm across her lap.

"It looks like Lek captured another one."

Brian turned to face the man at the next stool. He was hunched over his beer glass, almost as if protecting it. He looked in his late forties and there was more black than white in his wavy hair and thick mustache—but just barely. His well-lined and darkly tanned face sprouted about two days' growth of heavy beard. Deeply etched forehead wrinkles and a deep, puckered, magenta scar on his right cheek appeared and disappeared in the intermittent streaks of red from a nearby search light.

Chest hair sprouted above his brown shortsleeve shirt and a slight stomach bulge protruded above his belt buckle. Yet his burly frame was large, muscular and brawny, and he projected an image of strength, power and virility. He held out his hand to Brian. "Webb's the name. Roger Webb."

Brian shook his hand briefly. "Brian Mason. You a friend of Nalin? I mean, 'Lek'?"

"I'd like to be. But so would about a hundred other guys." The man laughed and took a long drink of beer. "You just travelin' through on business or plannin' on stayin' awhile?"

"I guess I'll stay awhile. I want to look up some old friends. Then it's back to New York."

The man turned on his stool to lean against the bar, his beer held tightly in his lap. "The Big Apple, uh? What line of work are you in—if you don't mind my askin'."

"I'm a publisher. I thought I'd check out Bangkok's printing."

"Well, Brian, old buddy, as you can see, the City of Angels— as this place was named by somebody long ago—is flooded. I bet you most of the printing presses in this city are three feet under water." He took another long drink and belched. "But this town can be under ten feet of water and I still ain't goin' no-where else. I'm just gonna' sit here, drink my beer, and watch pretty girls dance. Hell, I'll build 'em an ark to dance on if I have to. Anyway, I'm also an owner of the place, and the show must go on as you New Yorkers put it."

"You're the owner of the Horny Tiger?"

"Well, if you're doin' business in Thailand, you got to have a Thai partner who owns more than half. Of course, that don't mean nothin'; just keeps the government happy. I actually own about thirty percent. Somebody else owns the rest."

"Bob Donnelly?"

The man's eyes suddenly drained of their merriment. "That's him. You know him?"

"We used to be in the army together out here."

"That a fact?"

"Yeah. In the Sixties. You happen to know where I can reach him?"

The man scribbled out a number on a pack of matches and handed it to Brian. "Bangkok phones have improved a lot but during the rainy season you may or may not get through."

"Thanks. Does Bob come here every night?"

"Nope. He sure don't. You'll seldom see him in here. I kind of run the place along with Maew behind the counter and Nit the cashier and Boonsom. He's the disc jockey. And Oy helps me out. Of course, she cain't dance for shit. None of 'em can—except for Lek there. Or 'Nalin' as you call her. She shore is something, ain't she? We had some pretty ones back in Alabama but nothin' like that."

Brian swivelled on the stool to face Nalin. A well-built man in his mid-forties was leaning against the counter with his face close to hers. He was speaking to her and gesturing. She stared back at him with little expression on her face.

Suddenly, Brian felt Roger's hand grip his shoulder. He was already standing and starting to walk. Come on. I'll take you over to meet Lek."

The hand on Brian's shoulder was strong and insistent. Brian made a split-second decision to go along with him. He stood up but held back until Roger turned back to him. "If you don't mind, Roger, I'd rather you didn't give her my real name—not just yet."

Roger shrugged. "Well, I didn't figure you for the kind of schmuck that uses phoney names with bargirls but, if that's what you want, you got it."

Brian walked slowly, allowing Roger to approach Nalin first. Roger stood beside her, one hand gripping his belt, the other holding his half-empty beer glass, rudely interrupting and completely ignoring the man talking to her. "Lek, honey, I want you to meet a friend of mine; and a close personal friend of Bob's. All the way from New York. His name's . . . Gatsby. Jay Gatsby."

Brian glanced quickly at Roger but Roger's deadpan expression gave no indication that he was perpetrating a practical joke.

Brian remained aware of the seated man's angry face out of the corner of his eye but gave his attention to Nalin. She stared at him without changing expression and said nothing. But suddenly she shook her head as if shaking hair off her shoulders and thrust her hand out. Brian took it and held it for several seconds before letting go.

The man stepped forward and spoke angrily. "Hey, Tex, if you don't mind—"

Roger spoke without looking at him. "I don't mind at all, partner, but seein' as I'm from Alabama, I'm not really a 'Tex', now, am I?"

"Yeah, well, I—"

"Let me tell you, Jay, old buddy, Lek here is the best dancer in the Horny Tiger and that means the best on Patpong Road and that means the best in all of Bangkok, City of Angels, and that means the best in the world. And since I cain't git nowhere with her, maybe you can. But, remember. As the Bard of Avon said, 'Drink, sir, provokes the desire, but it takes away the performance.'"

"Look, asshole, I already asked her to go with me tonight. So how about you and your buddy just—"

Roger placed his beer glass down on the bar and threw his arm around the man's shoulders in comradely fashion which belied the firmness of his grip. He now spoke in his conspiratorial tone to the man as he led him off toward the front of the bar. "Well, now, I figured that but, you see, you and me are a bit long in the tooth for a pretty little thing like Lek there, so why don't you and me just go off to Soi Cowboy or some other place and see what we can find?" Both men were of medium height and of similar build, and to anyone across the bar they would have appeared as two remarkably alike old friends who had one too many and who willingly supported one another as they walked.

The man's angry words were lost in the music. Brian turned to Nalin. Her dispassionate stare was now completely replaced by a winsome, engaging smile; a bright smile of perfect white teeth, full lips and tiny crinkles surrounding lively dark brown eyes.

Now that Brian was up close, he saw that her round cheeks, playful grin and slight tilt of the head gave her face an elfin even puckish quality, a pixy planning her next mischievous prank. It was easy to see in her the young Suntharee.

Brian now saw the number pinned to her bikini was '18.' Beneath it the edges of several 'lady's drink' bar chits were visible, indisputable proof of her popularity with customers. At the end of her silver neck chain, a finely wrought gold case held a tiny meditating Buddha encrusted with the wear and patina of age. Her smooth, light brown skin was still covered by a thin layer of sweat. On her right leg, just above the knee, was a tiny 'L'-shaped scar.

She gestured toward the stool beside her. "Sit down."

"Thank you. I'm sorry we interrupted. This Roger is—"

At the word 'Roger' her smile disappeared. "You know him long time?" Her voice was pleasant but deeper than he had anticipated. "Actually, I just met him. He saw me staring at you and brought me over."

"Why you stare at me so much?"

Brian couldn't help thinking how beautiful she was. "All the men stare at you."

Her smile returned. "Not like you."

"The truth is I'd like to talk to you."

Nalin quickly put her cigarette out and sat with exaggerated primness, her chin propped on her fists, her elbows on her legs. "O.K. I listen."

"I didn't mean here. I thought we could go somewhere quiet." She gazed at him with an expression he couldn't read but one unnerving enough to keep him talking. "I won't keep you long, Lek."

For the first time, Brian felt—beneath the facade of insouciance—Nalin's lack of confidence. "I don't . . . I don't know. . . ." She let the sentence trail off and took a drink. She looked across the bar toward Roger and then back to Brian. "Roger say you close friend of Bob. True?"

"Yes. Bob and I. . . ." Brian took a drink of his beer. "Look, I just want to talk to you for awhile."

"O.K., I go. You pay the bar three hundred baht. Give to Maew. I go change." Before he could say another word Nalin jumped off the stool, grabbed a white purse from a shelf full of purses and shoulder bags inside the disc jockey's area, and walked into the back room. The disc jockey's smile gleamed in the darkness of his booth.

Brian looked toward the front of the bar. Roger was leaning against the bar with a beer in his hand. He smiled in admiration, raised his glass, and nodded to Brian. Brian noticed the man who had spoken with Nalin sitting sullenly in a booth near the door, head down, eyes staring at his beer glass.

Beside the door the photographer was taking pictures of Oy, who had changed into a green-and-blue bikini and black mid-heel shoes with green studs. On her head was her Liberty crown and in her outstretched hand she clutched a styrofoam Statue of Liberty torch. She held a book under her arm in the manner in which the Statue of Liberty held her tablet, and from time to time she would check a postcard photograph of the original statue to ensure that her expression and posture matched that of the one in New York harbor. She waved her torch to Brian and smiled happily.

Brian walked to the stool next to Roger and took out three hundred baht. "I guess it's all set. Thanks for the introduction."

Roger slapped him on the back and laughed raucously. "That's all right, old buddy. You just be sure to report to ole Roger how things go. I'm dyin' to know if what I cain't get is worth what I think it is." He turned to the middle-aged woman behind the bar. "Maew, take this gentleman's money, will you?"

The door opened as a dancer tried to coax tourists to enter the bar. An elderly Caucasian couple smiled uncertainly and continued walking. Taxis and samlors sped through the flooded streets. The door closed. "Where you stayin', Brian?"

"I'm at the Oriental."

"Whoops! Oh, scuse me, that hotel is my very favorite. It's just that you can't bring any playmates back there. A few of the hotels here in Bangkok like to play up-market, you git me? And, unfortunately, that's one of them."

"I'll think of something." Brian handed the three hundred baht to Maew. "I'm taking Lek."

Roger called for his bill. "I think I'll see what's happening over at the Superstar. I shore would hate to go home alone on a rainy night."

Brian watched the photographer approach a booth with several tourists. He took their refusals politely and moved on to the next booth. Brian glanced about the crowded bar and stood up.

"Roger, thanks for the beer."

"My pleasure, pardner. We'll most likely see each other around again. In fact—"

Brian noticed the grin on Roger's face widen as he stared at something over Brian's shoulder. "You picked a winner, amigo. No doubt about that."

Brian turned to watch Nalin walking quickly toward him. She had changed from a bikini and high heels to a red-and-white T-shirt, blue jeans and white sneakers. Without the high heels, she appeared much shorter than before. Her right hand held onto the strap of her purse hanging from her shoulder. Her hair was tied in a rubber band behind her and she wore only a minimum of makeup. She could have passed on the street as a young girl on her way home from secretarial school.

She stopped briefly near Brian, said, "O.K.," and started for the door. Brian looked toward Roger for one final wave but before he could bring his hand up, Roger shoved him roughly toward the rear of the bar just as someone's fist grazed Brian's ear. Brian caught a stool and jumped to his feet just in time to see Roger Webb hit the enraged and inebriated customer in the groin with his knee and finish him off with a right to the jaw. Bathed in pulsating lights and constantly changing iridescent patterns, bargirls ran, beer glasses and ladies drinks fell and customers ducked. The man lay completely still, sprawled face down across the table of a booth.

Nalin stood at the door. She turned, pushed it open and disappeared. Roger spoke to Brian while nodding toward the door: "Go!" Brian moved past Roger and walked quickly to the door. To Roger he said: "I owe you one."

"No problem, partner. Just enjoy, that's all."

Brian spotted Nalin getting into a samlor, a small, open, canopy-covered, three-wheeled vehicle with blue-and-yellow coachwork. He waded through several connected puddles of water and jumped in beside her, not sure if she had been planning to wait until he got there or, because of the unpleasantness, to leave without him.

Brian turned to Nalin, one hand clasped to his aching ear. "Look, Lek, I'd like to go somewhere and talk. It's important. We could go to the Oriental. The coffee shop, I mean."

She turned and stared at him with a level, penetrating gaze, then turned away. Brian couldn't decide if she thought his suggestion insincere, facetious or—considering the situation—insulting.

Nalin hesitated, then almost whispering, gave the driver an address. Brian understood enough to know she was asking him to take them to the nearby Suriwongse Hotel. The driver roared off immediately giving Brian a stab of pain near his ear. They both gripped the side of the samlor. A row of five bulbs inside the samlor behind the driver's head flashed back at him every time the driver hit his brake: red, orange, blue, green and yellow.

He fell silent for the rest of the short journey; past the bars on Patpong and around the corner onto Suriwongse Road. The samlor made a sharp right down the dark, partly flooded, narrow lane leading to the outside rooms of the Suriwongse Hotel.

One of the hotel's boys detached himself from a group and, waving his flashlight vigorously and urgently as if directing an aircraft away from its disastrous course, guided the samlor into a car space, then immediately drew a large curtain behind them. Brian paid the driver twenty baht, twice what the ride was worth, and turned to find that the boy had already opened the door of the room and let Nalin inside.

Brian moved ahead of him into the doorway and turned to block the door. The boy's face broke into a happy grin at the large tip and he *waiied* Brian politely.

Brian entered the small room. Nalin had put her purse down on a bedside table and stood uncertainly near the bed, glancing about. When she noticed Brian watching her, her expression immediately changed to one of nonchalance; but Brian was certain that she found her surroundings as unfamiliar and distasteful as he did.

The Mitsubishi 'Bear Globe' air conditioner banged away in grunts and groans and suffused the room with a foul odor. The room was dominated by an extremely thin, well worn, pink bed coverlet and orange painted walls. A spittoon was squeezed in between the queen-sized bed and a chipped table. A plaintive Thai love song came from a wall speaker near the bed. The grey telephone offered no buttons or dial or any device for calling outside.

As he started to move, a sudden movement caused him to look up. A wall lizard scampered across a ceiling mirror placed directly above the bed. When he looked again at Nalin, she had sat on the bed and was lighting a cigarette. Brian walked toward her and stood, looking down at her. "You're new at this, aren't you?"

His remark seemed to both anger and embarrass her. "What are you talking about? Many men take me here before." She drew smoke into her lungs and immediately began coughing.

Brian held her wrists. "Lek. Listen. I don't really want to talk with you in a place like this."

She tilted her head and stared at him for several moments with slight indignation and genuine puzzlement. Finally she shrugged. "You no want to talk to me, O.K., I go." She put out her cigarette and reached for her bag.

"How much face will you lose in the bar if you go back now?"

She looked toward the door, uncertain of her next move. Brian gently pushed her onto the bed and spoke softly. "I just want to talk to you, Little Tadpole."

Her eyes grew wide and her mouth opened. "How you know my name? Nobody know that name. Only. . . ."

She stared at him in a silence broken only by the intermittent groans of the air conditioner.

"I'm Brian, Nalin. Paul's brother."

Her facial expression ranged from disbelief to fear, from anger to respect. Finally, she threw herself face down on the bed, her hands covering her face, and began crying.

Brian sat beside her on the bed. "Nalin, I'm sorry. I didn't mean to meet you like this. Here, dry your eyes." He handed her a towel but she merely clutched it tightly in her hands. Her sobs grew louder and more insistent. "Nalin. Hey, Little Tadpole, can you remember what Paul and I used to do when you cried? Remember the funny faces we made when you fell down and hurt your knee?" After several seconds of silence, Nalin's sobs grew softer and more regular. "You don't know how happy I am I found you. Your mother was so worried. She wants you back home. She spoke to me in—"

Nalin suddenly pushed herself up and stopped crying. She sat facing him, staring angrily through wet eyes surrounded by tiny smears of blue and black. "Do you actually think for one moment that I would ever again return to Ayudhya to live with my . . . *mother*? Do you?"

Brian was equally shocked by the perfect grammar and by the depth of hatred in her voice. His hands gently gripped her shoulders. "Nalin, your mother didn't raise you to . . . to be a dancer on Patpong Road."

For several seconds she stared at him and said nothing. the anger drained from her eyes and a new determination came into her face. She quickly wiped her eyes with a tissue from her purse and stood up. "I have to go now."

Brian again put his hands on her shoulders and turned her around. "We have to talk, Little Tadpole. I came all the way from New York to see you."

She stared into his face as if searching for something then looked down. "You came to see her."

"Of course, I'm happy to see her too. But she's worried about you!"

Hatred again flooded her eyes. "I'll never go back there."

"Look, let me take you somewhere and we'll get something to eat. OK?"

She finally looked up at him again. "If you promise not to talk about her."

Brian wiped a tear from her chin. "OK, Little Tadpole. I promise."

They left the room and slipped through the curtain. As they walked down the dark lane leading to Suriwongse Road, Brian turned to see the boy detach himself from the group and saunter with towels and soap toward the vacated room. The dim light illuminated the boy's grin like that of Alice's Cheshire Cat.

# 18

IN the restaurant setting, she had successfully—at least on the surface—put her emotional upheaval behind her. She had collected herself admirably and, except for the subject of why she had run away from home, she discussed events with perfect calm. She smoked Brian's Salems but only infrequently inhaled. She poured hot Thai chilies on her food as if they were merely sugar over strawberries, and drank several glasses of iced tea.

Brian waited for coffee to arrive before finally agreeing to pay ten baht to the persistent shoeshine boy for a shine. He lit up a Salem and leaned back. "So, if I may sum up, you were attending Fine arts School in Bangkok, then moved to Thammasat University to study Drama. You visited your mother on a holiday. For some reason, possibly connected with some of your mother's mail, you suddenly packed your bags and returned to Bangkok—not to school, but to become—using the name Lek—a go-go dancer." He gulped some coffee and continued. "Nalin, it might be my time of life for a sudden change of career and mid-life crisis, but it certainly isn't your time yet. Am I right?"

Nalin smiled politely but stared at him as if trying to decide whether or not to take him into her confidence. "Yes, Uncle Brian."

"Nalin, please no more 'Uncle Brians.' It makes me feel old. Just 'Brian' will do."

"All right. Brian."

"Thank you." Brian felt someone tug at his trousers. He examined his shoes as the boy slipped them back on. He had done a poor job possibly because he needed to save on polish. Brian handed him 20 baht and returned his *wai*.

"And then you approached Bob Donnelly about working in his bar and he eventually agreed."

"Yes, Uncle—I mean, Brian."

"Will you tell me how long you intend to stay there?"

She hesitated and looked away; then looked directly into his eyes. "I'm not sure." She lit another cigarette and after one puff left it to burn in the ashtray. Brian began to suspect she never actually inhaled tobacco.

"How do you get along with Bob?"

"He seldom comes to the bar. I almost never see him . . . I think I remember my mother telling me you didn't . . . get along with him." Her carefully phrased statement was spoken more as a question. Brian watched her study his face attentively as he replied.

"Your mother was right. I always found him too full of himself." Brian suddenly remembered the black army sergeant nicknamed 'Unicorn' saying that for Bob, getting invited to a full-bird colonel's house for dinner seemed to give him the same kind of thrill other men got from "getting it on with a fifteen-year-old virgin."

"But you worked with him in the army for almost two years."

Nalin's question drew him back from his reverie. "What? Oh. The army. Right. Well, Bob did help Paul and I shift some army provisions over to your mother's school. On the sly. And when she most needed them. I suppose he's all right. I guess I just could never understand people with upper-class pretensions; and Bob was the worst example I've ever seen of a thoroughly middle-class man with a desperate need to be upper-class."

The bass of the music from a nearby go-go bar rumbled through the restaurant's walls, muffled but constant. Outside the window, through the thin gauze curtain, Brian could see deaf mutes along both sides of the narrow enclosed sidewalk exhorting passersby to purchase their cheap Chinese silk embroideries, rice paper drawings and leather cutouts.

"Do you like working there?" he asked.

Again she hesitated. "I don't dislike it. I like to dance and there is a sense of freedom and . . . independence."

Oy spotted Brian just as he noticed her at the door. She had changed her bikini and crown for T-shirt and jeans, but her wide black belt was ornamented with an enormous statue-of-liberty belt buckle. She squealed and ran over to their table pulling the hand of a burly young American with a sloping forehead and beady eyes. "Hi, Blian! Hi, Lek! This is Larry. He's taking me for *all night!*"

The man looked confused. "Who's Larry? I'm George."

Oy squealed again and slapped his well-developed shoulder. "OK, Jorch, never mind. Larry, him long-time before boyfriend. He go Switz."

Brian shook Larry's hand. "She means Switzerland, George."

George looked befuddled. "Yeah?"

In one hand, Oy clutched a bag of mangoes, with a still smaller bag inside of fish sauce, chilies, red onions and dried shrimp. With her free hand she strained to pull her date toward an empty table as a tiny tug might try to tow a liner. "Come on, Jorch, leave lovers to eat alone. They no want us aloun—you bet your ass!" She squealed again and tilted her head, accidentally ringing her bell earrings.

Brian waved to Oy. "Nice meeting you, George."

"Yeah."

Nalin laughed silently. "I like Oy. We are like sisters now. Her father died last year. She supports her son and three sisters in school."

"In Bangkok?"

"Yes. She lives on a canal just outside of Bangkok. Her mother runs a restaurant beside the canal. Oy stays with me in my apartment a lot. Sometimes. . . ." She paused as if undecided on whether to continue, then finished her sentence quickly. "When I don't use my apartment for a night or two I let her sleep there. At least she doesn't have to worry about mosquitoes." Her dark brown eyes narrowed in thought. "Brian, if you don't mind I'd like to go back to the bar. They might need me. If too many girls are bought out, there aren't enough dancers. I want to tell you more but I can't. Not now."

"All right. I'm going to the hotel and get some sleep." He called for the check. "But answer me one question first. It was you who wrote the letter and signed your mother's name. Correct?"

Nalin's face slowly relaxed as she continued to stare at him. "Yes, Uncle Brian, it was me. Just give me some time . . . before I explain. I'm sorry to bring you all the way to Bangkok by deception. But I knew you'd come for *her* . . . I'm sorry."

"But how did you know I wouldn't write to your mother before coming?"

Her face lit up with an embarrassed smile. She reminded Brian of the young Rita Hayworth in a movie he had nearly forgotten. "The maid who takes in the mail. . . ."

Brian finished the sentence for her. ". . . had instructions to intercept my letter."

"Yes." She grew thoughtful. Her eyebrows, which slanted inward at exotic angles, slanted still more.

"What's wrong?"

"But I gave her instructions to call me as soon as a foreign man arrived at the house."

"The phones went dead. I don't think they're fixed yet."

They remained silent while Brian paid the check. As they stood up, Nalin spoke again. "Brian, I hope you forgive me for bringing you all the way to Thailand. Please be patient with me. But the letter was the only way to make sure you'd come."

He placed his hand briefly on her shoulder and squeezed. "It's all right, Little Tadpole. I've been away too long. Far too long. I feel like I've come home."

# 19

THE petite secretary walked back to her desk from the open doorway of Bob Donnelly's inner office. Her voice was almost lost among the sounds of typewriters and telephones. "Please go in." Brian walked toward the door with the large white letters against a dark grey background: Robert Donnelly—President.

The two men nearly collided in the office doorway. Up close, Bob's well-lined face appeared far older than his 44 years. His mustache was thin and well-trimmed, and resembled those on the faces of Thai soldiers in temple murals. Beneath his slightly thinning blond hairline his fleshy face and confident smile reflected prosperity and success. His paunch reflected his sedentary, desk-bound way of life. Bob clasped Brian on the shoulder and then shook his hand up and down several times. Brian returned the smile. "Been a long time, Bob."

"It certainly has Brian. But you look good—not even a paunch." As the handshaking stopped, the smile faded. After a briefly embarrassing two or three second hesitation, Bob gestured toward his office. "Well, come on in. Ladda, coffee, please."

Bob's spacious fourth floor inner office looked out over a noisy traffic jam and a row of gaudily painted concrete shophouses across the street. Each shophouse had been painted a different color. Behind them, Brian could just catch a glimpse of a canal. The office walls were covered with pictures of a smiling Robert Donnelly shaking hands with Thai clients, Thai officials and Thai military officers. A Van Gogh print and a large, original and very colorful painting of a Balinese temple-dance added color to an otherwise staid, conventional office.

Brian sat in an armchair in front of the desk. A large, slightly over-exposed, photograph of an attractive Western woman and two young children faced him. All three were well-dressed and they stood squinting into the sun. A temple's wall of broken porcelain tiles glittered beside them. Behind their smiles, the wife seemed haggard or worried and the children bored and petulant, impatient for the photographer to finish.

Bob sat behind his desk in a large leather swivel chair and adjusted his blue-and-white club tie, its sailboat motif identifying the wearer with sporting activities enjoyed by the upper classes. Although nearly three inches shorter than Brian, Bob now appeared taller. "When did you say you got in?"

"Just a week ago. From Hong Kong."

"You certainly surprised me with your phone call. The last time we corresponded was, let's see. . . ."

"Nearly fifteen years ago. You were still working for a public relations firm. I had just joined Barron Books." Brian looked around. "From the looks of thing now, you've done very well."

Bob's smile broadened with unconcealed pride. He clasped his hands together as he looked around the room surveying his domain. "Not bad. Forty-five employees in three companies: Public relations, import-export and interior decorating."

Brian smiled. "Three companies and one bar."

Bob's smile faded then reasserted itself. "Oh, yes. I have an interest in a bar on Patpong. Someone couldn't pay off a debt so I ended up with it."

"You and Roger Webb."

Again, Bob's smile faded. Brian noticed that without his smile, he seemed far more weary and much older. The secretary brought in a filigreed silver tray with coffee, briefly interrupting their conversation.

As she bowed slightly and left the room, Bob leaned back in his chair and put his palms together. "Yes. Roger and I met some years ago. We were about to go into business together. It was fortunate I found that we were ill-suited to be business partners before I got in too deeply with him. Roger *is* a *minor* partner in the bar. He seems to have little else to do but sit around in it. I'm afraid he has a drinking problem. A lot of Bangkok bar managers become their own best customers. How he manages to keep his Thai resident visa despite all that he's into is a mystery to me."

After a few awkward moments of silence, Bob continued in a jocular voice. "Well, we've got to get you out to meet the wife and kids. Fay has heard a lot about you. You said on the phone you're here to meet with writers?"

"Right. I plan to meet with the SEA Write award winners while they're in town. I should be in Thailand for a few weeks."

"A few weeks. . . ." Bob quickly studied his appointment book. "What about Friday for dinner? Say, six o'clock? We'll send a car to pick you up. The Oriental, you said, right?"

"Right. Sounds fine to me."

Bob closed his appointment book. When he again looked at Brian he spoke in a jovial manner but Brian detected the caution in his voice. Bob seemed to understand that any subject which might lead to mention of Paul's death in front of Brian still required discretion and circumspection. "Have you heard from anyone in the old unit? I had a letter years ago from Jackson that he was working in a bank somewhere in the Midwest. You know Stanley was wounded in Vietnam. Jackson said Stanley had a lot of flashback problems about the war. Last I heard he was in Key West."

"Yeah, I heard that from somebody. He was wounded the same day Paul was killed; in the same firefight. Only three of our unit went to 'Nam: Stanley, Jackson and Paul. One physically and mentally disabled and one dead—I guess people in the Intelligence business don't do so well on a real battlefield."

Bob frowned, then stared at the papers on his desk. "God, Brian, I've never really gotten over Paul's death myself, so I'm sure you haven't. For someone like him to. . . ."

Brian broke the silence. "You do know Nalin is working in your bar."

Bob's eyes widened but then he grew thoughtful, leaning on his soft, clasped hands. "Yes, I know. She called me and said she wanted a job at the Horny Tiger. At first I thought she was joking. I tried to find out what the problem was between her and her mother but she wouldn't tell me anything. So I offered her a job in the office but she insisted in working in the bar. She started as a waitress, but now she's a dancer. With her education and she's dancing on Patpong! Have you seen her?"

"Yes. I had a talk with her but I can't get much out of her either." Brian stared briefly at the sailboats. "I went to Ayudhya last week."

"You saw Suntharee?"

"Yes."

"I haven't seen her for years. I guess she spends a lot of time teaching children. I think she feels that as long as she keeps busy with the school, she won't have time to think of the past."

Brian finished his coffee and stared into the cup. "Right after Paul died, Suntharee was living only to bring up Nalinpilai. Something happened recently to turn her daughter against her, but she wouldn't say what either. Just asked me to try to get Nalin to go back to the house." Brian rose. "Listen, this isn't the time or place for swapping old stories. Let's do it in your Patpong bar some night. I'll let you get back to work."

Bob rose and walked around the desk. He put his hand on Brian's shoulder and walked him to the door. "I'd like that. So, Friday at six. In front of the Oriental. Don't forget."

Brian shook hands. "I won't; and thanks. I'm looking forward to meeting your family." Brian passed through the bustling outer office and walked out into the hallway. Despite his exit from an air-conditioned office into the heat of the day, he felt relieved. Any prolonged contemplation of Paul's death could even now bring him close to despair and actual nausea. He hailed a taxi, named his destination, accepted the price without bargaining, and sat back against the torn fabric, bathed in sweat.

In the midst of an endless traffic jam, Brian reflected on his meeting with Bob Donnelly. There had been the expected uneasiness between two men who—beneath the surface—had never gotten on well. But he had felt something more significant than that: an inexplicable anxiety, even wariness in Bob's demeanor. But if Brian was correct in assuming that Bob Donnelly was apprehensive of his arrival in Bangkok, he had found no clue as to why.

When a newsboy held up a local English language newspaper just outside the taxi window, Brian bought a copy and flipped idly through the pages. He looked at the photographs of barefoot residents wading through the dirty water of their flooded lane; heroine smugglers hanging their heads in chagrin when caught in the act at Bangkok's Don Muang Airport; and a grinning man proudly displaying dead snakes which had invaded his house on the flood waters of an October deluge. The images of local color had an invigorating effect on Brian's spirits and, despite the traffic congestion, he felt his tension gradually dissipate.

# 20

IT was after midnight when Brian walked into the Horny Tiger and up to the bar. Roger was sitting on a stool facing away from the bar with his thick arms around the narrow waist of a dancer with a voluptuous body. She was standing with her back to him; Brian had a sudden image of a musician with his double bass waiting quietly for the next string passage to commence. Roger suddenly spotted Brian. "It's about time, old buddy. I thought you and Lek—I mean, 'Nalin'—must have run off and got married." He motioned for Maew to bring Brian a beer. "So, how's your ear?"

Brian suppressed his irritation at the suggestive way in which Roger defined his relationship with Nalin. "Great! Only hurts when I listen."

Roger's speech was slightly slurred. Brian noticed several ladies drinks around his beer glass and a wad of chits in the cup beside it and wondered how many he'd had. He looked around the bar but failed to spot Nalin.

Roger nodded toward the back. "She's in the changin' room." He leaned back against the bar and smiled knowingly. "Well, pardner, how did it go?"

Brian grimaced at the still unfamiliar taste of Thai beer and at Roger's interrogation. "You should know a gentleman never tells."

"Aw, shit, they ain't no gentlemen in Bangkok."

Brian felt his temper rise and made an effort to speak matter-of-factly. "Look, Roger. I was close to Nalin's mother many years ago. My brother married her. He died and now I'm trying to help Nalin with whatever problems she's got. I'd appreciate it if you'd stop suggesting that I'm trying to take her to bed."

Roger stared thoughtfully at Brian for two or three seconds, then shook his head and smiled a sheepish grin. "Hey, pardner, my apologies. Workin' in here ever' day"—he gestured about the bar—"sometimes I forget people have other relationships than sex. Apology accepted?"

"No problem. Forget it."

"I did hear from Oy that you were a monk in Thailand once and speak pretty good Thai. And when I heard you call Lek 'Nalin' I figured you weren't just some horny tourist on his first trip to Bangkok. And it's pretty obvious Nalin don' belong in a Patpong bar." Roger waved a flower-seller away. "You gettin' closer to solvin' the mystery of what she's doin' here?"

"Not yet. I did manage to catch up with Bob Donnelly though."

At the mention of Bob's name, Roger's eyes narrowed and his smile hardened. The music stopped and the dancer pried Roger's arms from her waist. "I go dance now." Roger patted her on her buttocks. "All right, sweetheart. Shake it, don't break it." Roger stared after her. "So how *is* Bob these days? I cain't say that I've seen him lately."

Brian noticed the same cautious undertone he'd felt when he had mentioned Roger's name to Bob; barely concealed animosity underneath an attitude of nonchalance. "He's doing fine. Busy with all kinds of business deals."

Roger chugged his beer and signaled for another. "I'll bet."

"I get the distinct impression you and Bob have had a bit of a falling out."

Roger lit a cigarette. "Bulls-eye! Except, we never really had a falling in."

"Any particular reason—even though it's none of my business?"

"If I told you what I don't like about "Uncle" Bob it would take all night. But for starters after I arrived in Bangkok a job I had lined up fell through. I ran into Bob at a couple of get-togethers with foreign correspondents and Vietnam vets. He approached me about starting up a company with him. I didn't have anything else going so I agreed. At the time I thought it kind of strange that somebody like that would approach me to join him in business. It just didn't figure. But later I realized that old Bob likes to associate with 'colorful' people; people he sees as men of action. He gets some kind of charge out of it."

Roger stroked his cheek scar. "Anyway, let's just say I didn't like much about Bob or about the way he does business. I may be just a dumb Alabama hillbilly that loves his female flesh soft, succulent and young but there are some things *I* call obscene."

Brian glanced at the fishtank in which tropical fish swam amid coral formations, colored stones and vegetation. Like the girls themselves, they had been uprooted from their natural environment and released as part of a display in which they were to cavort, entertain and please the onlooker.

The dancer who had pried herself from Roger's arms threw Roger a kiss as she danced. Roger saluted her with his glass. "Dang, darlin', you're beautiful!" Roger glanced at Brian as if seeking confirmation.

"She is pretty," Brian said. "Also the only one I've seen without a Buddha around her neck."

Roger chuckled. "Yep. The Horny Toad's only Catholic. Somebody started a rumor that she transmits lots of VD. Probably a jealous dancer. Anyway, until I put a stop to it, customers were referrin' to her as 'Our Lady of Perpetual Aids.'"

Brian began to understand that, not unlike the young people of Manhattan's East Village, the dancers of Patpong belonged to an outcast society, a demimonde in which provocative dance, insistent rhythm, ebullient music, bawdy humor and daring dress were all elements of a common language, a common sanctuary and a common armor.

Roger shook his head in admiration. "She got some figure for a girl pushin' thirty and she's parlayed it into a pile of money. Been married to three guys—American, French and then an Aussie. She got one house in Pattaya and an apartment in Bangkok. That's one little number that won't be goin' back to the ricefields when her tits start to sag, let me tell you."

"*You're* not married are you, Roger? If you don't mind my asking."

"I don't mind at all. I was married to a girl from Baton Rouge. Divorced." Roger suddenly stood up. "Got one son with a Thai lady, though. Come on, I'll show you."

Roger led Brian through a narrow hallway at the back of the bar, its darkness almost untouched by flashing lights. On the wall of the hallway was a bulletin board of brown cork backing to which were pinned announcements, photographs, newspaper clippings and postcards from former bargirls now working abroad.

The first door had plastic white letters pasted unevenly across which spelled out, "Changing Room." The letter "C" had accidently or intentionally been removed and the sign now read, "hanging Room." Roger's office door had a drawing above the doorknob, a caricature of a sleeping Roger, his belly, chest hair and beer glass greatly exaggerated. Neatly printed letters spelled out: Lips That Touch Liquor Shall Never Touch Mine.

Roger's office was tiny and cluttered. Along one wall photographs of various sharpness and size depicted dancers and waitresses who had long since left the Horny Tiger. Still older photographs of Roger and his helicopter crews lined another wall. The scenes progressed from Ft. Wolters, Texas and Ft. Rucker, Alabama, to Qui Nhon, Vietnam. A large photograph of several men in fatigues grouped before a helicopter had been signed for Roger by the men of the 92nd Assault helicopter Company. It was in that picture that Roger's facial scar first appeared. Brian guessed it to be a shrapnel scar of battle.

Roger picked up a photograph on his desk and handed it to Brian. It was a snapshot of Roger and a child about three or four years old sitting on Roger's shoulders. The child was laughing and pointing to whoever was taking the picture. Brian returned the photograph. "Very nice."

Roger replaced it on the desk. "Yep. Four years old and already overweight. Just like his daddy. Shows you what can happen when the Bible belt meets the bikini belt."

Brian noticed that Roger failed to volunteer the name of the mother. But it seemed less from any feeling of shame than from a traditional Asian attitude that the mother was less important than the son.

Roger plucked a bottle of Mehkong Whiskey from the shelf. "Drink?"

"No, thanks. I've still got one sitting on the bar."

Roger poured himself a drink and slumped into his chair. "Well, you go on along, then. I've got some bookkeeping to do. I'll be there eventually."

Brian stopped at the bulletin board. The board was cluttered with photographs of bargirls sitting on the laps of men or clowning with customers at a bar party. Brian recognized Dang, Oy and others now working in the bar. It was only after he had glanced at all of them that he realized he had been looking for

Nalin. He felt a genuine sense of relief that she wasn't in any of the photographs.

Just as he again sat at the bar Nalin appeared and stood beside him with her hands folded on the counter. "Hi, Uncle Brian." Brian swiveled on his stool to face her. "Hi. You certainly are busy tonight."

"Too many customers and they all like to talk to girls."

"Stop being modest. They all like to talk to you." Brian waved to Maew. "Maew. A drink for the lady. What would you like?" Nalin sat on a stool. "You don't have to do that, Uncle Brian."

"I *want* to do that, Little Tadpole. What time does the bar close?"

"One o'clock."

"I'll drop you off on the way back to the hotel. If that's all right with you."

"Sure, it's all right. I mean, it's fine with me." Brian reflected that she seemed genuinely pleased. She raised her glass. "Cheers. And thanks for the drink."

As a Whitney Houston number was replaced by the sounds of Carly Simon, Nalin drank a sip and stood up. "I have to dance now. See you after I change."

"I'll be here."

Brian stared at the Buddha shrine, a small shelf crammed with symbols of Buddhism and objects of popular superstition. They reminded him of Suntharee's Buddha room. His sudden memory of her was so vivid and detailed that he felt both guilt and longing in equal proportion. He knew he should be more persistent in his attempts to solve the mystery of her daughter's behavior so that he could return to her. Yet not only did he feel himself enjoying Nalin's company but his tolerance of Bangkok's nightlife was turning to fondness and the realization made him slightly ill at ease.

The constant passage of bikini-clad dancers—complete with physical contact—as they squeezed past customers to climb onto or off stages served as an effective aphrodisiac. Glasses and ashtrays jerked and clinked the length of the bar in encouraging response to the dancers' energetic steps. Fish swam faster and, possibly, more warily.

He noticed a Lionhead Goldfish staring at him as if in interrogation and he began to think about what he was going to tell

Suntharee. He had found her daughter. She was indeed a bargirl. She was also in good health, intelligent, beautiful, popular and—for no reason Brian had yet discovered—she despised her mother. Nalin's place on a stage had been taken by a half-black, half-Thai dancer gyrating to the music in a wet-look nylon bikini, dinosaur earrings and brown boots. The girl, no doubt the product of a GI father and Thai mother during the Vietnam War, suddenly caused Brian to think of his brother and the way he had died. He felt something gnawing at him, as if he should be remembering or recognizing something important.

Nalin had not danced the last two numbers so as the music ended, she emerged from the changing room ready to leave. She wore a white blouse tucked into a pair of jeans. Her long hair bounced behind her as she walked quickly to Boonsom's cubical and took her handbag from the shelf. She waved to Oy and stood beside Brian. "I'm all ready, Uncle Brian."

Brian finished his beer and stood up. The fast music and flashing lights died abruptly and in the silence and the bright, unflattering lights of regular but powerful tungsten bulbs, the Horny Tiger changed in atmosphere from a bewitching, seductive and infamous lounge into a very ordinary room smelling of garlic, Thai beer, nicotine and sweat.

# 21

A S their samlor sped erratically through Bangkok's streets, Brian kept one arm around Nalin and one braced against a metal sidebar. Along the wider streets and lanes, the facades of squat, concrete buildings with dark interiors were illuminated by fluorescent lights; concrete and fluorescence—Bangkok's twin symbols.

They stopped the samlor in a lane near Nalin's apartment building. Nalin bargained with the driver to return to the Oriental, then thanked Brian for taking her home. As she prepared to leap from the samlor, Brian again tried to question her. "Nalin, I still don't know what it is that attracts you about that bar, but the point is I can't remain in Thailand forever. If there's something I can do to help you, you've got to let me know soon."

She slid closer to him, a subtle movement which made his arm around her seem like a sign of intimacy rather than a gesture of protection. "Do you still love my mother?"

Brian felt unnerved by the question and by the directness of her stare. "Hey! I'm asking the questions here. It was your letter that brought me here. So, you owe me an explanation."

"But you thought the letter was from her. I need to know you're not. . . ."

"Her puppet? Look, you're getting damned personal this evening so let me ask you something personal: What is your relationship to Roger?"

She stared at him in genuine surprise and amusement and then laughed loudly enough to cause the driver to turn and grin. "Roger is nothing to me. He is like a big brother to Oy; can't you see that?"

"That may be but he'd certainly like to take you out."

Nalin climbed out of the samlor and stood facing him. "Roger likes to take all the girls out. And Oy wants to go to America to live. Roger feels he should help her out."

"He owes her something?"

She walked a few paces toward her apartment, then turned. Light from her concrete apartment building silhouetted Nalin and a row of banana trees behind her. "Don't forget tomorrow at eleven." She gestured for the driver to go, waved to Brian, and crossed her arms over her chest. The samlor swung around and Brian heard her words from behind after he could no longer see her. "Roger is the father of Oy's baby."

# 22

**B**RIAN sat inside the lobby of the Oriental Hotel waiting for Nalin to arrive. He reread the copy of his telex he was about to send to John Adelman in New York, detailing printing and shipping costs and turnaround time for both guide-books and novels.

The low costs and quality printing more than justified his proposal to print in Asia and he felt the success of a fiction program was now a very real possibility. Yet he also perceived that something in Thailand was accelerating a change in him, a change which had begun even before he had left New York. He could feel something within him slowly building, something that might prove powerful enough even to overshadow his interest in the success of his publishing goals.

The night before he had written a long letter to his son. He had also called Ayudhya and, over a very bad connection, had spoken to Suntharee. He spoke about his meetings with Nalin in as upbeat a manner as he could and then mentioned his meeting with Bob Donnelly. The poor quality of the connection and the necessary shouting made any attempt at intimacy impossible. He had promised to do his best to persuade Nalin to return home and then return to Ayudhya himself.

The public relations people of the Oriental were helping him set up meetings with Thai novelists as well as with other Asian writers who were flying in for the ASEAN awards ceremony. As he reflected on their writing, he settled back into his chair and relaxed. He had found three writers for his series: one Chinese, one Thai, one Indonesian, and he felt pleased with himself. Whatever was keeping him unsettled and apprehensive had nothing to do with his publishing program.

He watched Nalin walk toward him through the lobby, wearing a red belted white dress and a red ribbon tying her long black hair in a pony tail. The colors enhanced the beauty of her light brown skin. He could see several men in the lobby turn to stare at her as she walked. She plopped herself down in the chair opposite him and let out a long sigh. "Hi, Uncle Brian. Sorry I'm late. Traffic is bad again."

Brian knew from long experience that suggesting to Thais that they allow enough time for traffic-clogged roads—i.e. a Western logical approach—would elicit only puzzled and slightly amused stares.

"No problem, sweetheart. Would you like a drink before we go?"

"No, thank you." She picked up a guidebook someone had left on a table.

Brian finished his drink and looked at the last line of his telex to New York: "I should be back in NY by the end of next week."

He looked at Nalin and suddenly realized his 'indigestion' was in fact irritation at the thought of leaving and that he simply was not ready to return to New York. He knew he could not yet articulate what personal realization he had to experience in Thailand, but he was certain there was one, and that, if he left now, he would feel dissatisfied for the rest of his life.

He felt a growing confidence that, if he could only stay long enough, something would yet happen which would clarify everything, leaving him fulfilled and certain that he had done what it was he had come to do; that he had found what it was he had come to discover.

He wanted to be able to look back on this period of his life—on this journey—on Suntharee, Nalinpilai and on Thailand itself, with pleasure, nostalgia and a sense of accomplishment. The emotional needs that Suntharee's—or rather, Nalin's—letter had unleashed had to be satisfied or at least understood before he returned to resume his former existence.

Brian crossed out the last line of the telex and printed carefully: "Work with writers going well but am not yet able to give firm date for return. However, after next week my expenses here will be charged to my personal account not company's; also, time spent will be charged to personal leave."

Nalin thumbed through a guidebook. "Are you writing a letter to someone?"

"I'm sending a telex to New York telling them that I'll be

staying in Thailand a bit longer than I thought."

"Really! That's wonderful, Uncle Brian. But . . . why don't you just call them?"

"Because then I would have to explain my actions and the truth is there is no real business reason for me to stay here beyond next week."

Her eyes narrowed and her lips lengthened into a smile. "Another reason?"

"Never mind. It's just that, for now, I would like to avoid speaking with anyone in New York about my trip. And a telex is just the answer for one taking the coward's way out." They rose and began walking through the lobby.

"Do you always take the coward's way out, Uncle Brian?"

"Only when I can find it, sweetheart, only when I can find it."

# 23

BRIAN sat beside one of several mythological animals on the upper terrace of a Bangkok temple. He leaned into the shade of a banyan tree to avoid the glare of the sunlight as it poured out of a dirty blue sky to reflect off the shards of Chinese porcelain embedded in a nearby wall.

He watched Nalin carefully place a square of gold gilt onto the chin of a Buddha. She stared at the statue for several seconds, then turned and walked to Brian. As he watched her, Brian reflected that she seemed to combine aspects of an ingenue and a sophisticate in equal proportions. Together they walked beside a wall mural depicting scenes from the Tale of Rama, King of Ayudhya.

Nalin stopped in front of a scene depicting Rama about to shoot an arrow at a graceful gazelle in a forest. "You see how Rama was tricked by sorcery into believing an evil demon was actually a beautiful antelope?" She turned to face him. "Would you be able to tell the difference, Uncle Brian?"

Brian smiled. He had given up any hope of breaking her habit of calling him "Uncle." He had also begun to sense a certain flirtatiousness in the way she spoke the word to him. "I might. If I knew what you were talking about. Am I under a spell?"

To Brian's surprise, tears welled in her eyes and she hugged him briefly but with surprising strength. He placed his arms around her but she stepped back and hailed a taxi. "I'm going to the university to meet some friends, Uncle Brian."

She squeezed his hand, then released it. "Are you coming to the bar tonight?"

"I seem to be spending every night in the bar."

"And why is that, Uncle Brian?"

Her mischievous smile caught Brian off guard. As he stared

at her, he began to suspect, perhaps for the first time, that at least part of his interest in her predicament (and his willingness to spend time in the bar) had been a convenient pretext. While he inwardly wondered if he was deceiving himself about his own motives, he smiled as nonchalantly as possible and answered. "Maybe I love to watch tropical fish while listening to Roger's war stories. Now, no more questions. There'll be enough of those when Barron Books gets my telex."

# 24

BOB Donnelly's dinner had cleared away the layers of nostalgia and warmth through which Brian had remembered him and forced him to focus sharply on Bob the man rather than on Bob the memory.

There had been eight couples at dinner including a Japanese businessman and his wife, a German businessman and his wife, a Thai diplomat and his wife, and Bob and his wife. A wealthy Chinese-Thai widow had been invited to keep the sexes evenly balanced. Bob had been a gracious host and attentive to detail but for Brian the dinner had proved not only boring but interminable and irritating.

It was a gathering at which people had little in common except a penchant for collecting Thai antiques and for collecting gossip about the various affairs of well-placed persons in the kingdom. Brian found them not only unkind, snobbish and unpleasant but they also seemed to combine the worst traits of certain expatriates—greed and ignorance. Much of the conversation was given over to undisguised envy and admiration for acquaintances who had made a great deal of money by smuggling antiques out of Thailand to Europe or America or Japan. Brian felt he was surrounded by grasping philistines who did not so much live *in* Asia as *off* Asia.

It soon became clear to him that Bob was using his 'New York publisher friend' to impress his acquaintances and using his successful, upper-class business associates to impress him. At dinner, little had changed. Only now Bob boasted not about his contacts with full bird colonels, but about how many 'important' paintings he owned and how many employees he had.

Brian's irritation led him to leave shortly after and to head for the hotel. Inside the taxi, he thought of how unpleasant it was to admit that a former friend had become a pompous, social-climbing snob. Or, as Unicorn had said, "Everybody bullshits but Bob is the only man I ever seen who believes his own bullshit!"

While the taxi was trapped in the inevitable traffic jam, Brian began examining his feelings toward Nalin; feelings about which he was becoming more and more uneasy. He was supposed to be helping her if and when she would let him and then sort out his relationship with her mother. Yet, he knew that his feelings for Nalin were becoming less avuncular and more romantic. Perhaps Roger—shrewd judge of people that he was—had read his motivation better than he could himself. And he considered the possibility that, despite her denial, Roger was the reason she had taken work in the bar. When he thought of the bar, he remembered Roger's solitary drinking in his gloomy office, Oy's fascination with the Statue of Liberty, Dang's flirtatious behavior with any man who entered the. . . .

Even before he had finished the thought, the bulletin board photographs of Dang formed in his mind with perfect clarity. He suddenly realized what it was that was bothering him; what it was that he had overlooked.

He leaned forward and asked the driver to take him to Patpong Road. Fast.

## 25

BRIAN opened the door of the Horny Tiger and walked straight to the bulletin board. He quickly removed a snapshot and brought it to the disc jockey's cubicle. He slipped inside, sat on a stool and shined Boonsom's flashlight on the photograph: A bikini-clad Dang sat on the lap of an extremely thin and very drunk customer who smiled aggressively out at the camera. The man's hair was thinning and he appeared to need a shave. He held a beer glass high above Dang's head with drunken abandon. Dang made no attempt to mask her bored and sullen expression.

Brian replaced the flashlight on the shelf beside Boonsom's stereo equipment. He spotted Nalin among a group of dancers at the bar dutifully listening to Maew's lecture on proper bargirl behavior with customers. She gave him a puzzled smile but Brian had already turned away to search for Dang.

He spotted her standing beside the bar, dropping the leftovers of a spicy Thai snack into the fishtank. Piscicidal bits of red-and-green chilies made their way to the bottom of the tank falling upon the diver and among darting splashes of fish like manna from heaven. The offering was quickly devoured in a frantic rush of fins and tails. She saw him approach in the mirror and turned to greet him. "Hi, Blian."

Brian leaned across the bar and held the photograph out for her. "Dang, can you tell me anything about the man in the picture?"

Dang stared at the picture and wrinkled her nose as if at a bad smell. "Him no good. Cheap Charlie. Butterfly every girl. Always get drunk then have big mouth."

"When was this picture taken?"

She scratched at her raised vaccination welt lining one shoulder like an epaulet. "Maybe three, four months ago."

"Does he come in here often?"

"No. He tell me he work for Chinatown big boss. Him no good. He—" Dang paused, suddenly aware that she might be insulting Brian. "He your friend?"

Brian shook his head. "Do you know his name?"

"I think he say 'John.' No, wait. I think . . . 'Phil.' Yes. 'Phil Johnson.'"

Brian sighed audibly. "Would you know where I can find him?"

"Chinatown. He make big talk how he take care Dragon Club. On Yaowarat Road—big road in Chinatown, you know?"

"I know."

Dang reached into a small bag on the bar and extracted a crisp brown locust recently fried in oil. She snapped off its head and legs and popped the remainder of the rainy season delicacy into her mouth like popcorn. Brian noticed the nearby ashtray overflowing with tiny wings, claws, knotted antenna, twig-like tibia, flattened femur, compound eyes and mashed mandibles. The scene reminded him of a Khmer Rouge killing ground. "Everybody know Dragon Club for do drugs."

"Thanks, Dang."

Dang gripped her side with both hands. "It hurt here."

"What does?"

"No. Not mean now. When he squeeze me. It hurt too much! So I say to him why you have gun inside shirt?" Dang spoke while continuing her snack: 'snap,' 'crackle' and 'pop' and, finally, a very noticeable, blood-curdling 'crunch'. "At first, he too much angry me then he jus' laugh."

Brian handed Dang the photograph and walked out of the Horny Tiger. As the door closed, Roger stood beside Dang. He took the photograph from her and studied it in the flame of his cigarette lighter.

"Blian I think him want to find this man."

Roger thoughtfully rubbed the shrapnel scar on his cheek, the result of an enemy bullet ricocheting inside his chopper over 20 years before. He remembered thinking how, as he had flown over hostile territory, the VC and their AK-47's had been right under his nose. He put the photograph in his pocket.

Dang popped another locust into her mouth and stared up at him. "Ploblem?"

"Nope. It just may be that once again I didn't see somethin's that's been under my nose all along."

# 26

BRIAN walked into the Dragon Club and waited briefly by the door for his eyes to adjust to the room's semi-darkness. The nightclub's spacious area was filled with layers of circling cigarette smoke and forced feminine laughter. Its plush leather booths, brass table tops and velvet curtains had been manufactured in the favorite Chinese color scheme: red and green. Gaudy but lucky. Heavily made up Chinese-Thai girls in glittering evening gowns sat beside Chinese-Thai businessmen who paid for their company.

Brian followed a waitress in a clinging cheongsam to a seat at a long wooden bar which served as the body of a dragon. At one end, a carved dragon's head extended toward the door. Its eyes stared out at new arrivals from a gold head complete with horns, tongue and teeth. If the carver's intention had been to create ferocity, it had been thwarted by someone's decision to paint the neck an incongruous pink. At the far end of the bar, the tail jutted out to complete the beast's ludicrous appearance.

Brian leaned back to look down the bar. Besides himself, there were only two customers. A Chinese man sat drinking and talking in a drunken slur to a bored bartender, and beyond him, on a stool nearest the fierce red eyes of the dragon, sat the man in the photograph.

Brian picked up his beer and sat beside the man. He was even thinner than when Brian had known him. The man stared at his drink without acknowledging Brian's presence. Brian lit a cigarette and looked at the man's reflection in the mirror. "Phil Johnson?"

The man spoke without looking up. "Who wants to know?"

"I was told you were working in a bank somewhere in the midwest."

"You were told wrong. Now fuck off."

From somewhere behind them, a Chinese singer began pouring her heart into a Mandarin Chinese rendition of *Greensleeves*.

"You always were a mean drunk." The man slowly lifted his head. Brian saw his eyes narrow and focus on his own reflection in the mirror. "Even when you were known as Bill Jackson."

The man turned to face Brian. His thin, pockmarked face was that of an alcoholic. He took a long drink from his whiskey glass and spoke into the melting ice cubes. "It can't be you because you died up there."

"No. My brother died up there. Paul. I'm Brian. Remember?"

Brian noticed the man's hand begin to shake. A small tattoo of a four-masted sailing ship caught in rough seas decorated the back of his hand. Brian guessed that when he rolled his fingers, the ship tossed in the waves. "Brian. So you're back."

"I'm back."

Bill Jackson seemed to weigh certain possibilities carefully. Finally, he sighed. "So, you want to talk about it."

"So I want to talk about what?"

He looked again at Brian and then stared at the red-and-green wall pennants with Chinese characters of good fortune. After several seconds he seemed to come to a conclusion. "OK, first things first. If I don't take a piss, I'll go blind. Then, you want to talk about your brother, we'll talk."

Ten minutes later, Brian entered the men's room. Bill Jackson had disappeared.

# 27

OVER the next several days, Brian continued to meet with writers arriving from ASEAN countries as well as with local expatriates. Several seemed promising but, to his surprise, he found his thoughts straying from the task of locating writers of quality fiction, and more focused on his relationship with Nalin.

Almost as if by unspoken agreement, when inside the Horny Tiger, they seldom spoke beyond basic pleasantries and humorous comments on bar life. It was as if they were involved in a clandestine love affair and had decided to show no intimacy when in the presence of anyone they knew. And, yet, with the exception of holding hands when crossing a street or climbing into a boat, their occasions together had, on the surface, never gone beyond affectionate friendship.

Yet Brian knew there was a growing emotional attraction between them. He felt both confusion and unease at its presence, but, as he reluctantly admitted to himself, an undeniable anticipation at something yet unknown to him, something both undefined and uncertain. He also wondered if whatever was developing between them, though still lacking in shape and definition, could lead to a betrayal of his promise to Suntharee and even of his responsibility to Paul himself.

They had spent most of a bright Wednesday afternoon with Oy and her son at her mother's canalside-restaurant to the north of Bangkok. Just after dark, during a long taxi ride back into the city, Nalin had invited Brian to her apartment for coffee. Brian had accepted.

An elderly Thai watchman opened the gate. The light from the building fell across his brown crinkled face and open mouth filled with gold teeth. His enormous belly drooped over his beltless shorts like an overripe papaya. He briefly shined his flashlight to guide their steps.

Brian passed through the small living room and walked onto the tree-shaded balcony which allowed a partial view of well-kept houses, spacious lawns, shrubbery and trees. It was almost as if modern Bangkok with its highrises and traffic jams had disappeared and been replaced by what had been years before.

Nalin stared at Brian quizzically as he returned from the balcony. "Sit down, Uncle Brian. I'll make some coffee."

"Coffee will be fine. I like your apartment." She made no reply and disappeared into the kitchen while Brian wondered how many times he said that meaningless phrase to women in New York.

He walked slowly around the living room. One wall was covered with several rows of books, in Thai and English. English primers lay beside Hawthorne's *Scarlet Letter* and Flaubert's *Madame Bovary*. A disintegrating, one-eyed teddy bear sat propped against a stack of Thai magazines. Cassette tapes lay sprawled beside a recorder. The tape already installed was Barbra Streisand's *Memory*.

Brian pressed the start button and sat on the couch facing the opposite wall. There, above a rowing machine and several potted plants, was a large surrealistic oil painting of Buddhist symbols transformed into phantasmagoric silver and gold images of bright suns above gilded temples and meditating monks on lotuses nearly as high as the temple roofs. The emaciated skeletal form of the fasting Buddha dominated the scene.

The decoration and every item in the sparsely furnished living room gave evidence of belonging to someone of intelligence and daring. The decor and choice of books and music might reflect the inchoate personality of youth but there was not one item in sight to suggest that the occupant of the apartment was—or ever had been—a girl who worked in a bar.

Nalin returned with a tray of coffee and Thai fruit. While Brian held the tray, she pulled out a small metal table from under the couch and unfolded it. Its painted design was that of an idealized Teutonic town of centuries ago where men of the arts in quaint dress gathered at cafes to create and exchange ideas. "You take sugar, right?"

"Sure. Two lumps and milk as well. Here, I'll do it."

She sat in the chair facing him. Each of them took up toothpicks and began eating small wedge-shaped pieces of pineapple.

Brian felt slightly embarrassed at the situation but still more unnerved because of his growing confusion of emotions toward her. He wondered how much his unease showed. "I see you kept the teddy bear. Can you still remember when you fell?" "I remember. And I remember when you gave it to me." She looked toward the teddy bear as someone might gaze upon a terminally ill friend. "I had to buy you something to keep your mind off the pain." She lifted up her dress and examined her knee. "There was more blood than pain. Anyway, the scar is almost gone." "There isn't much left of the teddy bear, either."

They listened in silence to Barbra Streisand finish singing *You Don't Bring Me Flowers, Anymore*, followed by the loud backfiring of a samlor turning in a nearby lane.

Brian spoke softly. "Nalinpilai Wanpen."

She stopped suddenly just as she was about to bite on a slice of pineapple. "Yes?"

"Oh, nothing. I was just saying your name. 'Beautiful Lotus in the Full Moon.' Thai names are incredible. But yours fits very well."

She stared at him thoughtfully for several seconds. "Do you think I'm beautiful?"

"Very beautiful. I always knew you would be. Just like. . . ." Brian let the sentence trail off.

Nalin spoke harshly. "I am not like her." Then her voice softened. "And I am not a little girl now. I'm as old as she was when you met her; when daddy married her."

Brian thought about the fact that she referred to Paul as 'daddy.' "You're the same age, but I'm not. You've still got a lot of growing up to do and I've got a lot of growing old to do. That's the big difference."

"You talk like you're an old man. You're still young. I. . . ." Nalin stared at him and left the sentence unfinished.

Brian realized that the character of their relationship was about to be settled and he knew he had made a mistake in accepting her invitation. He had been flattered by the apparent infatuation of a beautiful, young woman, and he could forgive himself for that; but now was the time to avoid doing anything he might later regret. He quickly finished his coffee. "Well, I'd better be off." Nalin crossed over to him and moved the tray aside.

Brian started to rise. "How easy is it to get a taxi out here? I'd better—"

Nalin suddenly leaned into him, threw her arms around him and kissed him hard. Brian held her and then gently took her face in his hands and pulled her away. There were tears in her eyes. "I don't want you to go. I want you to hold me and love me like daddy loved her."

"Little Tadpole—"

"I'm not 'Little Tadpole'. Why can't you see me as I am?"

They stared at each other for several seconds. Barbra Streisand sang about fairytales and love.

"You can sleep on the couch. But don't go. Not tonight."

"Will you tell me why you've become a dancer in a—"

She shook her head. ". . . I can't. Not yet. But I will."

Brian smiled. "OK, I'll sleep here. Now, dry those beautiful brown eyes and get me some pillows."

Brian was awakened by neither noise nor light but by the presence of someone near him. He opened his eyes and saw Nalin standing beside the couch staring down at him. She was dressed in bra and panties and an open bathrobe. As he stared up at her she sat on the edge of the couch and held his head in her hands.

"Nalin?"

She brought her face closer to his and stared into his eyes. Her hair cascaded around her face, framing it as a portrait. Finally, she stopped a few inches from his face and spoke softly but with determination. "I am a *woman*."

He sat up and stared at her impossibly exotic eyes, delicate nose and generous mouth with full, richly curved lips. Then she was kissing him, first tentatively and then more insistently. He held her shoulders lightly and then gently began pushing her away. When she responded by clinging to him more tightly, he embraced her head and shoulders . "Nalin." When he heard his own voice he realized it was more a voice of passion than a voice of protest.

Her only response was to run one hand over his face with her fingers lingering on his lips. He felt his resistance waver and a surge of desire passed from her fingers onto his lips and through his body. She looked up at him and then put her head down again, still holding him. She suddenly stood up and took his hands and tugged. He let her pull him to his feet and lead him into the bedroom.

The room was lit only by the digital clock of a video machine and a small bedside lamp. He stood by the bed in his underwear. Nalin lay on her back and looked up at him. "I am a woman. I love you. I want you to make love to me."

Brian knew he wasn't going to resist but some sense of guilt toward someone or something—whether to a real person or to his own impossible dream—made him want to be the one seduced.

She unhooked her bra revealing the perfect form of her breasts and raised her arms to him. He knelt beside her on the bed and stroked her from face to knees and back to her face. Then he lay beside her and kissed her face and cupped his hand over one of her breasts.

As she turned and hugged him he slid down and kissed her neck and breasts. She began to moan softly and as he moved his hands over her body he could hear her calling his name like an invocation.

Some of her awkwardness in the final act of undressing was transferred to him but when she again held him, clung to him, he felt a great surge of both tenderness and passion for her. They held each other for at least half a minute, kissing and looking into each other's eyes.

Brian gently pushed her down on the bed and began making love to her. His movements were slow and tentative, then, once certain she was not in pain, firm and regular.

When she climaxed she arched her back, turned her body away from him and gripped his shoulders—all with the surprising strength that sexual consummation bestows.

He lay beside her on the bed and held her in his arms. She glanced up at him and stared into his eyes for several seconds, then slid even deeper into his arms. "I want you to hug me. Hug me a lot," she said.

Brian hugged her and whispered to her to sleep, but they lay awake together for a long time. After she finally fell asleep, Brian glanced about the room, still unevenly lit by the weak bulb of a desk lamp and by the eerie green digital numerals of the clock. He held her for a long time, surprised at the depth of his own joy at being with her like this and irritated by the difficulty of understanding his own emotions. He knew beyond any doubt that the tender affection he once had for her was gone, now replaced by something much stronger than simple fondness. He was still trying to analyze what had taken its place when he fell asleep.

# 28

WILLIAM Jackson sat at the bar of the Dragon Club speaking angrily into the bar phone. In the mirror along the wall, his red face stared back at him from between imitations of traditional wine jugs lining the counter. "You should a fuckin' told me he was in Bangkok. *That* is the point. . . . No, asshole, I didn't say anything to him. I got the hell out of here. But how long before he finds me again? I can't stay out of this place forever . . . Yeah, well, you *better* fix it so I don't have to worry. 'Cause it's your ass as well as mine . . . that's good. that's real good. You just keep on remembering that. . . Yeah, the canal house, but when . . . ? Yeah, well, don't 'wait and see' too long, asshole. He starts sniffin' around, we both could. . . . Hey, I know how to keep *my* mouth shut. I been doing it for twenty years. And my mouth stays shut as long as the payments keep coming. You better remember that!"

Jackson slammed the phone down and took a long drink. He spoke to his mirror reflection. "He should have told me Brian was in town. . . ." Jackson stared at the amber liquid in his glass and let his memory drift lazily back to the Bangkok he and Brian had known during the war, and then to the reconnaissance team firefight in the Vietnamese Highlands and how Paul died. He took another long drink. "I got nothing against you, Brian. But you should have stayed away. . . . What the hell." He unsteadily raised his glass in salute then lowered it without drinking and spoke angrily to his mirror image. "Christ, don't this fuckin' war ever end?"

# 29

BRIAN woke to the melancholy sounds of Bach's *Concerto for Two Violins and String Orchestra* coming from the living room. He glanced about the bedroom. A calendar with scenes of Thai classical dancing hung above shelves filled with stuffed animals, books, tapes and various brands of cosmetics. Next to the bed was a white jar of Mudd Mask. A typewriter had been placed on a shelf with a stuffed monkey propped into position as a typist.

He straightened the colorful hilltribe quilt, turned off the floor fan, put on his underpants and squeezed into the robe Nalin had left on the bed. He walked to a sunlit shelf of photographs and picked them up, one after the other: Nalin as a baby being held by her Thai father, a handsome man with a kind face; Brian and Paul, both barechested and in shorts, holding aloft a beaming three-year-old Nalin; a teenage Nalin with a seductive stare in a one-piece bathing suit lying on a huge floating pad of a Royal Water Lily. The circular leaf was a glossy green, its edges turned up to reveal a rusty red pattern which closely matched Nalin's bathing suit in both color and design. Nalin, about 20, dressed in a traditional silk Thai outfit surrounded by friends at a party; Nalin with no makeup and short hair standing beside a girlfriend—both were in cap-and-gowns and holding diplomas; Nalin and other performers from Bangkok's Fine Arts Department posing in front of a mosque in Kuala Lumpur and again in front of Jakarta's National Museum; a photograph of Nalin and other actors on stage in what looked like a dress rehearsal of Romeo and Juliet; Nalin sitting at the bar of the Horny Tiger with Oy on her lap—both were making faces at the camera; a photograph of Roger at New Year's Eve surrounded by over a dozen bargirls in Harlequin masks and party hats. The girls pressed close to Roger's smiling, lipstick-smeared face. There was no photograph of Suntharee.

He walked into the living room. Nalin sat stiffly upright on the rowing machine, deep in concentration as she slid forward and then rowed herself slowly backward while exhaling loudly. She was dressed in a pair of light blue shorts, white T-shirt and white socks. Brian watched her complete several repetitions. "You getting ready for the next Olympics, Beautiful?"

She turned to him and quickly looked away. As she did so her face flushed and the speed of her repetitions increased. Brian could sense her nervousness beneath her attempt at insouciance. "You finally get up, lazy man?"

"I finally got up, early riser. I didn't know you were an exercise nut."

"Forty-one. Wait a minute, OK? I want to do fifty. I don't want to get fat . . . forty . . . two."

Brian walked to stand beside her. "Take your time. You look more exciting doing that than when you're dancing on stage."

"Forty-three. Maybe I'll bring this to the Horny Tiger. If I get bored with dancing, I can row." She laughed in a slightly abandoned way with her head thrown back. Brian stepped forward and managed to kiss her just before she slid forward again. She stopped rowing, threw her arms around him and kissed him passionately. When she released him, Brian nodded toward the kitchen. "The coffee smells great."

She looked up at him coquettishly and began rowing slowly. "I went out this morning and bought some things while you were asleep, lazy man."

"You did? I didn't even hear you get up. Or go out." Brian walked toward the bedroom. "Oh, nuts. I can't shave without a razor." He watched her row one repetition and spoke jovially. "Maybe you *should* take the rowing machine to the bar. Ask your Uncle Bob."

At the sound of Bob's name, she seemed to stiffen. She stood up and walked toward the kitchen. "I'll get the coffee; you shave, OK?" She smiled mischievously. "There's a razor in the bathroom."

"Thought of everything, did you? All right, sweetheart, I'll shave while you exercise. Take your time."

As Brian passed by the bed, Nalin suddenly jumped on him from behind and together they fell onto the bed. She ended up lying on top of him. He held her tightly and kissed her. "I thought you were making coffee."

"I will. I just wanted . . . you." They kissed again for several moments. Brian looked at the clock. "Hey, Little Tadpole, I've got to get ready. I've got an appointment to see some writers at the Oriental in forty minutes."

Nalin rolled quickly off him and jumped onto the floor. "OK, I'll get coffee. You shave." She threw on a blouse, slipped into sandals and disappeared into the kitchen.

While Brian shaved in water which changed from hot to cold and back again in seconds, he felt the first pangs of conscience and then guilt form and expand inside him, but the truth was when he thought of the night before and of Nalin in his arms, he felt a happiness he had not known for years. He tried to analyze what he felt for Nalin. Was it simply a combination of affection and lust? Was he falling in love with her? Could he love someone as a woman whom he had loved as a child? He had loved Suntharee deeply and in Ayudhya had felt that love stirring again, yet now he made love with the daughter she had sent him to find. To Nalin the situation seemed perfectly acceptable: No one had been hurt and they had enjoyed each other's company. It was fun, *sanuk*, pleasurable. Very practical. Very pragmatic. Very Thai. But what did she *feel*?

First the mother, then the daughter. He felt the razor nick the skin on his neck. His emotions swung back and forth like the temperature of the water itself. No, he wasn't sorry about last night but as he shaved off the foamy lather, each pass with the razor seemed to reveal a deeper guilt and self-loathing than he had ever felt before; not a measure of blame for a specific act, rather the knowledge that he had not conducted himself as he should have according to his own standards, according to that demanding inner voice which dictates each person's understanding of character.

Brian finished shaving quickly and splashed aftershave onto his face and neck several times in a futile attempt to efface the small dots of blood which broke through the surface of his skin like signs of stigmata.

In the kitchen he found the coffee on the table beside a long slice of papaya. Brian sat and squeezed the lime over the soft, pinkish red pulp.

Nalin turned from the sink to place her own breakfast of Thai-style congee on the table. She reacted with shock to the cuts on his neck. "You never shaved before today?"

"Must be the Bangkok weather. It makes my skin tender."

She left the room and reappeared in seconds with a box of tissues. She stood before him with her breasts nearly touching his forehead. "Don't move while I do this." She tore a small piece from a tissue and carefully applied it to his chin. Then she repeated the process several times. Brian watched the delicate, almost reverential, way she placed the bits of tissue to his face and neck, the total concentration in the act itself, and felt an urgent, enormous, inexplicable surge of love for her. He suddenly realized it was the same intent absorption he had seen on her face when she had applied squares of gold leaf to the Buddha statues in the temples they had visited. He pulled her head down to his and began kissing her fervently.

She struggled at first and then sat on his lap responding. He stopped long enough to look at her. A tiny, blood-soaked bit of tissue now stuck to her chin. He kissed her tenderly and any doubts that he loved her were over.

# 30

TWO days later, Brian rented a car and drove to Ayudhya.
He had found it impossible to tell Suntharee the truth
about his relationship with Nalin over the phone—it had
to be discussed in a face-to-face meeting. It had been less than
three weeks since he had promised to help her daughter and
yet, from the moment he arrived at the house, nothing seemed
the same.

Brian had explained that he would be returning to Bangkok
the same afternoon as he had scheduled meetings with writers
the following day—a convenient grain of truth to camouflage a
larger evasion. He felt that his excuse had been blatantly trans-
parent and yet he sensed something in Suntharee closer to relief than disappointment.

They had walked about the grounds of the school and sat
for nearly an hour on a stone bench in the Kingdom of Make
Believe. Sounds of children singing drifted over the diamond-
shaped enclosure but, whether because of his own inner turmoil or because of Suntharee's circumspect behavior, the near
rapture Brian had felt on his first visit had vanished.

He could feel cautious reserve between them and he wondered if it had been there on her part the first time he arrived as
well; and if he had simply been too blinded by nostalgia to see
it. Hadn't she warned that things always get spoiled? What had
she meant?

He spoke of his attempts to question Nalin and his failure to
find out what was wrong. Then he had taken his hand from hers
and finally managed to begin what he had rehearsed in the car
on the way up to Ayudhya. "Suntharee, I'm . . . I'm seeing a lot
of Nalin . . . ."

She had stared at him for just a few seconds and then smiled.
"I'm glad, Brian. She shouldn't be alone now. When you see her

please tell her I love her."

Before he could continue, she had abruptly stood up and together, without touching, they had walked to the house. He had kissed her cheek before getting into the car and tried again to make himself clear. But as soon as he began, she had hugged him and whispered, "Take care, Brian." And then she was a receding figure on a verandah beneath the spreading branches of a breadfruit tree staring at his car as it sped off down the driveway.

On the way back to Bangkok, Brian tried to determine if she had understood him completely. He had wanted to clear the air but it seemed he had only succeeded in complicating matters still further.

As he pulled into the driveway of the Oriental, he remembered his phone call to John Adelman just before leaving New York. Brian had apologized for being moody and preoccupied. He had said he needed a change and the trip to Thailand might give him a second chance at something he thought was lost in the past forever.

John had replied that he hoped it worked out, then he had added, "but be careful of what-might-have-beens; they're usually pretty painful."

# 31

THE buzz of long-tailed boat engines rose and fell as the craft skimmed past the Oriental's seawall. The tinkling sounds of a waitress sorting silverware drifted across the hotel's terrace just reaching Brian's table. He had been sitting for nearly an hour with the three most talented Thai writers he had met since his arrival and was just concluding his briefing on the type of writing he was looking for. ". . . so your question is well taken, Khun Vinai, but don't worry—what we don't want is the cliched novel with Westerners in an Asian setting in which Asians appear only as background. We want Asia involved as an active, integrated—"

Brian looked up at the deep red hair, green eyes and wide belted green summer dress. The three men rose. "Karen! What are you doing in Bangkok?"

"My paper sent me over to cover the latest border flare-up. I just stopped by to say hello. Please sit."

Brian made introductions and a waiter offered Karen a chair. "No, thank you, really. I have to check in with the A.P. office for some advice on getting to the border. Please continue."

"You're staying here?"

Karen laughed. "On my paper's per diem? No way. I'm up the street at the Trocadero."

"Well, stop by tonight for a drink. Dinner if you can. The barbecue here is the best deal in town."

"You've sold me. What time?"

"See you right here at 7:30."

After Karen had left, Brian answered questions on royalty arrangements, Thai translation rights, copyright, advance and deadlines. Brian began an energetic discussion, sometimes debate, by suggesting that their Buddhist beliefs were so much a part of their existence that they colored everything they experienced and also the ways in which they attempted to interpret their experience in their novels. He welcomed the intellectual stimulation as a breath of fresh air.

Finally, the eldest of the three looked to his companions. "Yes?" Both smiled and nodded. "Mr. Mason, I think we have just made a deal. I sincerely hope that you will not be disappointed with what we send you."

Brian shook his outstretched hand, then the others. "Khun Vinai, after having read your work and that of Khun Wattana and Khun Borivat, and after meeting with the three of you, I feel an enormous confidence in my decision to go ahead with this program."

As they rose, Brian returned their *wais* and signed the bill. The atonal music of the tourist show's Thai boxing match increased in rhythm and volume and Brian watched sparrows hop away from the path of camera-laden tourists rushing in the direction of the exotic sounds. He waved goodbye and smiled broadly, even as inwardly he felt his unease grow at Karen's unexpected arrival.

# 32

BRIAN had just finished his shower when the phone rang. He sat in the chair beside a hotel room window and picked up the receiver. Through the window he looked down on waiters in long-sleeved white tunics and black trousers serving tourists colorful drinks in tall glasses. "Hello?"

The voice on the other end of the line was slurred. "You really don' know anything, do you?"

"What happened to you the other night?"

"I had to run an errand. Listen, Brian, ole' friend, you want to talk, I'm your man. What the hell, huh? Bangkok warriors got to stick together. Hey? Ain't that right?"

"That's right, Bill. Or would you prefer 'Phil'? Hey, why the name change?"

"Path of leas' rezistanze, you know wha' I mean? Pub-blicity don' always pay out here, ole' friend."

Brian could hear music in the background. "Yeah, I think I understand."

"Brian, my man, you don' unnerstan' a goddamn thing! hey!"

"What's wrong?"

"Nothing. I jus' spilled my drink. But no need for panic, lots more where that came from. . . ."

"Hello? Bill, you still there?"

"Yeah, I'm here. I was jus' thinkin' 'bou' your brother."

"Yeah, but you never answered my letters about why your patrol—"

"Hey, you know what?"

"What?"

"I don' think you understan' a goddamn thing."

"About *what*?"

"About how it all wen' down."

"Make some sense, Bill."

"Look man, *listen*! I am making *sense*. Just *don't trust anybody*! This call . . . this call is my way of giving you a fair chance. God knows he never had one."

Brian lit a cigarette. "Look, Bill, how about meeting me later tonight?"

"Meeting you?"

"Sure. I'll wait for you in the Horny Tiger bar. On Patpong."

"The Horny Tiger. That's *per*fect. That is perfect."

"What's so perfect about our meeting in the Horny Tiger?"

"Just relax, ole' buddy. Even . . . even if you don't have the questions, I'll give you the goddamn answers. It's just that I'm drunk enough that I thought, bein' you so fuckin' innocent and all . . . fuck it!"

A sharp click and then the dial tone sounded in Brian's ear. He hung up the phone and stared out at the river trying to make sense out of William Jackson's remarks.

# 33

A T 7:15 Brian placed his razor on the marble sink and answered the knock at his room door. He had half expected an inebriated, slovenly William Jackson. Instead, Karen stood in the hallway, looking fresh and summery in a white halter-neck blouse and baggy blue slacks. She leaned back, hands on hips, and gave him a big smile. "Maid service, sir. Make down your bed?"

Brian moved aside and bowed her into the room with the sweep of one arm. "Well, come in. If this is a typical maid, this hotel deserves to be rated first in the world." He held her shoulders and leaned forward to kiss her cheek. She reached up and kissed him on the mouth.

Brian wiped lather from her cheek and chin and went back into the bathroom. "One minute; I'm almost ready."

Karen sat on an armchair near the bed and looked down on the river traffic below. Tangled islands of water hyacinth floated into reflected lights on the river and then disappeared in darkness. A police boat's searchlight snapped on to light up the far shore. Wooden structures swayed and tremored in the unsteady beam of its powerful light. Abruptly, the light went out. "I hope you don't mind that I came early, Brian. I know it's a bit unusual in Thailand. I thought we could have a drink here before we go."

"No problem. Help yourself to the minibar."

"Thanks. But I'll wait for you."

Bright white lights of a river ferry lit up the water and among the passengers Karen could see the saffron robes of several monks standing at the stern. "Have you found much changed since you were here?"

"I haven't seen much yet. Hell of a lot more traffic in this city; I can see that. A lot less green. And some of the strangest architectural creations in the world have replaced beautiful old houses along once quiet lanes—not a very encouraging trend. Too soon to tell though."

"You really love this place, don't you?"

"Thailand? I suppose I do." Brian finished patting aftershave onto his face, put on his shirt, and went to the mini-bar. "So what are we drinking?"

"How about a gin tonic?"

Brian pulled out the small bottle of gin and began mixing the drinks. "Well, you are in luck because I just happen to be the best gin-tonic mixer this side of the Mehkong Delta."

"Not enough to put me to sleep this time, OK?"

"Not to worry." He handed her the drink and sat on the bed facing her. "Cheers."

Brian took a drink and began speaking immediately. "Well, you'll be happy to hear that I've found four additional candidates for the Asian writer's series. An ex-monk, an ex-communist, and two full-time writers. I'm finally beginning to feel confident about finding the talent we need. I may have sounded confident before but . . . ." In the face of Karen's wry smile, Brian let the sentence trail off. "Why am I talking so much?"

"Probably because you're worried about how you'll avoid my question."

Brian took a long drink and stared at her. "Question." He repeated the word softly and slowly as if it were an unfamiliar word assigned to him in a spelling bee.

"The question I came to Bangkok to ask. If you still love her."

Brian finished his drink and looked at his empty glass. "That kind of question deserves a stronger drink. How's yours?"

"Mine is just fine."

He moved to the minibar, mixed a gin tonic and sat down again on the bed. Karen handed him a cigarette she had lit for him.

"Thank you." Brian returned her stare. "All right. I took the train and went up to Ayudhya. I saw her again. It was a nostalgic, bittersweet and, yes, romantic, reunion. She's even more beautiful than before. Lovely."

"So you're saying—"

"But she hadn't sent me the letter. Her daughter, Nalinpilai, sent me the letter pretending it was from her mother because she knew that would get me back here." Brian sat up against the bedboard, took a drink, and continued. "Suntharee was—and is—very worried about her daughter, formerly with the Fine Arts School and with the Drama Department of Thammasat University, who now dances in a go-go bar in Bangkok's nightlife district. She asked me to find her."

After Brian said nothing more, Karen spoke. "And did you find her?"

"I found her and I've spent time with her but she still won't say why she hates her mother and why she left home so suddenly and why she wants to dance in a go-go bar."

"But you do love Suntharee?"

Brian let some time pass before answering. He studied the light sparkling off Karen's diamante earrings. "I thought I did when I first saw her."

"And now?"

"Now I know I'm not in love with her. Only fond of her and all that she represents: Thailand as I knew it—before townhouses, shopping centers and traffic jams; before my brother died; before I grew older."

Karen tapped her fingers gently and repeatedly into the fingerbowl as if in time to an unheard melody. Finally, she spoke. "Then what about us?"

Brian looked into his glass and then stared into Karen's eyes. "Karen, I've fallen in love with her daughter, Nalinpilai."

As Karen's eyes widened, the green of her irises seemed to deepen. She sat motionless in thought, looked toward the floor, then back to Brian. "You probably thought that about now I'd be making some artfully phrased wise crack to put you in your place. Well, I'm resisting but . . . now *I* need a stronger drink."

Brian got her one and sat down again.

"I know. She's 23 and I'm 43. She's young but quite intelligent. And well educated. There seems to be some purpose for her pose as a go-go dancer."

Karen rubbed her glass between her palms and then stared silently into her drink. "May I say something rather personal?"

"Shoot."

"At San Francisco State you couldn't make up your mind whether to go out on strike or not. You didn't wear the red *or* the blue armband. And you took a long time to make up your mind between Janet and me. Now you've fallen out of love with your brother's widow and in love with her daughter. Is it possible you're one of those people who really doesn't know his own mind?"

"It's not really that simple."

"Sorry if I sound upset; I have no right to be."

"Karen, I decided at San Francisco State that the leftists and SDS and all the rest of them were as totalitarian and manipulative as the school system they claimed to be fighting. I wish I *could* have joined one side or the other; commitment to some cause would have made things a lot easier for me. I did take a long time to decide about more personal matters, but in the end I did choose—I chose Janet. And I know my own mind where Nalin is concerned."

"Would you still love Nalin if she were only a go-go dancer?"

Brian weighed the question before answering. "I think so. Love is love."

Karen fingered a rose petal floating in the fingerbowl. The bowl was set in a napkin folded to represent a lotus. On the table beside it were Thai bronzeware and another cellophane-covered basket with fruit. "Do you remember Mr. Mak, the ex-policeman you met?"

"How could I forget? Don't tell me someone has agreed to publish his manuscript?"

"He threw himself off the roof of his building two nights before I left Hong Kong."

Brian let out a long sigh. He stood up and walked to the minibar. "Oh, God. I need a stronger drink myself. Want one?"

"No thanks."

He fixed himself another drink and sat down on the edge of the bed facing her. "How well had you known him?"

"Not well. He gave me background on some stories I was writing for the paper on drug smuggling in Asia. I just wish he had been able to clear his name. His life was ruined because he was honest and idealistic. Some of his bosses made millions dealing in drugs and some are still respected members of Hong Kong's business community."

"Or living quietly abroad."

"Living luxuriously abroad . . . the bastards."

Brian suspected the last bitterly spoken accusation was more directed at him than at any corrupt former police officers living abroad with their ill-gotten wealth.

Karen toyed with a vase of Madame Pompadour orchids then set it back on the table. "Brian, what you do is your business. And if you insist on making a fool out of yourself over someone young enough to be your daughter, well, hey, you're a big boy, I can't stop you." She took a long drink and continued. "But if you weren't so head-over-heels you might just consider the possibility that you most likely see the young Suntharee in her."

"And I've fallen in love with a memory? With what I couldn't have when I was young? I've thought of that. Time will tell."

"Oh, good. You've thought of that and time will tell. . . . Sorry. I didn't mean for that to come off quite so bitchy. . . . Which bar does the girl work in?"

"Which bar? The Horny Tiger."

"Oh, God."

"You know it?"

"Who doesn't? I told you I did a story on Asian nightlife. The Horny Tiger's a macho mecca for every horny lowlife on the prowl."

"Is that right? Well, the fellow who runs it—"

"Let me guess. The fellow who runs it is actually a sensitive soul right on the cutting edge of male-female relationships. He even believes women should be *educated*!"

"I wouldn't know what he believes about male-female relationships but he is an expert on the border camps and he's on good terms with the Thai military honchos in charge at the border. He's been there many times. With food and blankets. I guess it's a guilt trip for his chauvinism, right?"

"Ouch! You sure know how to make a girl feel small."

"You're doing fine all by yourself. Anyway, his name is Roger Webb. I thought we'd drop in after dinner and I'd introduce you."

Karen tilted her head and gave him an incredulous look. "You were going to take me to where your new love dances in a bikini and high heels to introduce me to her boss?"

"You make it sound a bit different from what I intended."

Karen bit her lip and stared at him. She finished her drink, picked up her purse and rose. "I think I'll take a rain check on that dinner."

"Karen. . . ."

"Hey, don't worry, Karen will get over it. And I think I *will* see your bar buddy about the border. I can use the help. I just want to meet him on my own terms—as a journalist on a story, not as an also-ran for your affections. Fair enough?"

"Fair enough." Brian rose and followed her to the door. "I will see you before you go back to Hong Kong, won't I?"

"Oh, sure. I'm here for quite a while." Karen stepped out into the hallway. "I actually took a leave of absence from the paper. I guess I was thinking. . . . Hell, who knows what I was thinking?"

Brian watched her step around an elderly Asian couple and disappear into the elevator. Leaving him with feelings of guilt and memories of the two of them at San Francisco State College.

# 34

**P**UMMELED by both the relentless downpour and by powerful gusts of wind, the banana tree fronds flailed and tore at each other like Siamese Fight Fish. The tattered fronds of the betel nut palm resembled a withered spider shaking violently in its final death throes.

Brian stood beside Nalin on the wet and windy balcony of her apartment as brief but torrential showers turned roads into rivers, ricefields into marshes and hotel lobbies into tourist sanctuaries. It had turned the yard below Nalin and Brian into a growing and muddied collection of fallen branches, twigs, fronds, leaves and bottles.

After a few minutes, the rain lessened and the banana fronds drooped and sagged over the wall—outstretched arms of pitiable beggars. Brian could smell mint leaves and rotting wood below the balcony. Fronds and leaves dripped water from one to the one below as if passing on secret messages.

It was a late afternoon, the time of day which, in the tropics during the rainy season, was meant for love-making. Brian and Nalin had just made love and, dressed in a robe, he stared at Nalin as he had so many times before. She was draped in a *paong*, which covered and clung to each curve of her body. Her long black hair fell well below her bare shoulders. He found her allure most compelling when she dressed in traditional Thai dress and wore no makeup; when she seemed to look and act and think more like a traditional Thai.

The night before she had teased him about becoming addicted to the Horny Tiger—its ambiance, its comraderie and humor, its comfort and its spirit of fun. He had merely laughed, but he realized the truth in her words: He *was* experiencing the soporific, deactivating effect of the Thai way of life on a Western mind. He had heard the Thai belief spoken many times: "If it's not *sanuk* (fun or pleasure), it's not worth doing." And beneath the onslaught of the languor of a tropical milieu, he felt his Protestant work-ethic crumbling to dust.

While Nalin entered the bathroom to get ready for another night at the Horny Tiger, Brian walked to the balcony and watched the activity in the lanes below. His thoughts kept returning to Jackson's words about his brother. He had been in the same firefight with Paul when he died. Yet when he spoke of it his words seemed to imply something more. Did he harbor some sort of important message or was he just a hopeless drunk spouting nonsense? But if it was nonsense, why did he disappear? And why hadn't he come to the Horny Tiger as promised?

The night before, the night of October 30th, Brian had returned to the Oriental to find a message from Bob Donnelly and two letters in his box. He had returned Bob's phone call and had managed to get out of yet another invitation to another dinner party for himself and Nalin. He had then phoned Karen at the Trocadero and learned that she had met with Roger webb who would soon be accompanying her to the border. They had agreed to meet for a drink in the near future.

The first of the letters was from his son with little news of school in London but with many questions on Brian's activities in Asia. The second letter was from John Adelman, telling him that, for the first time in his career, Richard Collins had taken sick leave and advising him to return to New York as soon as possible.

Brian's brief reply to New York spoke of his progress in locating expatriate writers who showed promise of doing some intelligent writing on Asia. After debating with himself on how to respond to his son, he wrote a letter replete with details on Thailand but omitting any mention of his confused personal involvements. As an afterthought, he had written of Karen's appearance with a brief explanation of who she was. It was only after he had mailed the letter that he realized that his mention of Karen was intended not for his son's eyes but for the eyes of his ex-wife. His discovery that he still had some unfocused desire to inspire jealousy in his ex-wife was not a pleasant one.

He also realized that the stormy patches in his love affair with Nalin were becoming more frequent and more heated. Particularly now that the SEA Write awards were over and writers had returned to their respective countries, he felt pressure to return to New York. He knew he felt deeply about her but he felt confusion about their relationship and guilt toward Suntharee. Nalin still refused to talk about her mother or about her reasons for becoming a go-go dancer, and Brian knew his patience was running out.

It seemed that the more violent their arguments the more passionate their lovemaking. As a way of avoiding unresolved and volatile issues, Nalin had taken to tearing long banana fronds from nearby trees and, lying on the bed wrapped only in the smooth green blade, she would wait for him as he came in the door and ask coyly and demurely, "Uncle Brian, would you like a banana?"

While Nalin was in the bathroom, Brian phoned a nightclub and made reservations for that evening to celebrate Halloween. He hung up and reflected on the argument that they had just thirty minutes before. A discussion of Halloween's origins had led into a discussion of Thai folklore which in turn had somehow led to a fierce argument over Suntharee and the way Nalin was treating her. Then, once again, their impassioned lovemaking had healed all wounds. But Brian decided the time had come to get the truth from her or to leave for New York.

He watched her walk into the room and slip into her dress and shoes while carefully avoiding his eyes. He took a deep breath and began. "Nalin, I think this morning is as good a time as any to find out what the problem is between you and—"

"I hate my mother."

"All right, you hate your mother. How about if I pin a scarlet 'A' on her chest. Will that satisfy you?"

Nalin stood tensely in front of a vanity mirror and stared hard at his reflection. "She should not have made love with anyone else. Especially. . . ." She let the sentence trail off.

Brian lit a cigarette, exhaled and sighed. "All right. I'm sorry. I thought . . . I don't know what I thought. We made love once, shortly before I left Ayudhya. It was a mistake and I'm sorry. I didn't know I was going to fall in love with you."

Nalin's body tensed still further and she turned to face him with her brown eyes opened wider than Brian had ever seen them. Then he saw them flare in anger and disbelief. "*You?* You made love with my mother?"

"Yes. Isn't that what you were accusing me of? You mean you
didn't know? So who were you talking about? Who did you mean?
I don't—"

Nalin grabbed her purse and ran to the door and flung it
open. She looked back at him with eyes filled with fury and an-
guish. Brian sat up on the bed, preparing to rise. "Nalin, I'm
sorry. I don't understand who—"

The door slammed.

Brian felt stunned to the point of immobility. He roused himself, put out his cigarette, and walked slowly to the balcony. Within
seconds he could see her running headlong away from the apartment, never once looking back.

He lit another cigarette and stood motionlessly staring out at
the end of the lane where she had turned the corner and disappeared. In his mind, the vivid brightness of her white summer
dress had streaked against the russet and tawny patches of earth
and cracked stretch of black asphalt like something pure and
unblemished struggling to escape from something sordid and
tainted. He stood lost in thought, mired in confusion and consumed with guilt long after his cigarette went out.

# 35

SHORTLY after 6 p.m., Brian stepped from a samlor onto Suriwongse Road and walked toward Patpong. He had planned to arrive at the Horny Tiger early in hopes of having a quiet talk with Nalin, but as he approached the bar, he began to fear the very real possibility that she might not forgive him. He grew increasingly angry at himself—not only for his culpability but for his growing vulnerability as well.

Crossing the street, Brian glimpsed monks blessing the newest Patpong bar with holy water. One of the things that had attracted him to Buddhism was the way sensuality and spirituality could be effortlessly and guiltlessly combined. No Catholic cardinal in New York or any other city would have sent priests to bless such dubious establishments as bars and massage parlors; but Buddhists understood that, whatever the enterprise, all was simply a part of the World of Illusion. It seemed to Brian a wisdom denied those brought up in the mindset of Judeo-Christian tradition with its obsession with instilling guilt in the faithful and fear of a vengeful God's wrath.

As he entered the bar he was immediately confronted with the face of a witch mask to his left and a goblin mask to his right. The dancers who wore them briefly held up their arms above their heads in menace even as they laughed, then abruptly turned their attention to other customers.

As Brian walked slowly to the bar, he tried, without making it obvious, to spot Nalin, but the bar was already crowded, mostly with locals stopping off for a drink on their way home.

He could see that the outrageous, eccentric and shocking elements of Halloween quite naturally appealed to girls whose behavior was often described in exactly the same terms, if not worse; and both the outre spirit and bizarre paraphernalia of Halloween were well in evidence.

Maintaining a pretense of nonchalance, Brian gazed about the bar in search of Nalin. As far as he could discern through the boisterous crowd, flashing lights and thick smoke, she was neither on a stage nor in a booth. At the far end of the room, a dancer emerged wearing the black-and-red mask of a vampire. As she walked toward him, her body was hidden by the crowd and by the time she was only ten feet away, Brian was sure it was Nalin. He swiveled to greet her, smiled broadly and was about to speak when she raised her mask to the top of her head and Brian recognized Dang. She smiled at him and went on to stand by one of the bar's small windows looking out at the street.

Brian spotted Roger at the bar handing over ten baht to a teenage girl selling orchids. As she left, he spoke to Brian. "Brian, my friend, take a note: there ain't nothin' in this world more seductive or more irresistible than a very young girl with very knowing eyes." He gulped a vast quantity of beer and looked around the bar, not without distaste. "We better have a good night to pay for all this Halloween bullshit."

Brian looked about the bar as if in admiration of the 'Halloween bullshit' while again searching for Nalin. Again, there was no sign of her and he was certain she would not have been in the changing room this long.

Maew stood smiling at him while standing beneath a mobile of a spiny globe fish, its puffed-up body as round as a ball. "Some girls say 'ma'am phom dang' be your before ladyfriend. True?"

Brian struggled for a few seconds with the Thai phrase before it suddenly hit him with full force: "Ma'am phom dang." Madam Red Hair. So, inadvertently or otherwise, Karen had let it slip that they had once been lovers. Just the right rumor to ensure that Nalin would break their relationship once and for all. Brian forced a smile. "That's a long story, Maew." He glanced at Roger's watch. "Where's Nalin tonight, anyway? We're going to a Halloween party and we're already late."

Maew and Roger exchanged glances. Brian looked at each of them. "What's going on? Something I should know about?"

A dancer squeezed by Roger on her way to the stage. Roger placed a hand on her buttocks and gave her a push up onto the counter. "Well, she *was* here but she left."

Maew moved away to serve customers farther down the bar. Brian felt both his temper and his anxiety rising. "Left? When?"

"About an hour ago."

"Where'd she go?"

"Alex Greene's studio. He's a photographer. He's got a studio on Patpong Two near the Superstar Bar. He came in and they went out together. Nalin's modeled for him before. He must have—"

Brian threw a hundred baht bill on the bar, got up and headed for the door. Roger called after him: "Be careful; he's a nasty piece of work."

Brian pushed through the sidewalk crowd of tourists, vendors, bargirls, beggars and pimps, ignored taxi horns and reached the far end of the street. In less than two minutes he had walked the two blocks to the building. Amid several faded signs stuck carelessly over the doorway, he saw one marked, "Alex Greene, Photo Studio."

In the dim light provided by naked, flickering bulbs, he ran up several flights of stairs. He banged on a door. After a second round of impatient banging, the door opened to reveal a Caucasian in his early thirties, dressed in jeans, sneakers and a tight-fitting 'Bottom Up Bar' T-shirt. Above his muscular physique, the man's beetle-browed, narrow-eyed face reminded Brian of an angry ape.

"Yeah?"

"I'm looking for Nalin."

"Yeah, she's here. But I'm in a photo-session with her now."

"I'd like to speak to her."

"Can't it wait?"

Brian returned the man's glare. "No, it can't wait."

After several seconds, the man stepped back and pointed toward the open door of an adjoining room. Brian walked through the disordered living room and through the doorway of the small room. He noticed the cord running from the power pack to the flash head too late to avoid tripping over it and he fell onto his hands and knees. Alex's voice boomed behind him. "Hey, man, watch it! You know how much these things cost?"

The room was cluttered with light stands with electronic flash and umbrellas, a white reflector board and trunks of photographic equipment. Several potted plants provided a background for the photographic session. On the table in front of Nalin was a hand-held Hasselblad 500 C/M with a 150 mm. lens.

Brian rose to his knees. In his overworked imagination, he had expected to see Nalin's abundant charms revealed in full erotic display, but the woman he saw on the platform in front of him took his breath away. She was fully dressed in the role of the heroine of a Siamese classical drama. Her oval face was perfectly framed by a gold and silver crown. Her right side was highlighted by the glow of an orange gel filter. Curved ornamental pieces extended down behind her ears from the lower part of the crown. A string of red-and-white flowers hung from the crown almost touching her left shoulder.

Thai classical dance garments covered her completely except for her arms and hands, ankles and feet. Light winked back at him from the jewelled collar, necklace, bracelets, armlets, anklets and rings. With each of Nalin's slightest movements, sudden, bright reflections and brief sparkles coruscated along every part of the costume.

Her face was thickly powdered but only a faint trace of red remained on her lips. She stood with one foot raised inward pointing off to the side, hands stretched outward, one curving up from below and one curving toward her shoulder. Her long fingers arched in backward curves, a position impossible for anyone not having practiced the movement from early childhood.

Her eyes stared back into his with an emotion impossible to read. Not anger, not annoyance, certainly not apologetic. Then Brian realized it was pride. She knew the effect she was having on him. She stood in the full angelic form of a classical Thai dancer, adorned with all the trappings of the spiritual beauty derived from the creators of the ancient Khmer empire and transformed by the Siamese.

Brian thought of Nalin's very sensual form as it had appeared in her bikini now dressed and posed as this glittered seraph and he felt the anger drain out of him. And he knew that she felt the love and admiration and desire that she stirred in him. He stood up slowly, still staring at her. He mustered what anger he could. "Remember, we're going to a Halloween party?"

She stared at a spot above his head and spoke in a crude bargirl accent, succeeding in her attempt to irritate him. Other than placing her foot on the platform, and relaxing her arms, she remained in position. "Oh, sorry 'bout that. Next time we go."

"Next time? What next time? There isn't any next time."

Alex spoke up in explanation but not without a touch of menace in his voice. "Hey, man, I got a last-minute call from a client, you know? He needs this shot for a brochure and he needs it like yesterday, you know?"

Brian spoke to Nalin. "You're coming with me."

Alex moved closer. The dull yellow in the corners of his eyes seemed to deepen with anger. "Hey, man, *after* the session she goes with you. Not until we're finished here. You saw where you came in, right? So make it."

Brian stepped forward to grasp Nalin's wrist but felt himself spun around. He managed to lean backward with enough speed to avoid the full force of Alex's large fist aimed at his face. But in his awkward position he felt himself again tripping over the cord. The light stand toppled over, smashing the flash head and its tube.

Brian sat on the floor and felt his chin, trying to keep his mind clear. He knew Nalin was gone but light and shadows seemed to dance around him. He heard Alex's voice screaming about the cost of a new head for a Broncolor.

Brian shook his head to clear it and looked up. "I'll pay you for your goddamned light equipment."

Alex stood above him menacingly, his left hand holding the fist of his right hand. In the play of light and shadow, his face appeared even more simian than before. "You'll pay, all right, man. Get up!"

Brian quickly placed his left foot on the man's knee and his right foot behind the ankle of the same leg. Holding Alex's foot in place, Brian pushed out with his left leg. Alex shouted a loud "Hey!" and tumbled over backward. As he rolled over to push himself up, Brian leapt on his back with one knee and bent the man's right arm sharply and painfully up behind him. His anger at Nalin, at himself, at whatever was threatening his idealistic image of Thailand Past was now focused on the man beneath him.

He used both hands to hold it in place while he waited for his own breathing to calm down. "Now, listen, asshole. I don't have time to fight you so you send an invoice for your equipment to the cashier at the Horny Tiger. But get one thing straight: Nalin is mine and I'm getting up now to go after her. Now do you understand that or do I break your arm?"

Alex grunted. "Yeah, yeah. I got it. Just get the hell out. You'll sure enough get a fucking bill for this mess, you son-of-a-bitch."

Brian jumped up and walked quickly to the door. He stepped over items of Nalin's discarded costume and walked down the stairs two at a time, half expecting the man to follow him. Outside the building he looked up to see Alex peering down at him from a tiny window. His angry face was bathed in magenta from the nearby neon advertisement of the Charming Moon beauty Center. Brian was painfully aware of the unexpected depth of jealously he had displayed in the studio but decided there would be time later to analyze the character failings of a middle-aged man who acted like a teenage street tough.

He ran into a light breeze, past noisy samlors and motorcycles, down Patpong Road, past talking, laughing, shouting tourists sitting beneath parasols around outdoor tables, past partly open doorways revealing glimpses of bikini-clad flesh, past the constantly moving neon lights and arrows of bar advertisements and finally reached the Horny Tiger.

He stood before the closed door for over a minute, then turned and began walking toward his hotel. His stomach seemed to have turned sour. The taste of guilt was metallic and as pungent as Thai chilies. But he'd be damned if he'd make an even larger fool of himself than he already had. He walked back to the Oriental beneath a sky filled with heat lightning, feeling drained of energy, pride and self-respect.

# 36

BY the time Brian had reached his room, he felt disgusted with his behavior. Words such as 'self-abasement,' 'blatant immaturity' and 'mid-life crisis' forced themselves into his consciousness. Against his own will and common sense, he had fallen in love with the daughter of the woman he was supposed to be in love with, and she had made him vulnerable and he was ashamed of his own vulnerability. He felt that since his arrival in Bangkok there was less of him than before and that he was somehow less in control of events—as well as of his own emotions.

He dialed the Trocadero and was finally put through to the right room. Karen picked up on the first ring. "Hello."

"Karen. This is Brian."

"Hi, Brian. You sound upset. But, don't worry. I still feel bad about how I acted. In your room, I mean. I shouldn't—"

"Forget it. That's ancient history. Anyway, you apologized on the phone. And that's not why I'm upset."

"Something else then."

"Right. I'm upset because the word is out at the Horny Tiger that 'Madam Red Hair' and I used to 'get it on' as we must have said in the Sixties. And I'm upset that Nalin is upset, and I'm embarrassed at my obsessive and puerile pursuit of a girl nearly half my age and angry at myself for acting like a schoolboy smitten by the charms of his first girlfriend. Not to mention that I'm upset with Nalin for being able to make me feel this way."

"Wow! Now *that's* upset. I can't help you with the schoolboy part but I can tell you that the only person I said anything to about us was Roger. So if the cat's out of the bag, and you thought an angry, jealous redhead tried to piss on your parade, you're wrong. Try asking a bar boss who says a lot of things to anybody who will listen when he's drunk—which is pretty often."

"Forget it. It's my problem. Anyway, I should have known you wouldn't have."

Karen sighed. "Look, Brian, I won't pretend I'm happy about the way things have turned out between us, but I'm not the insanely jealous type. In fact. . . ."

"Go ahead."

"Well, Roger said something else I think you should know but I haven't said anything because I'm certain you won't want to know."

"Which is?"

"OK. According to him, your girlfriend has been sleeping with his partner."

Brian tried to keep his voice steady. "Bob Donnelly? But Bob is—"

". . . totally plastic, as we used to say in the Sixties."

"You've met?"

"More or less. He came into the bar. Wallowed in getting his pompous ass kissed by some of the employees, then left. A real snob, that one. . . . Look, Brian, I'm sorry. I should have shut up."

"No. Not at all. I'm glad you told me. It's something I've got to deal with. And I appreciate your telling me."

Brian hung up the phone and sat lost in thought for a long time. Then he walked out of the hotel and headed for Patpong Road.

# 37

BRIAN reached the bar shortly after closing, just as the girls were coming out. He saw Oy and Nalin across the street, bargaining with a samlor driver. As he approached, Oy spotted him and backed away. Brian managed to take hold of Nalin's arm before she turned, and he lifted her up and into the samlor. He jumped in beside her and ordered the driver to the Oriental.

As Nalin struggled to pull away from him, he turned to her and said, "We're going to discuss your relationship with Bob Donnelly. In my room. Now." She freed her arm from his grasp but remained in the speeding samlor, angry and sullen, rubbing her wrist where Brian had held her. They sat silently, hands braced on the grillwork at the sides and feet against the grillwork behind the mirror, carefully avoiding physical contact with each other.

Even though he thought Roger's claim might actually be true, Brian suspected the anger he felt toward her would dissipate. What she had done before they fell in love was, after all, her life. It was 'Uncle Bob' Donnelly he felt a growing anger for; if this was true, it was yet another display of his lack of character. He couldn't imagine Nalin being attracted to him and he speculated on what power of persuasion he had used to get her to bed. He suddenly remembered the phrase from a book he had edited: "A man tolerant of everything and committed to nothing." He thought, not without a certain satisfaction, of how accurately that phrase described Bob, and then, with growing uneasiness, he remembered Jung.

What was it Jung had said? "Everything that irritates us about others can lead us to an understanding of ourselves." With that thought—and no doubt partly thanks to the amount of alcohol he had consumed in his room after speaking to Karen—Brian began to see some irony in his own situation and in his own attitudes. Here he was in Bangkok sitting in a speeding samlor—lights flashing, leis swinging wildly from mirrors—with the daughter of a woman he once loved condemning a man he had long disliked for behavior not so far removed from his own.

This insight into his own hypocrisy seemed to roll over him in waves—warming, comforting, consoling and strangely liberating. Hypocrisy was the sun and while Uncle Bob passed deeply into its gravitational field, and was far more influenced by it, perhaps a powerful telescope would reveal that both men were in fact in orbit around it. And who then did Nalin orbit? What were the influences on her?

Brian chanced a glance at her. Nalin, however, was turned away from him looking out at the nondescript buildings and poorly lit sidestreets flashing by, her face a mask of insouciance carefully hiding her emotions.

# 38

ONCE inside the room Nalin disappeared into the bathroom. Brian slowly undressed and slipped into a hotel robe. Underneath, he wore jockey shorts and over-the-calf socks. Nalin had chided him for 'dressing like an old man' by wearing boxer underwear and shortly after assuring him he would look sexy in jockeys, she had bought him a pair as a present.

He stood by the window, watching the river traffic through partly open curtains. A gibbous moon hung over a colorful night sky lit up with brilliant bursts of fireworks displays which reflected on the water below. The river itself was crowded with boats and along the waterfront, hotel guests and their friends were celebrating the landmark 96th birthday of an elderly Thai statesman. Huge shadows of Thai classical dancers swayed and darted mysteriously across the lawn.

Brian could hear the sound of Thai music and the soft explosions of fireworks through the glass, but his thoughts were on Bob Donnelly. He had been genuinely shocked by Roger's accusation and couldn't for the life of him think of a reason Nalin would sleep with Bob. Despite his growing disillusionment and smoldering anger, he knew Nalin was still suffering pain from his relations with her mother. He wondered who it was who now had the high moral ground—who was to be the injured party and who was to seek forgiveness.

Nalin returned to the room dressed in a blue silk nightgown and sat in a chair looking out at the river. She poured herself a glass of ice water and sat with her hands in her lap. At first, neither spoke, neither wanting to broach the actual issues between them as it might lead to the very argument both wanted to avoid. Brian moved pillows aside on a sofa facing her and sat down. Her eyes met his and she waited patiently for him to begin.

"OK, Nalin, we have to talk. That's pretty clear, right? Nothing is solved by silence." When she didn't respond, he continued. "I would like to say something and I'd appreciate it if you wouldn't interrupt me. All right?"

"May I have a cigarette?"

"All *right?*"

"Yes! All right! Now may I have a cigarette?"

Brian realized he had to calm down. He wondered if his hand would shake if he tried to light it for her. He handed her the cigarettes and the matches and then sat down again on the sofa. "I'm sorry I raised my voice."

Nalin lit a cigarette, nodded, and said nothing.

Brian made an effort not to fidget. "OK. First of all, I want to say that I deeply apologize and I can only ask that, whatever we decide tonight, you will forgive me for the pain I caused you."

Nalin said nothing but glanced away from him, inadvertently silhouetting her face against the warm glow of a bedside lamp.

"All right. I've said what I wanted to say about that." Brian shifted his position on the sofa and stared into the ashtray for several seconds before beginning again. "Now, about Bob Donnelly, I don't know if you really went to bed with him or not, but the way I see it, if it happened before we fell in love, it's not really any of my business. If you've been to bed with Bob for fun or for money—"

Nalin drew her arms tightly around her as one might don a suit of armor before battle. She spoke quietly but with dignity. "I have never been to bed with any man for money. Never."

"All right. Fine."

"Never!"

"All right. I heard you." Brian lit up another cigarette. "I won't pretend I can understand why you would get involved with someone like Bob, but I know I have no right to accuse you."

"Someone like Bob? I thought he was your friend."

Beneath her casual manner, Brian detected a serious interest in his reply. "Acquaintance. Bob is the most pompous, pretentious man I've ever met. In any case, we grew completely apart. We had nothing in common to begin with but that we served together in Bangkok in the army. And that he knew Paul, your mother and you as a child. But he still invites me to lunches and dinners as if we're two of a kind." Brian hesitated as he saw a strange look pass over Nalin's face. He couldn't decide if it was skepticism, irony or ridicule. "I need to say also that I don't understand you in other ways as well. I still don't understand why you left home and took up work as a dancer and I think it's time you trusted me; but first you have to forgive me for what happened in Ayudhya between your mother and myself."

Nalin stiffened her fingers and interlocked them, palms down, in her lap. She raised her arms slightly but seemed unable to pull her hands apart. For the first time she seemed near tears. Her voice thickened. "It would be so much easier to forgive you . . . if it were anyone except my mother."

"I know. I know I've hurt you. Very much. Tell me how I can get you to trust me."

She glanced out the window and looked down at the river lights then stared straight at him. "Do you still love me?"

"You know I do."

"Would you like to know why I ran away from Ayudhya?"

"Of course."

Nalin took a drink of ice water and sat the glass down. "If you really wanted to know, you could have asked my mother."

"I did ask your mother. She was . . . vague. I could see that the subject gave her a great deal of pain."

"And you think it doesn't give *me* pain, Uncle Brian?"

Brian had never heard her speak the words 'Uncle Brian' with bitterness. He was beginning to see his action from her point of view. "I know it does. I only—"

"Then why? Why is it all right to insist that I explain, but not her? Because you still *love* her."

"That's not true."

"But you still have feelings for her."

Brian leaned back and sighed. "I have *feelings* for her, yes. Friendship. Respect. Even fondness. But I don't *love* her; I love *you*." He leaned forward again and took her hand. "Sweetheart, I'm too old for a stormy relationship. I need some peace of mind. Love means trust and you're not trusting me enough so that I can help you. Your mother has worked very hard for many years to make a success of the school. So whatever the grievances you have against her, however she may have wronged you, please remember it couldn't have been easy for her, alone and on her own, all those years since Paul's death, making a success of—"

"She hasn't made a success of it."

"What?"

"And she hasn't been alone or on her own."

"But, sweetheart, I saw—"

"My mother has borrowed a great deal of money to keep the school going. It was a bad investment."

Brian stared at the fruit bowl, the unfolded napkin, the fingerbowl and a selection of glossy magazines. "Well, a lot of businesses borrow money to—"

"She borrowed money from Bob Donnelly; a lot of money."

Brian sat up straight. He picked up a sofa pillow, held it as if guessing its weight, then tossed it to the other end of the sofa. He attempted to keep any hint of shock or distress out of his voice. "Your mother borrowed money from Bob?"

"Yes. More than once."

Brian lowered his gaze to the carpet. The phone rang. Neither moved to answer it. He spoke without looking at Nalin. "They met at the house in Ayudhya?"

Nalin placed her feet behind her on the chair. "And in Bangkok."

Brian used his hand to brush the carpet where his ashes had landed. He put his cigarette out and when the phone had stopped ringing he looked directly at her. "Are you suggesting that—"

"Yes. I am." Brian detected the deeply felt pain and anger driving her words. "So, you see, you do have something in common with Bob. Both of you slept with both of us! Two of a kind."

Brian stood up. "Stop it!"

Nalin stood up, tears flowing freely. "No. *You* stop it! You hurt me! You hurt me emotionally! You—"

Brian tried to hold her but she resisted and ran to the door. He followed her and stood beside her blocking her attempt to leave. Her eyes stared into his like the accusing eyes of a child who has been horribly betrayed by an adult. He could feel guilt gnawing inside him like a cancerous growth. He wiped tears from her cheeks with his finger. "Nalin, I'm sorry. Deeply sorry. I don't know what more I can say."

He held her shoulders and kissed her forehead, eyes, nose and lips. They stood for a while without speaking. Brian cradled her in his arms, and kissed her; but despite his love for her and feelings of guilt, and his fear of losing her, thoughts of Nalin with Bob and Suntharee and Bob's secret relationship penetrated into his inner recesses and stirred his emotions almost beyond endurance. Finally, she kissed him gently on the lips. "I'm sorry, too."

He let out a long sigh. "All right. We'll take it one step at a time, OK? But I intend to return to New York in the near future so you'd better remember what I said about love entailing trust. Now let's get ready for bed and see if things look any brighter in the morning."

Twenty minutes later, as he stepped out of the shower, the bathroom door opened and Nalin, wrapped in a white cotton robe, stood facing him. For several seconds, they stared at each other. Nalin moved forward, picked up his bath towel and fastened it around his waist. As she began stepping back, as if uncertain of his reaction, Brian reached out, held her chin and one shoulder, and kissed her tenderly. She threw her arms around him and pressed her cheek against his chest.

Although they were together again, they both displayed the caution and anxiety and emotional turmoil of lovers after a quarrel; neither wanted to be the one to make too sudden a move. Once in bed, Nalin gave in to exhaustion and fatigue and fell asleep almost immediately. Brian turned to stare at her. All makeup had been removed and, except for the area around her eyes and lips, her face was covered with the white cream of a mask pack. The rough texture of the cream reminded him of his school days in Monterey when he and Paul had scraped paint from the clapboards of his grandmother's house. He realized that since he had come to Thailand, too many things reminded him of Paul.

Long after Nalin had fallen asleep, Brian lay awake, listening to the intermittent roars of long-tailed motor boats. He thought of himself as mired in confusion and helpless to pierce a carefully constructed, omnipresent veil of deception. It seemed that nothing in Thailand was as it first appeared; as if in the country's tropical heat and lush surroundings, duplicity or at least deception flourished as abundantly as exotic flora.

As Nalin lay sleeping, cradled in his arm, Brian remembered her remark about his toilet kit. She had picked over the items he kept in it including Tiger Balm ointment, Anacin, Tums, Lomotil and Visine, and she had asked why he needed so much medicine. He had laughed and advised her to stay young forever. But he realized that over the years he had unconsciously been adding several 'just-in-case' items to his kit. It had suddenly made him feel very old and now as he looked at her smooth brown face, he was astonished at her youth and at his own temerity in being involved with her.

He had not told her that he had called her mother that morning. Brian had begun several sentences with the intention of learning something from Suntharee about her relationship with Bob. Each time he had changed the subject or not finished the sentence. He decided it was simply not something he could discuss on the phone.

Toward the end of the conversation, she had asked if Nalin had said anything about coming home. He had told her no. Then she had asked him to take good care of her. After a pause, Brian had said that he needed to talk with her about personal matters. There had been a long silence and then she had said, "I'm sorry, Brian, I seem to be having trouble with the phone. We'll talk again soon." And then the line went dead.

Brian had begun to realize just how simple and uncomplicated life in New York had been. He fell asleep and dreamed of Tantalus, son of Zeus, condemned forever to stand beneath succulent fruit which moved out of reach as he tried to touch it. But as Tantalus turned it was Brian himself who was standing beneath a tree of exotic and colorful tropical fruit that glittered in the moonlight like stars and burst open like fireworks as he tried to touch them.

# 39

A S Brian entered the Horny Tiger, Maew handed him an envelope embossed with Alex Greene's company logo and address. Inside was a bill for the damaged equipment. Brian made a mental note to change more traveler's checks into baht, folded the bill and put it in his pocket.

He spotted Nalin dancing on a rear stage, her lissome figure undulating about a pole, her long hair and neck chain flying. Sweat glistened on her back and light played off her neck and shoulders. Her feminine contours created by her brown skin stretched over shoulder blades and collar bones to engender an exciting sensuality. Brian wondered again at how painlessly and how completely she seemed to have adapted to the world of Bangkok nightlife. It was with a sobering shock that he remembered the same thing could be said about himself.

He thought again of the Brian Mason who lived and worked in New York City and of the Brian Mason presently ensnared, or, at least, enmeshed, in an almost Jekyll and Hyde existence in a kingdom ten thousand miles from his Greenwich Village apartment. He thought again of how easily the country could attract and disorient whoever ventured within its boundaries. In the brief and relatively quiet interval between songs, the door opened and Bob Donnelly walked in.

Although his anger toward Bob—for his tryst with Nalin, for his relationship with Suntharee and for his infuriating snobbery— had not dissipated, Brian was convinced that the key to Nalin's bizarre actions of the last several months somehow involved Bob and possibly the Horny Tiger in ways he did not yet understand; hence, he made a quick decision to swallow his true feelings and reluctantly forced a smile.

During his brief appearances inside the Horny Tiger, Bob packaged himself as an affectionate, sympathetic uncle to whom

one and all could tell their troubles and receive advice and bene-
diction. And yet there was also evident a clear desire on his part
not to be touched or fondled by the girls in any way, an unspoken disdain for close proximity with his bikini-clad employees.
Owning a bar on Bangkok's Patpong Road might provide that
dash of color for his otherwise staid personality, but he was not
about to give of *himself* or to become involved in any real problem the girls might have, be it drugs, abortions, or the sickness of
a child. There was about that smile always a certain condescen-
sion, the amused tolerance of a jovial but aloof father listening to
his children speak excitedly about the day's events.

After the usual fuss over his presence had died down, Bob sat
at the bar next to Brian and ordered an Amarit beer. For several
minutes they spoke of Bangkok in the Sixties and how it had
changed. Then, as Bob signaled for another round, he abruptly
changed the subject. "Have you learned anything about Nalin's
leaving home?"

"Not much. It seems she found an old letter which belonged
to her mother. I don't know who wrote it or who received it or
what was in it, but whatever it was, it was enough to cause her to
leave home and school. And come here."

"It must have been quite a letter to accomplish that."

"Well, whatever was in it, it turned Nalin completely against
her mother. But I'm getting closer to her. I think I'll have gained
her confidence soon. I'll take a look at the letter myself. There
may be more than one. In any case, if I'm lucky, I can help
straighten it out between them and your bar will lose its best go
go dancer."

Bob seemed about to speak but changed his mind. Brian continued while looking at Bob for his reaction. "Would you believe
I ran into Jackson the other night?"

"Jackson? In Bangkok?"

"Yes. It seems he's been living in Bangkok all along. I guess
you must have missed him."

Bob allowed himself an indulgent smile. "That wouldn't be
difficult. We must travel in very different circles."

Brian noticed Nalin now wrapped in a thin, diaphanous robe
sitting alone in a rear booth, intently observing the two of them
together. He turned back to face Bob. "That must be it."

"How's he doing?"

Brian speculated on the odds that Bob had not known Jackson was in Bangkok; about the same as winning the Thai lottery. "Not so well. A bit too fond of the bottle, I'm afraid. I wanted to talk to him but he seems to have disappeared."

"Doesn't surprise me." Bob nodded toward a booth. "They all end up the same."

Brian turned to see two middle-aged men drinking with two dancers about one-third their age. Before them on the table were two bottles of beer, two carmine-colored ladies drinks and peanuts.

"Friends of Roger," Bob continued. "Retired Air Force sergeants. leftovers from the war. Thailand's full of them. The bargirls probably have higher IQs than they have. Guys like them would love to go back to the States but they wouldn't fit in. And they know it."

"How about you?"

Bob gave him an indulgent smile. "I couldn't live in the States again. Besides, people here depend on me."

Brian thought of Suntharee's dependence on Bob for money and companionship. And of Nalin in bed with him. Fueled by his anger toward Bob and annoyed at his own decision to avoid a confrontation on personal matters, Brian raised his voice. "That's right. they do, don't they? You always did provide help when it was needed—even in Ayudhya."

Bob began tugging at his thin, well-trimmed mustache. "I'm not sure I understand your point." Bob's tone finally showed annoyance. Brian noticed once again his habit of puffing up his cheeks when angry or upset and he began to realize the globefish above their heads was the perfect symbol for him—not only all blown up and full of himself but the fish also was known for puffing itself up when under attack.

Brian stared at him, stood up and picked up the cup holding the barbills. "My point is—"

Bob reached for the cup. "I'll get that."

"No, you won't. *I'll* get that. I guess my point is that a guy who owns a bar shouldn't look down on the people he sells his beer to."

# 40

BROWN-and-black sparrows hopped about on the hotel's three-tiered marble terrace like tiny mechanical toys. As the sun set, a delicate slice of pink spread hesitantly above the Thonburi side of the river like a line of watercolor drawn by an indecisive artist. In the relaxed calm of early evening, even the boat engines seemed more subdued, less angry—a kind of purring growl had replaced an incessant whine. Bangkok was emerging from the grip of the rainy season.

Roger watched Karen's hair catch the last glow of the sun and hold it in place, as if prolonging its warmth. He stared for a few moments watching Karen sip her Grasshopper. "Now that's pretty."

"What is?"

"The way the green of your drink compliments your red hair."

"Thanks. Just don't call me 'Red,' or 'Carrot-top' or any of those. And please continue with your story."

A waiter began placing censers with mosquito coils under each table. Roger ordered a gin tonic for Karen and another beer for himself. White running lights, red port lights and green starboard lights crisscrossed the river. A pleasant breeze sprang from the river and caressed them like the ministrations of an expert masseuse.

"Hell, nothing more to tell. When I first came out here I'd been married just over four years to a lady from Baton Rouge. She got off the plane and took a look at the way Thai girls move and talk and smile and I could tell she felt she was bein' out-charmed and out-sexed. So she did what she always did when she wanted something: She gave me an ultimatum. Said we either go back to the States PDQ or else it was divorce time."

Roger fell silent while a waiter placed a lampshade-covered

candle on the table. "Well, I guess she figured it would work again. But this time I said, 'Honeybunch, you know the Thais believe they gain more merit by buildin' a new temple than by restorin' an old one. So I'm gonna give you your chance to gain more merit by buildin' a new marriage, then rebuildin' an old one. You go back to Baton Rouge and send me divorce papers whenever you've a mind to. As for me, I like it here just fine.' And that was that."

Karen laughed in reaction to Roger's monologue and from the effects of the gin. She rose, just a bit unsteadily, and mussed Roger's hair. "All right. Let me go to the ladies' room first and then I want to hear more of your chauvinist adventures, OK?"

Roger reached up and held her hand for a few seconds before releasing it. "Shouldn't someone of your persuasion have said, 'Women's Room'?"

Karen threw up her hands in surrender. "Touché, El Chauvinisto! Touché!"

# 41

THE watchman had swept the mud and shrubs near the back fence with his flashlight for several minutes before he spotted the padlock. He picked it up, wiped the mud off it and examined it in the light. The lock's shackle had been forcefully pried from its steel body. Whoever the intruder was, he had taken the trouble to cut through a chain lock as well as to pry open the padlock.

He concentrated the light on one of the footprints near the gate and then placed his own foot carefully inside it. He realized the man had worn very large shoes—perhaps because he was a large man or perhaps to fool anyone on his trail into thinking he was large. It had been less than two hours since his last check of the perimeter but he knew he would have to check each apartment to ensure that none had been broken into.

He moved around the building to his tiny shack near the front gate. He turned off his radio, reached under the counter and withdrew his smooth wooden club. As he walked toward the front stairs of the building, the front gate opened and Brian, arms full of groceries, walked carefully over the mud toward the driveway.

The watchman knocked on the first of the apartment doors and gave Brian a gold-toothed smile which glittered in the light of a bare bulb. Brian nodded as he passed him and began climbing the stairs. The watchman thought of telling the foreigner about the break-in, but he still wasn't certain how much Thai the *farang* spoke and he decided it would be easier to communicate with the girl once he reached her apartment.

He heard Brian drop something on the stairs and saw his shoes reappear as he backtracked to pick it up. He was about to approach him and tell him of the broken locks when the door to the downstairs apartment opened and he turned away to begin his inquiry.

# 42

U PRIVER the huge letters spread across the nearby Shangrilla Hotel were bathed in a yellowish-orange light. Roger finished his comments on feminism, saluted Karen with his beer bottle, and took a long drink. Karen stared at him in disbelief. "Roger, you can't seriously believe that a woman working in a massage parlor is not being degraded."

"Well, in Thailand, buffalos trampin' back and forth over harvested crops is known as 'massagin' the rice.' So it seems ever'body in Thailand is massagin' somethin', anyway."

Karen laughed loudly then stopped abruptly.

"What's the matter?"

"Why do I always end up fighting with men I've made love with?"

Roger leaned forward and took her hand. He opened his mouth to speak, then suddenly stopped to stare stonily toward the coffee shop. Karen turned to follow his gaze. Bob Donnelly and two well-dressed Asian men were just turning to go back to the hotel. Bob saw them and waved to Karen. Karen returned the wave while Roger turned away. Karen turned back to Roger and started to speak. "Bob Donnelly—"

Roger interrupted while staring out at the river. "Now that is one man I couldn't get to like for all the gold in Maew's teeth."

Karen remained silent.

"All right, so you don't agree. Fair enough. No law says you have to make my enemies your enemies."

"I do agree. It's just that you articulated my thoughts better than I could."

Roger laughed and called for the bill. While they waited, he avoided Karen's eyes. Finally, after he had paid, he looked directly at her. "Karen, about what happened at the border."

"Don't worry. We made love but we're not lovers. I'm not chasing you."

"That's not what I meant. I meant you were in an emotionally vulnerable state after seein' what you saw. Most people who visit the border areas for the first time usually are. Wounded and dying teenage Cambodian kids . . . I don't know, maybe I shouldn't have—"

Karen reached across the marble table and took his arm. "Hey, big boy, let's just say *I* laid *you*, OK? And no regrets."

"You're all right, you know that?"

Karen rose. "Sure. I'm fantastic. I've known it all along. But I never could convince Brian of that."

# 43

BRIAN knocked perfunctorily on the door of Nalin's apartment as he unlocked it. Inside he could hear playing the most recent tape he had bought her: Mozart's *A Little Night Music*. He kicked off his shoes and dropped the grocery bags onto a chair. "They can probably hear your taste in music all the way up in Chiang Mai." He turned the volume down and shouted toward the bedroom while stacking tapes lying in disarray into a neat pile. "In fact, a representative of the Cambodian government was having a beer in the Horny Tiger and he told me to tell you they're moving their troops back from the border area because they can't stand the noise from your tape deck."

Brian noticed a chair overturned near the balcony. The glass door was open and the wind was ruffling papers on the floor and newspapers on a small table. He walked out onto the balcony and looked over the banana trees and areca palm fronds swaying in a slight wind. From far away a siren wailed but there was no sound or movement in the dark lane below.

Two thoughts came to him almost simultaneously. The small brown figure impaled on a fence below was that of the teddy bear he had given Nalin as a child; and he suddenly remembered that the same music he was listening to had been played by and for doomed prisoners at the gates of Auschwitz.

Brian felt the fear forming in his stomach as he walked quickly back into the living room, slid the door closed and uprighted the chair. It was then that an overturned table drawer and still more papers in disarray caught his eye. He walked into the short hallway and called again toward the bedroom. "Nalin? Are you here?"

Inside the ransacked room, he stepped over discarded desk drawers and a jumble of books and approached the silent and immobile figure sprawled across the bed.

# 44

INSIDE the walled-in garden of a comfortable Bangkok home, Yuen Sheung-fuk moved his wicker chair a few feet closer to a bamboo screen and sat once again within the welcome shade of a large mango tree. Several feet above the marble table before him baskets of wild orchids hung from the tree's branches. Yuen could feel rivulets of sweat coursing down his back and chest and he shifted uncomfortably. He suppressed a sigh of impatience and reflected that if he could finish here quickly, he might still make the evening flight, thereby escaping the damnable heat and humidity of Bangkok for the relative coolness of Hong Kong.

The man before him—a brother of a Golden Triangle warlord who sometimes fought with and sometimes fought against General Li—sat motionlessly in his own wicker chair staring at a line of red ants crawling up the leg of the table. His excessive corpulence and extreme caution were in sharp contrast to his brother's reputation for physical fitness and daring offensives. Finally, he turned back to Yuen and continued his questioning in a northern Thai dialect. "And you're certain General Li told no one else except you and his son?"

Yuen responded, also in Thai. "That's what he said. One caravan will be carrying the opium and the other will be merely a diversion. And he trusted no one except his son and myself."

"And when will you learn which is which?"

"Soon. And as soon as I know, you will know." When the man again grew thoughtful, Yuen glanced at his watch and pressed on. "General Li will be only lightly guarded so as not to draw attention to his caravan. It seems to me this is the opportunity we have all been waiting for."

The man's fleshy lips widened into a rueful smile. "I have no more love for General Li than you do; but he has not survived all these years in the Golden Triangle by being careless or stupid. I have lost count of the times I thought he was finally finished only to see him victorious in the end. And I have paid a price for underestimating him." The man held out his left hand. the greater part of three fingers were missing.

For several seconds, he seemed lost in a hypnotic swirl of bitter memories, then, as if suddenly reaching a decision, he nodded. "All right. You learn what you can and if my brother agrees your information is sound and the time is right, then it just might be that General Li's luck has finally run out."

# 45

HER still body was clad only in bra and panties. The panties were decorated across the front with a small figure of a cartoon character resembling a cross-eyed duck. The bed was still made but the covers were rumpled and the hilltribe quilt had dropped to the floor. Her hands lay stretched out at her sides. The fingers of her right hand had fallen near the bedside table next to a white jar of Mudd Mask. One of the pillows lay exactly in its proper place at the head of the bed and one lay across her face and neck. Brian reached for the pillow covering her face and pulled it away.

The white Mudd Mask paste on her face had dried to form a thousand tiny cracks across her skin. He bent over her body, and with all the will power he could muster he ignored the message of her eyes. He quickly placed his fingers on her neck, feeling in vain for her carotid artery then grabbed her wrist and, refusing to acknowledge the significance of her bluish fingernails, felt frantically for a pulse. He moved his hand along her stiffening arm and, in growing panic, shouted her name and slapped her face.

Finally, holding her own cold hands in his own, he allowed himself to look directly at her fixed and dilated pupils. The opaque and fissured paste had pulled her skin and distorted her features, giving her face a twisted and pained expression. From his throat emerged an inhuman sound, a slowly forming, steadily rising explosion that would soon fill the apartment.

# 46

NEARLY two hours after Roger had entered his office, he re-emerged and, fortified with several glasses of Mehkong whiskey, carefully wended his way from his office into the bar and sat on a stool facing Maew. He looked around the room. "Damn! I fell asleep! That's what I git for mixin' my drinks. Oy get in yet?"

Maew spat out a tiny piece of lotus pod into her hand and dropped it into the fish tank. "She here before. I think she go shopping with the new dancer—Pla (fish)." She pointed the pod toward the changing room. "Pla went to change. She and Oy came back late."

Roger knocked once on the changing room door and opened it. "Pla? You in here?"

Pla was standing in red-and-blue pumps, tying on the bottom part of her blue-and-white bikini. She made no attempt to cover her small breasts while she concentrated on tightening the string to her satisfaction. Shallow creases of concentration lined her forehead. She stood beside a wall pierced with nails over which hung plastic bags with articles of girls' clothing. The top of her bikini was draped over the wall's fire extinguisher. She looked at him without guile or embarrassment. "You call me?"

"Have you seen Oy, sweetheart? We've got a date tonight."

She adjusted her bikini's extra loops of string as she wanted, then turned slightly away from him, embarrassed by the subject, not their situation. "I think she angry you."

Roger smiled, folded his arms and leaned against the door. "You think Oy angry *me*? Now, why would my favorite girl in all the world be angry with me?"

Pla snatched her top from the fire extinguisher and placed it around her breasts. While she tied it she looked up at Roger.

"Uncle Bob came here. Say too much about you and a lady."

Roger could feel a tight fist of anger forming in his gut. "What lady?"

"*Ma'am phom dang.* He talk same you butterfly Oy. He say you in love with foreign lady; maybe take her to America. I think Oy angry you."

Roger clenched his fists and emitted a long sigh. "I see. So where did she go? Where did *everybody* go?"

"Many girls go to Kung's house. Kung have new baby just get born last week."

Roger started to turn away. "So she went to Kung's."

"No. She see before baby of Kung. Oy say Nalin not stay home tonight. Nalin stay with Kung. So Oy say she go house Nalin. Oy sleep there tonight."

# 47

**B**RIAN recalled the rest of the night as if remembering a blurred hallucination through which isolated images of absolute clarity had been woven at random: Thai police in uniform moving constantly and erratically about Nalin's apartment, their .45s appearing absurdly large on their small frames. Overweight detectives in somber, short-sleeved shirts and crumpled trousers carbon dusting for fingerprints, photographing, questioning, taking notes. A brief dispute over whether the case should be handled by the Tumahamek or Lumpini police stations, the trip to the Lumpini police station. Questions and answers and the signing of a statement. At some point the realization of someone crying and the figure of Roger Webb—his eyes swollen and red—sitting beside him.

Brian remembered nothing of the ride to the morgue set inside the sprawling police compound except that the police car turned in opposite Siam Square where the four of them had once had lunch together and how it seemed important that he try to remember what each had for lunch. He remembered other images with varying degrees of clarity: a group of women sitting on benches along the building's covered but open-fronted waiting area—some sitting in silence and some weeping—and only gradually recognizing them as Nit, Maew and dancers from the Horny Tiger. Nalin held onto one of the dancers who leaned against her shoulder to weep. Nalin stared at Brian with puffy eyes and he could see the sorrow, pain and fear mingled in her expression. She began rocking the dancer slowly back and forth and whispering to her.

A long, dimly lit hallway, and the bright white walls of the morgue itself; a police pathologist introducing himself and telling him something irrelevant about the Scientific Crime Division; the incredibly lined, broad brown face of Oy's mother—her thin lips fixed in a mirthless smile—lighting incense and a candle in front of Oy's body as it rested on an open refrigerated shelf, so that when Oy was taken to a temple for cremation her spirit would follow her to the cremation ground.

And etched in his memory forever was the face of Oy, small, childlike, yet already somehow unearthly and unfamiliar; her eyes closed and her shiny skin now washed clean of all traces of makeup. She seemed to rest in undisturbed slumber, as if she had once again fallen asleep in a booth inside the Horny Tiger while waiting for customers.

And the diminutive figure of Oy's mother approaching Roger, gently taking his hand, and in a kind and consoling voice, telling him that Oy was happy and, as Brian himself had once been told so long ago, telling Roger not to cry because the spirit of the dead would have to swim through his tears to reach its journey's end; and the distraught hulk of Roger Webb embracing and being embraced and partly supported by the tiny calm figure dressed in a worn blouse and sarong, his convulsive weeping almost drowning out her quiet words of compassion.

# 48

Jackson's face contorted with anger. "I *told* you: I *had* to snuff her. She knew who I was!..Yeah, you also said the place would be *empty*. . . .You're damn right it's time. . . .Yeah, well, *you* figure out how to get him there and I'll take care of him once he's there. . . . Eleven sharp. . . . I said I'll be there! And my drinking is my fucking business!"

He slammed the phone down and poured himself another whiskey. He lay back on the bed and watched the lazy revolutions of the ceiling fan. After nearly a minute he turned to glance at the large wall banner surrounded by Vietnam War photographs:

SOUTHEAST ASIAN WAR GAMES

1960—75 SECOND PLACE

He took one last drink and set the empty glass on the bedside table. As he began drifting off to sleep, his thoughts turned to his next assignment. "Nothing personal, Brian, my man. Just business. But this is gonna' cost that bastard more. A whole lot more."

# 49

A S Oy had died a violent death, her body was taken not to her home for ceremonies but directly to a temple; a temple not far from her mother's restaurant.

Her body lay in an elaborate casket elevated and surrounded by incense, wreaths and other flowers. Next to it was a large, very grainy, high-contrast head-and-shoulders photograph that had been blown-up and carefully cropped to avoid revealing the interior of the Horny Tiger. Her eyes were open wide, but slightly unfocused, as if she had just woken up, but it was the only photograph anyone could find of her without a big smile or impish grin on her face. And this had only been possible because she seemed to have just turned to face the camera, unaware that she was being photographed. It was, perhaps because of this, slightly out of focus. The flickering light of nearby candles gave Brian the impression that her eyes were constantly looking about, as if even in death she wanted to see who in the room had a lady's drink in front of her.

There was the sonorous chanting of Buddhist monks and the atonal melodies on xylophones, cymbals, gongs and drums. Mourners poured water over Oy's outstretched hand before the coffin was nailed shut and, finally, the actual burning of the body in the flames of the furnace.

Men wore black armbands over white shirts and women wore black. But the outfits of the bargirls were not simply black but long-sleeved and immaculate and of the finest material; attire which had obviously cost a great deal. The girls of Patpong Road had dressed at Oy's funeral to give to one of their own in death— that which one in their profession would seldom if ever receive in life—dignity and respect.

Oy's son, Jiap, neatly dressed in a small blue suit, sat between Roger and Nalin, most of the time content to sit quietly and still. Only occasionally did he insist on walking about and, at those times, someone from the Horny Tiger would keep an eye on him. He would eventually come to a halt, and before sitting down again beside Roger, would cast a puzzled, slightly anxious glance at his mother's photograph, as if Oy's expression was reminding him to behave in her absence.

Throughout much of the chanting and the sobbing and the chatting of the mourners, Nalin sat in silence. She was dressed in black crepe and her light makeup was smeared with tears. At one point she returned Roger's embrace, but, for most of the ceremony, she stared at Oy's picture as if trying to explain that it should have been her in the bed, not Oy, and begging her spirit's forgiveness.

Three days after Oy's death her bone slivers and ashes were placed in a brass urn and taken to her mother's canalside house and placed on a shelf in the 'hong phra,' Buddha room.

# 50

THE small, dilapidated wooden-and-brick structure had once been a minor canal-side outbuilding on the estate of a wealthy Thai-Chinese importer of construction material. After the man's death it had been abandoned.

Inside, just beneath a window, William Jackson sat on the remaining section of wooden floor with his back against a wall. He glanced at his watch for the fourth time in four minutes: 11:35. The bastard was late. He had better have an explanation. And the money. Jackson took a long drag on his cigarette and thought about Brian and what he had to do; and he realized it was the first time he'd felt remorse since Vietnam, when he'd—

At the sound of a motor on the canal, he walked cautiously across the room and looked out a canal-side window. The narrow, shallow draught boat passed quickly beneath him, its long, partly submerged, rudder pole glittering in the moonlight. He watched until the boat rounded a bend of the canal and disappeared.

Just as he turned, he spotted the shadow of a man approaching from the estate side of the building. Jackson moved silently to stand in the darkness beside a pillar. He lifted his shirt and rested his hand on the wooden grip insert of his five shot .38 Special tucked into his belt. The shadow disappeared and then there was silence. Something was wrong. Very wrong. His hand gripped the revolver and he brought it slowly upward. If this was that asshole's attempt at a double-cross, it would be the last mistake he ever made.

His hand holding the revolver began to shake. He felt sick. If only he had a drink. Just one. He snapped open the cylinder, saw that each chamber had a round, and snapped it shut; then, walking in a crouch, moved toward the door.

# 51

BRIAN stood by the lobby door watching the diminutive translator from Chulalongkorn University walk slowly down the Oriental's driveway and into the bright sunlight.

He then crossed the lobby toward the elevators and felt pleased at the way the meeting had turned out. The translator was everything his Thai writer acquaintances had promised— and more. She had agreed to translate sample chapters of the novels written in Thai which Brian had chosen for his program and they would then have another meeting. Brian couldn't help smiling as he remembered her warning that translations, like mistresses, could never be both completely faithful *and* completely beautiful.

As was the case with many Thais, she had not considered exactitude and directness in negotiating a virtue, but she had translated the work of the ex-monk and Brian knew she was the one he wanted.

Just before the elevator door opened, Brian saw the boy approach him with his name on a sign. He followed the boy to the counter to take the call. Brian picked up the phone ready for Nalin's voice and instead—once the hotel operator confirmed it was him—heard the distant but clear voice of John Adelman.

"Brian?"

"Yes."

"John here. In New York."

Brian struggled to decide exactly how to respond.

"You remember me? John in New York? We used to publish books together. We even rowed a boat together once in Central Park. And when the Mets beat Boston we got drunk together. That ring any bells?"

"What time is it there, John?"

"What time is it? Forget the time, old friend, and look at the *date!* Twenty-six November. Less than 30 shopping days to Christmas! Where have you been?"

"I was in the coffee shop."

After a pause, John's voice crackled with sarcasm. "So you've been in a coffee shop for two months. Thai coffee must be great. Are you all right?"

"Yes. I'm fine. How was Frankfurt?"

"Screw Frankfurt. Frankfurt is always the same. We sold lots of titles and I caught lots of colds. And, hey, the fair wasn't even held on a Jewish holiday this year."

"Somebody must have made a mistake."

"Yeah. Listen, Brian. I have some bad news for you. You sitting down?"

"Sure. Go ahead."

"All right. Richard Collins had a heart attack. Friday. He was having lunch at the White Horse Tavern in the Village and they rushed him from there to St. Vincent's but he died on the way."

"Jesus." Now Brian wished he had been sitting down.

"Yeah. Just like Bob Dylan."

"You mean Dylan Thomas."

"Yeah, whoever." He continued in a more personal tone. His voice had grown louder as the connection had improved. "Brian, David Martin took over as acting chairman."

"Let me guess. He wants a meeting of directors about my book program."

"We had a meeting of directors about your book program."

"But that's ridiculous. We could have held a telephonic meeting or I could have appointed an alternate. The bylaws—"

"The company bylaws don't provide for alternates or telephonic meetings, Brian. Just 48-hour notice. You didn't answer our phone messages so we sent you a fax and a DHL letter. Don't you read your mail either?"

"I was . . . out."

"Yeah. The coffee shop. Brian, look. That's the point I'm trying to make."

"What point?"

"You're out. Your program was voted down. If you're not back at your desk in one week from . . . today . . . no, yesterday your time . . . then you're out."

Brian felt his pulse quicken. He thought for several seconds, made certain he had control of his voice and then spoke. "What was the vote?"

"Four to one."

"Thanks for trying."

"Don't."

"Don't what?"

"Don't thank me. Thank Eliot."

"Eliot?"

"Brian. Eliot's independently wealthy and he's got no kids."

Brian noticed several heads in the lobby turn as he began laughing. He felt his sense of dread, guilt and all of his tension dissipate.

"Brian?"

"Yes, John."

"I argued with them until I was blue in the face. I told them you were on leave and you had lots of leave time coming to you. I told them you were paying your own way. I told them, oh, hell, I don't know, maybe if I had voted differently—"

"If you had voted differently you'd be a complete fool. The day you had your first kid is the day you gave up your right to bet on lost causes. I was going to lose, anyway. You know it. I know it."

"So what's funny?"

"Life."

"So are you coming back to the Big Apple in six days?"

"I don't know. What else is happening there?"

"What else? It's snowing, I've got a cold, my kids have the flu, my car radio was stolen again, and the review in the *Times* just tore apart our latest guidebook on New England. He did everything but call us Communists."

"John, listen, thanks for the call. Go back to sleep, OK?"

"It's two in the morning. I can't sleep. Maybe I'll go shovel some snow. That always relaxes me. Look, come back in time, will you, Brian? Maybe we can work something out with David."

"Yeah. Let me think on it, John. And thanks again for the call."

"Hey."

"Yeah?"

John Adelman placed his lips closer to the phone and lowered his voice. "Is Bangkok really as great a place for single guys as people say?"

Brian conjured up an image of John Adelman sitting on the edge of his bed, his lips pressed close to the phone's mouthpiece, glancing furtively at his wife—sleeping on the other side of the bed. He answered immediately. "Not at all, John. Very strict laws here, strictly enforced, and almost no sex outside marriage. It's all wishful thinking."

"Glad to hear it. I'd hate to think I was missing something."

# 52

BRIAN folded the local English-language newspaper to page three and placed it on Roger's desk beside a half-empty bottle of Mehkong whiskey. As Roger leaned on his elbows reading the article, Brian splashed some whiskey into two glasses. Brian took a drink and stared at the photograph of police removing a 'badly decomposed body' from 'a little used canal' in the Bangsue area of Bangkok. Children playing in the filthy water had discovered the man, now identified as Philip Johnson.

The body had three bullet wounds and police speculated the victim had been dead for several days. The man's profession and address were not known but police were now searching immigration files and other records for further clues to his identity. A spokesman for the Dragon Club denied an earlier press report that the deceased was a part owner in the club, and described him as 'a member of the club who often used the club's facilities for business purposes.'

Brian wondered if Jackson's death had anything to do with his own arrival in Bangkok. He could muster little sympathy for the man—only disappointment that he hadn't made clear what, if anything, he wanted to say about his brother's death.

Roger folded the paper and tossed it into a trash can, then, with a swipe of his hand, sent the can tumbling across the room. "Good riddance to bad rubbish."

"He was in a photograph on your bulletin board. I was wondering if you knew him."

"Every foreigner in Bangkok been on that board one time or another." Roger took a drink, swiveled in his chair, then swiveled back to face Brian. "Jackson was a lowlife into drugs and anything else illegal that might offer him a chance to make a fast, untraceable buck. He'd just come here to drink. Usually a mean drunk. I had to throw him out a few times. He had a crush on Dang. . . . Friend of yours?"

"I knew him slightly in the Sixties. In Bangkok. He seemed to travel all over the region as some kind of military courier."

"That a fact?"

Brian decided to change the subject. "Any leads yet on her killer?"

"Nah. I been harassing the police and I got some lowlife friends of my own out asking questions. Still zero." Roger cleared his desk and stood up. "Come on, let's get some air. Too damn gloomy in here."

Inside the bar, Roger suddenly stopped walking. Brian followed his stare to see Bob Donnelly holding court in a booth near the bar. Roger walked slowly to the booth. By the time he reached it, the girls in the booth had left, the girls on stage had stopped dancing, and, except for the music, the bar remained silent.

The music stopped. Bob glanced nervously around the bar and then spoke. "I was terribly sorry to hear about Oy's death, Roger. I had business in Singapore and couldn't be here for the funeral."

Roger stared into Bob's eyes, his arms hanging loosely at his sides. Neither his posture nor his expression suggested violence yet somehow it was unmistakably there—an emotion beyond anger and hatred. His voice was gravelly and flat. "You know why Oy went to stay at Nalin's the night she was murdered? She wanted to let me know she was angry. You know why she was angry? 'Cause some back-stabbing son-of-a-bitch told her that Karen and I were serious about each other."

Bob squirmed in his seat. He cleared his throat and spoke with caution. "I had no idea she—"

"That back-stabbing son-of-a-bitch was you."

A note of fear and anger now entered Bob's voice. the anger was forced, the fear was real. "Now, look—"

"Get out of here."

"What?"

"I won't tell you a second time."

"I'll leave when I'm ready. I *own* this bar." Bob's attitude was one of indignation but his voice was scratchy and tremulous.

Roger moved two steps closer to the table, leaned forward,

reached under Bob's arms, and in one swift motion, pulled him to his feet and jerked him forward. Bob fell against the bar, his flailing arms knocking over a glass and a bottle of beer. Roger stepped behind him and, with one hand grabbing the back of his shirt collar and one hand tucked into his belt, rushed him to the front door. The door opened only inward but Boonsom just managed to open it as Bob was propelled through the doorway and out across the sidewalk, sprawling beside an elderly fruit seller.

Roger walked slowly, almost sleepily, past Maew. He spoke without looking at her. "You better see about your boss. I think he had a fall."

# 53

*The Golden Triangle*

NEARLY an hour had passed since the heavy rain had finally stopped pounding the banana trees and lush jungle foliage surrounding the slow moving caravan of over 60 men and 100 mules. Huge, particolored butterflies again darted over the muddy dirt path as it twisted across rugged mountain ranges and remote low valleys toward the Thai border. Ahead lay flooded streams, mudslides and the danger of ambush.

Li T'ieh Sheng stopped briefly to loosen the laces on his boots and wipe sweat from his face. Before him, moving cautiously in single file, men in mud-caked green army fatigues carried their M-16 assault rifles, M-79 grenade launchers, light machine guns and hand grenades. Behind him a long-haired half Shan, half Chinese shouldering the unit's only 57 mm recoilless cannon stumbled over a tree's enormous roots. Li smiled at the resemblance to a betrayed Jesus carrying his cross to his Crucifixion. The young man's fatigue shirt was stained with a dark oil patch from the constant pressure of the butt of an American-made M-16 or Chinese-made AK-47 rifle, pressed tightly against him during firefights with competing armies of opium warlords. Among opium armies, such oil patches were the only 'long service medals' a combatant could display.

His thoughts turned again to the incident that had occurred less than an hour before. One of their patrols had caught two Muser hilltribesmen spying on them, one with a walkie-talkie. They were quickly led to a clearing and pushed to the ground with their hands tied behind their backs. Above them, roots of an enormous banyan tree descended like ropes from the branches. His son and two other men had interrogated the two for nearly 15 minutes but could not get them to talk. Finally, his son had led the older of the two into the jungle and executed

him with his pistol. The second prisoner was very young, perhaps, only 19 or 20. When the shot had been fired he had belched
uncontrollably and then vomited from fright.

His son returned and spoke again to the boy. Why were they
spying? How many men were they traveling with? Had the Musers
joined with the others? How had they known their route? Did
they plan to attack? The boy shivered with fear but refused to
speak. When his son and another man led the boy into the bushes
the boy had looked at General Li as a son might reproach an
unjust father.

Long ago, General Li had ordered his son to kill an American
officer in the Vietnamese Highlands; the one who had changed
his mind about getting involved in drug smuggling. He remembered how reluctantly his son had carried out his order. Over
the years, he had watched him change into an obedient soldier
who would kill without hesitation or remorse. In the last few
years, he had felt his pride in his son's development tinged with
undeniable sorrow; and General Li grew angry at what he believed to be his own emotional betrayal.

General Li waited in the silence and stared at the bunches of
green bananas hanging above their thick purple-and-red phal-
lic-shaped flowers, so heavy that the stem drooped downwards
almost touching a bush of vivid red wildflowers. He heard the
boy's voice screaming and protesting and he knew the boy's nerve
had broken when he had seen his friend's body. General Li waited.
Now the boy would speak and live or remain silent and die. Three
men would return from the bushes or there would be a shot and
only two would return. Either way, the presence of the Muser
meant only one thing: someone knew their plans. His eyes followed the route of giant rattan climbers, their long, slender, tough
stems snaking their way across dense undergrowth, and clinging
and climbing their way upwards along trunks and branches to
reach the jungle's canopy. Then he heard the shot.

The memory faded as the column of men suddenly halted
and each turned to motion the man behind to stoop and be
quiet. Li was secretly pleased with the interruption. His decades-
old leg wound was bothering him more than ever before. At times
his leg felt it was on fire and, despite his painful efforts of will, his
limp had become more pronounced than ever.

General Li watched his son walk quickly and silently past the men and mules. His son knelt down on one knee beside him. He rested his walkie-talkie across his other knee. Bits of grass and plant tendrils clung to the binoculars which hung from his neck. His son spoke in Mandarin, almost in a whisper. "We've lost contact with our scouts at point. I've sent more up ahead but we've heard nothing from them either."

General Li looked toward the walkie-talkie as if it alone held an answer to the mystery of the missing scouts. "Someone has taken our bait."

His son took off his sweat-stained cap and used it to wipe sweat from his forehead. "I'd say they ran into an ambush." His sunburnt face crinkled into a lopsided grin. "Unless they lost their way, of course."

Behind them the young man with the recoilless cannon chuckled softly. Li's eyes followed the erratic path of a butterfly as it flew about the walkie-talkie. He smiled back at his son. "How often do Shan scouts lose their way in the Shan states?"

His son took his canteen from his belt and offered some to his father who refused. He drank in long gulps, rinsed his mouth and spat out a stream of water. He capped and replaced the canteen, nodded to his father and abruptly returned to the head of the column.

Li watched with a father's pride as his son moved out of sight. Seconds later, while he was expecting the order to move out, he heard the first faint rustling movement behind nearby trees. He turned slowly toward the nearest trees of the dense jungle. A snapping noise came from the same direction. A minute before, he had seen the crested head and brilliantly colored plumage of a frightened kingfisher and shortly before that, a gibbon had used its slender but powerful arms to propel itself in great leaps through the trees. But this slight sound in an awesome and unnatural jungle silence—this was different. He glanced over his shoulder and saw the man behind him looking in the same direction. Li reached for the pistol in his holster. Just as his hand touched it a series of explosions tore up the road and enemy bullets began sweeping up and down the path like gusts of heavy rain. The men in the column dropped to their stomachs and returned the fire as panicky mules burdened with saddlebags began running in terror.

Li crawled around a dropped saddlebag to the side of the

trail and took cover behind a man-sized rock. Keeping low, he drew his pistol, aimed carefully at a blur of motion, and fired several times. The retorts of his pistol were completely lost in the deafening thunder of rocket grenades, recoilless rifles, bazookas, 60 mm mortars and M-60 machine guns and he knew they were completely outgunned by their ambushers. He felt a sudden sting in his right shoulder and his left hand touched the viscous wetness of his own blood.

A volley of shots hit the rock and ricocheted in several directions. He turned again to the man behind him. He lay on his side with both arms flung above his head, his right arm lying across his recoilless cannon. His long hair fell across his face and, beneath it, his sightless eyes stared back at Li. A dark red chest stain spread slowly outward to merge with his oil stain. Beside him, bullets slammed into the remains of a mule's torso the man had been using for cover.

Suddenly an explosion uprooted the rock and a section of the trail was blown away. Li felt himself being lifted as by a giant hand and just as quickly released to fall heavily on his back. He knew he could not move. He could only look up at a patch of blue sky framed by leaves and branches perched high above him. The almost perfect circle of blue framed by the green of the jungle began to blur and within that blue mirror, for an instant, Li saw again the pale face of the young woman from the city, her thin lips shaping an enigmatic smile, her wide eyes focused on his own face, as she again explained with infinite patience why poor men must not fight poor men. She stretched out her arm toward him. Li's hand trembled violently as he painfully stretched his fingers to release his pistol and reach out to take her hand. Her eyes held him as an unbearable stab of pain shook his chest and the woman's face wavered and then disappeared into constantly darkening circles of blue.

# 54

THE heavy-set man quickly moved his cigar away from his shirt and wiped ashes off his red-and-yellow plaid tie which completely clashed with his ill-fitting blue suit. He put the cigar out, lit another one, and leaned against the filing cabinet. He stared at the tall, thin man sitting across the room beside the coat rack. "Flip, what time is it now?"

"Five-forty."

"Five-forty in the fucking morning. This better be good, I can tell you."

"Take it easy, Barney. He wouldn't have called if he didn't have something."

There was a loud knock at the door and the door opened. Both men stared at the casually dressed, powerfully built man who silently crossed the office to make himself coffee. When he had finished he sat on Barney Richard's cluttered desk and took a long gulp. "Goddamn. Lukewarm again. I hate to come when your secretary's not here. You spooks cain't make coffee for shit."

Barney moved to the chair behind his desk, took off his jacket, and sat down. He looked into the eyes of the man drinking coffee in front of him with open distaste. "Now just what in hell happened up there? We're getting reports comin' in talking about a warlord battle to end all warlord battles."

Roger Webb lit up a Marlboro from a pack on Barney's desk and blew smoke out through his nostrils. He moved to a chair and leaned back, his arms at his sides. "Right now, I don't think anybody's too sure." He took another drag on his cigarette. He knew the irritation he could cause bureaucrats by taking his own sweet time to relate things. "It appears that General Li and his son decided to move nearly one hundred tons of opium from the Golden Triangle to Hong Kong. For the first leg of their journey it was all packed on one hundred mules."

Barney pushed his wife's photograph aside and put his feet up on his desk. "That's bullshit! It would take one thousand mules to transport that much opium."

Roger allowed his slowly exhaled smoke to pass over Barney's desk and into his eyes. "Very true, Barney. You really know the drug business. But so does our wily General Li and his wily son who converted the opium to morphine in their own Shan States factories. With the help of a few expert chemists from Hong Kong, I might add. The ratio of opium to morphine—as you gentlemen well know—is ten to one. So they simply eliminated the need for nine hundred mules."

Barney crushed his cigar in a bathtub-shaped ashtray he had gotten from the Darling Massage Parlour on his last visit. Visions of a naked Thai beauty clad only in soapsuds sliding her smooth body across his own briefly entered his mind. "Wily, my ass! On the phone you said they were ambushed and practically wiped out. So the morphine is in the hands of God-knows-which opium army and General Li and his son are dead."

Roger leaned back in his chair and stared out the window of the American embassy into the inky blackness of an early Bangkok morning. He could make out a marine guard walking slowly past the window yawning. Maybe they were all sex maniacs in the daytime—what the hell. "Well, not quite. It seems to be a bit more complicated than that."

The thin man, Frank Johnson, nicknamed 'Flip,' spoke up. "Will you speak plainly, for Christ's sake?"

Roger eyed the DEA man and reflected that anyone that thin *must* be on drugs. "Anything for you, Flip. O.K. My sources tell me that General Li and his son knew they couldn't hope to keep the conversion of opium to morphine a secret so they decided to purposely leak information about the convoy with saddlebags full of morphine. Ripe for the plucking, come and get it! The ruse was that one mule convoy would have saddlebags full of black market junk like toothpaste and bubble bath, that sort of thing. The other convoy would have the morphine. There was the usual Golden Triangle double-cross and whoever set up the ambush had obviously discovered the plan."

Barney lit a second cigar. "And General Li and his son were with the real one?"

Roger picked up the bathtub-shaped ashtray and read it.

"'Feeling is Darling.' Now, ain't that sweet?"

"Barney asked you a question."

Roger glowered at Flip, then smiled. Even at six in the morning, he wore a white shirt with three pens lining his shirt pocket: Mr. Preppie himself. "Oh, yeah, that's right, Flip, he did. Thanks for reminding me. Well, it seems they suspected a double-cross but decided to stay with the real one, anyway. They were pretty well armed. And ready for trouble. What they didn't know was that several hundred hilltribesmen had joined up with several hundred of Khun Sa's men. So General Li's boys simply bit off more than they could chew. Not a bad plan though."

Flip snorted. "What the hell do you mean, 'not a bad plan'? They're dead and they lost the morphine."

Roger's hand briefly touched the puckered scar on his cheek and he leaned back still farther. "General Li's son seems to have bought the farm all right. But my sources say General Li escaped. Maybe wounded, maybe not."

Flip spoke defiantly. "*My* source says General Li definitely bought the farm."

Roger glared at him. "You interrupt me one more time and you're gonna buy the same farm."

Flip's face reddened. He looked at Barney who shook his head and, with a wave of his hand, urged Flip to drop it.

Roger continued. "As for the morphine, Li never trusted anybody with the plan but his son and a financier based in Hong Kong named Yuen. He's the real money-man for the big opium boys. It seems General Li suspected Yuen had been getting set to double-cross him. It looks like they were trying to flush him out. And they did."

"But Yuen won, anyway."

"Nope. Yuen lost. The real morphine had been taken out in small convoys disguised as insignificant, independent groups trying to smuggle jade and Burmese Buddhas into Thailand. Every bit of the morphine had been loaded onto a special train inside Northern Thailand and was on its way to the Thai coast even before General Li's convoy set out."

"Well, what the hell were the saddlebags in Li's convoy?"

Roger emitted a loud burp. "'Scuse me, gentlemen, somebody I ate, no doubt. What were in the saddlebags, Flip? Well, that's the good part. The saddlebags were full of peppers."

"Peppers?"

"Right. All the peppers the poor hilltribes couldn't get rid of anyway. Whoever attacked General Li has got himself enough peppers to spice up every meal for the next ten years."

Barney banged his fist on the desk and swore. "Goddamn it to hell! Once Li gets the drugs on a freighter to Hong Kong he's got all the money he needs to buy more arms."

Flip's voice was full of bitterness. "We could have had them last year, remember, Barney? But whenever we're about to arrest anybody who counts in the drug business we find out we can't touch him because he's a goddamned paid asset of the CIA."

The fat man's face reddened. He swung his feet off the desk and leaned forward menacingly. "Well, maybe if you holier-than-thou DEA people would provide cover for our agents we'd do something for you sometime." Barney reached into a desk file, drew out a sheaf of paper, and threw it into the wastebasket. "And the quality of your agency's source evaluation reports aren't worth the paper they're printed on. In fact—"

Roger belched. "Gentlemen, if we could cut the inter-agency rivalry bullshit, I'd like to get back to bed. A bed, I might add, in which I had to abandon two already very abandoned women."

Barney relit his cigar, puffed and calmed himself. "Where do you think Li will go?"

Roger's eyes focused on the huge map of Southeast Asia on the wall. He pushed himself to his feet, walked to the map and placed his finger on the town of Nakornburi. His finger circled the town. "This is one place," he began, "that—"

Flip clapped his hands together and spoke excitedly. "That's exactly what I thought. Nakornburi is a narcotics-prone city with lots of converging highways. Li probably has plenty of friends there."

Roger glowered at the boyish Yuppie-like face flushed with excitement and reflected that some people simply don't belong in Asia. "What I was about to say was that Nakorn Sawan is the one place he won't go. He's too hot; worth too much; and too cautious; especially now. Anyway, Nakornburi never was his style." Roger's eyes scanned the map more closely. "My sources think he was wounded in the firefight. He needs a safe place." He moved his finger slowly across the map to Ayudhya. "He's lost his base in the Golden Triangle; he's on the run. I think he'll head for the house."

"Then we'll know it." Flip's voice failed to conceal a mixture of professionalism and smug pride.

"You got a man there?"

Flip glanced at Barney and then fidgeted in the embarrassed silence of a bureaucrat whose agency has to reluctantly admit the successful coup of a rival agency. It was Barney who answered. "*We've* got several men there on loan from the Thai Narcotics Division. I'll alert them."

"You were *expecting* General Li to head for Ayudhya?"

"No. After Stanley started opening up, we thought the house might be a distribution point. Seems we were wrong. But, at least, for once, we were prepared. Our first lucky break."

Roger grew thoughtful. "I figured you had somebody at the house when you told me about Brian arriving. But how could you have 'several' men at the house without somebody gettin' suspicious?"

"Because, among other methods, we made sure the woman got a cock-and-bull story about a rich kid with threats on his life needing full-time security. Not that it's any of *your* business."

"And just what *is* my business in all this?"

"Your business is to help us spring the trap shut. What I need to do now is have a chat with your friend, Brian. Get him in here."

"He doesn't know anything. Why not keep him out of it?"

"Because if he *does* know, he'll want revenge and that can make him useful to us. He knows the exact layout inside the house and he's in love with the woman. More important, if she's sweet on him and he questions her he just might get something out of her." Barney allowed himself a lopsided smile. "And, just maybe, I can get my hands on General Li alive."

"Which would do your career a world of good. But I'd like to leave Brian out of this. You said—"

"I said *if* we get the green light to make a deal with Stanley, remember? He hasn't told us yet who set up the deal. And he won't until he's sure he can get a lighter sentence and that's too bad because time is running out."

"There's no guarantee Brian would do anything to help you, anyway. You sure ain't about to bring his brother back for him.

And if he does get involved, it could damn well put him in danger."

"We'll see to it that he stays safe."

"Just like Jackson stayed safe?"

"We weren't protecting Jackson. We didn't know who he was until it was too late. If we had we might not need Brian now."

Roger inwardly cursed his own stupidity in never suspecting that local drug dealer and drunkard Phil Johnson was actually Bill Jackson. He'd never even known the man called Bill Jackson was in Bangkok. Still. . . . "I'd still like to leave Brian out of it."

After several seconds of silence, Barney spoke through a clenched-teeth sneer. "And I'd like my next report on you to say that you've been a very good boy so you can get another visa extension. Bring him in!"

Roger glared hatred at the bureaucrat across the desk. He suddenly reached forward, grabbed the cigar from Barney's mouth and crushed it in the ashtray. "The next time you go to the Darling Massage Parlor I'll make sure the mama-san fixes you up with one who's got incurable clap." He stood up, left the room and slammed the door.

# 55

Yuen Sheung fuk looked resignedly up at the long series of narrow steps leading up the hillside. Raindrops, so fine as to be almost invisible, hit his face and hands. The island's famous Peak had completely disappeared inside a mass of clouds and heavy mist. Large, grey clouds tinged with black billowed even larger at the expense of an already ominous white sky.

Yuen had seldom been to this part of Hong Kong Island and he felt completely out of his element. Although only a few years younger than General Li, Yuen had always loathed exercise, and the prospect of climbing a steep-stepped path intensified his anger at the necessity for running such a mysterious errand. Finally, huddling in his suit jacket, he faced into the fine rain and began climbing between the grey, drab concrete buildings.

An old woman peered from behind a shabby window above which a pole, hung with clothes now soaked from the rain, extended part way across the narrow lane. The cool December morning was damp and windy and the lowery and stygian sky continued to threaten more rain at any moment.

Despite his betrayal of General Li, Yuen felt there was no real proof of his own involvement, and, however Li managed to do it, he knew the shipment had reached Bangkok safely. But then why had the trading company refused to recognize his Bangkok receipt and instead handed him an envelope containing this address. He had demanded to see the person responsible—to no avail.

By the time he reached the top of the steps, a coldness in his chest forced him to stand still for several seconds. He read his instructions again and started down the long, narrow alleyway. A gust of wind flung his tie over his shoulder and blew a Chinese-language newspaper across the lane toward him.

He pushed open the door of a building set at the rear of a dead end lane. From the outside, only its colorful door gods and faded Chinese calligraphy distinguished the dull, grayish brown three-story building from others just like it.

Inside, Yuen wiped his feet on a mat and hesitated. The room's darkness was punctuated by thin candles and red electric bulbs and Yuen could see that the temple was seldom used. An emaciated dog stretched lazily and moved slowly away from his path. The smell of incense was so strong Yuen began to feel sick to his stomach. He hurriedly crossed to the rear wall and drew aside a faded curtain with embroidered figures of the Eight Immortals. The wooden door's only decoration was a small painted square inside which two Chinese characters announced: Fortune Teller.

In answer to his knock, he heard the sound of a bar and chain being drawn open. The door opened inward and a heavyset, swarthy man of about 25 beckoned him to follow up several stone steps. Yuen waited while the man knocked on the door of the room at the top.

The inside was clean, sparsely but comfortably furnished and well-lit. The abrupt change forced him to shield his eyes. The room seemed to serve its occupants as office, place of abode and temple storeroom. A convertible sofa was against the wall near a metal office desk and a fax machine.

A dark-complexioned man about 45 sat at a desk working with a calculator. A young, well-built teenager sat near a wall sorting and stacking incense and still another dark-complexioned man in his early 30's sat in a chair reading a newspaper. Yuen thought the man reading the paper looked vaguely familiar. The man who had brought Yuen into the room left the room and closed the door.

Yuen stood by the door while the man reading a newspaper and the younger man seemed to appraise him as a valuable but amusing antique in a curiosity shop. Yuen felt his temper rising. He spoke in Cantonese. "If you gentlemen have nothing to say to me, I shall—"

The man at the desk continued calculating without turning around. "You shall do exactly what we tell you to do. From now on. Is that clear?"

Yuen could feel the perspiration on his forehead increase. The heat of the room, the threat delivered in so rude a manner, and, most ominous of all, the Yunnan-accented Mandarin.

The man rose and opened the liquor cabinet. He placed ice into a glass, poured vodka into it and then Kahlua. He walked to Yuen and handed it to him. "Black Russian. Your favorite, isn't it, Yuen?" The man stared at him with a cold gaze then returned to his desk and sat down. As he pointed to a chair Yuen noticed a tattoo on his wrist. His first thought, as he walked to the chair, was that these must be local Triads trying to muscle in on his operation. But that was impossible. His organization was far too large, too powerful. And local Triads were not dark-complexioned men with Yunnanese accents.

The man raised a cup of tea and offered a toast. "To the successful arrival of General Li's morphine into Bangkok."

Yuen lifted his glass and drank. He now switched to Mandarin. I think you—"

"And to the successful escape of General Li from ambush." Again Yuen followed the man's lead and drank.

The man's beady eyes now glazed over with an angry gaze. His small, thick lips began moving. The voice was low and contemptuous. He raised his cup again. "And to the failure of those who planned the ambush." He turned the teacup upside down over Yuen's lap.

Yuen started to rise and felt himself pushed down by the muscular teenager who had left off bundling stacks of incense and was now standing behind him.

"I can explain any—"

"There is no need to explain anything. You see, many of us had felt you were no longer needed in any case. But the elders always protected you. Now that you betrayed General Li, it makes our job easy. And quite frankly, if you had killed General Li it would have made our job even easier."

Yuen's lips began to quiver. "I don't understand. I thought—"

"You thought we were General Li's men. We were before; but not now. You see, Yuen, times have changed. Up until now, Yunnanese like myself and my colleagues here have only been involved in transporting opium from Burma to Northern Thailand. And our Chiu Chau friends in Bangkok such as Mr. Ma here always handled the arrangements until the shipments arrived in Hong Kong. Where it was handed over to those who made the real profit—Cantonese such as yourself."

In the silence Yuen cleared his throat. "If there is any—"

"Of course, you never dirtied your hands with drugs; your task was to use your skills to invest funds in Hong Kong and abroad. But now Yunnanese of our generation living in Thailand can get travel documents; we are now Thais, after all. The younger generation of Chiu Chau Chinese living in Bangkok also feel as we do; that the time has come for us to become involved in external trafficking of opium and heroin."

The younger, dark-complexioned man neatly folded his newspaper and walked slowly from the other side of the room. He sat in a chair facing Yuen. He was the best-dressed and the most soft-spoken of the three men. "As you know, Mr. Yuen, the process of producing opium becomes more expensive every year. And once General Li and his associates and you and your associates take your cuts, well, it does seem to us that we have been getting a bit short-changed."

Yuen felt his mouth growing extremely dry. He wet his lips. "If it's a matter of renegotiating. . . ."

The man laughed. "No. It is a bit more than that, I'm afraid."

Yuen suddenly remembered where he had seen the man before: sitting behind the counter of the organization's gold shop in Bangkok's Chinatown. Over a year before, Yuen had left the usual amount of drug money to be laundered, and the man had given him a Hong Kong telephone number and coded sentence. There had been nothing unusual about the transaction and Yuen had never seen him before or after. But Yuen remembered that at the time he had felt the man was staring at him, as if appraising his worth. Yuen ran his tongue over the dryness of his mouth and felt the sensation of cold sweat as it appeared on his forehead.

The man rose, took Yuen's glass and walked to the liquor cabinet. He spoke as he mixed the drink. "What has basically happened here, Mr. Yuen, is that your company, shall we say, is being taken over by a younger, more aggressive group. The days of the Kuomintang generals and traditional syndicates are over." He handed Yuen the glass.

Yuen took a long drink and tried to control his voice as he spoke. "And how do I fit into this 'new business venture'?"

"If it had not been for your betrayal, we might have had to wait years to make our move. Now, all is possible. I have an

MBA from a well-known American University, but what is that compared to what you know and who you know? And, most important, as they say, what you've got on who you know?" The man gazed for a moment at the wood-and-tin huts on the hills in the distance.

"Yes, Mr. Yuen, in a very different way, on a salary which we will pay you, you do fit into the new business venture. You are after all still one of Hong Kong's most important Red Capitalists, are you not? We have taken the liberty of having some of our people visit your flat this afternoon. Your passport is now with us for the time being. Our people at the apartment say your taste in women is excellent. But from now on you will travel outside of Hong Kong only with our people and you will receive your instructions from us. And, Mr. Yuen, any acts of disloyalty—such as you displayed to General Li—will be dealt with severely. Are we clear now?"

Yuen glanced at the teenager. The boy now straddled a chair against the wall, his thick, muscular arms resting on the back of the chair, staring derisively at him. He held his right fist in his left hand as if he had just struck a blow and in doing so had hurt his knuckles. The oldest of the three men was again busy with a ledger and calculator.

Yuen attempted to control his voice. "And what happens now?"

The younger of the two men spoke again. "What happens? Nothing, Mr. Yuen. We know where you are. When we have need of your service, we will call you. You are free to go."

Yuen saw that most of the tea stain on his trousers had disappeared. He rose quickly, turned and walked to the door. He took out his handkerchief to wipe his brow and turned to face the men. He again made an effort to control his voice. "You said General Li is alive?"

The younger man spoke again. "General Li's son was killed in the ambush. The General himself seems to have been mortally wounded. As our own group in the Shan States is now in control, General Li can never return to power, and his health doesn't worry us too much in any case. Rest assured, Mr. Yuen, we will guarantee your protection. For as long as you show you deserve it."

Yuen felt his handkerchief slip from his grasp. As he bent to retrieve it, he felt he was baring his neck for an executioner's blade. He straightened quickly, walked down the stairs on trembling legs, and walked quickly out of the temple. The rain had stopped and aureate rays of a late afternoon sun streamed through banks of clouds to illuminate the harbor.

He walked steadily down the steep steps of the hillside, but a hard ball of fear was growing in his stomach, his heart beat wildly, his legs seemed barely in control, and he realized he had never felt so old.

# 56

ROGER and Brian sat at a booth near a Christmas tree Santa Claus entangled helplessly in a mass of artificial snow. Both men had been drinking steadily for over two hours. After waiting patiently for an opportunity, Roger had brought up the subject of Paul's death and Brian had grown more morose with each round of beer.

Roger kept his eyes leveled on Brian's face while inwardly cursing the CIA, DEA and all intelligence agencies. A barely pubescent dancer approached the booth and poured the remainder of Brian's beer into his glass. She looked at him while holding the bottle. "You want one more?"

Brian glanced at the tiny scars of insect bites on her legs, tell-tale signs of an impoverished childhood of planting and harvesting rice. He spoke without looking up. "I want several more."

The dancer took the empty bottle away, moved to the bar and yelled to Maew: "Beer Amarit!"

Roger spoke cautiously in an earnest tone. "Look, Brian, your brother—"

"My brother was a fool who got his ass blown off when he could have avoided the whole rice paddy trip altogether."

"From what you tell me about him he didn't sound like a fool. I think he believed in something."

"And he died for nothing. Something for nothing, that's what he got. Lucky man." Brian pressed his thumb and forefinger to his eyes. "I'm getting drunk. Which is about all I've done since I came to this blasted city. And which I'm doing these days with more and more regularity. Staring into a mirror seeing my imbecilic, befuddled face framed by bottles of liquor and bikini-clad teenagers.

The room filled with the heavy-hearted lyrics of Bruce Springsteen; a forlorn tale by a man whose brother had died at Khe Sahn and of the woman in Saigon who had loved him.

Neither man spoke until the next selection began. The bar filled with, "Brown Girl in the Ring." Roger waved to a waitress for coffee. "I never know when you're serious. I wonder if you do."

"Oh, yes. As with infections and intelligence leaks, I too can be serious. And, I confess, even maudlin. Especially about a brother I loved."

"Yet you git angry ever' time I mention his name."

"Why the hell not? He could be sitting with us now, in a Bangkok bar, cold beer to drink, and a good life ahead of him. All he had to do was to stay with me in the Army Security Agency. Finish his enlistment and marry later. But, no, not Paul Mason. He had to marry right away; marry a foreign national as well so that he'd lose his security clearance; so they made him a foot soldier and sent him to 'Nam to fight jungle shadows."

Roger spoke again. "It must have been something he felt he had to do. He had no choice."

"Oh, there is *always* a choice, Roger. It may not be easy, but choice is always there. And Paul made his. Then he got separated from his unit and died fighting the communists. He made his choice and. . . ."

While a waitress placed a piece of birthday cake in front of him, Brian took several gulps of beer. He stared silently at the lights striking the Buddha wall shrine, as if the shrine's Buddha alone could calm his emotions.

Roger picked up the fork and cut into his cake with the care of a biologist dissecting a poisonous snake which still showed signs of life. He placed a piece into his mouth and chewed slowly. "He got separated from his unit, yes. And he was killed. . . . But we no longer believe the communists did it."

Brian lifted his head and stared into Roger's eyes. From somewhere out of a patch of darkness perforated by flickered bands of light he heard a girl's voice ask, "Why you no eat your cake: You no like?" The massive amount of foundation on her face gave her skin an almost preternatural sheen reminding Brian of a ghost staring at him from the darkness. Or from the past.

"We think he was involved in smuggling heroin out of the Golden Triangle and either tried to double-cross or was double-crossed. Or he may have wanted to get out. His—"

In one swift motion, Brian stood and grabbed Roger's shoulders. Several drinks toppled over as Roger was slammed against the bar. "For Christ's sake, Brian, they got one of the men who was involved in the operation. A guy named Stanley confessed. Do you think I'd say this if we weren't sure?"

Brian heard the sound of his own voice as if someone else were speaking for him. "We?"

"The DEA, Brian—the Drug Enforcement Administration. I . . . help them out from time to time. That's how I keep my visa."

After several moments, Brian relaxed his grip. The nausea began to engulf him. He lifted his eyes to stare at the revolving ball and tried to seal his ears with the palms of his hands. But the colors pierced his physical defenses and with them, painful, offending messages slammed into his brain and surged into his gut. The globe of light seemed to stand still just as the rest of the room began accelerating out of control. Red, smuggling heroin; blue, younolike; orange, Brown Girl in the Ring, tra la la la la; green, Happy Birthday to you. Heroin. Blue. Brown. Gold. Triangle. Communists eat your cake. Ricefield green. Laotian Reds. Why you no like? Orange. Saffron. Buddhist monks. Brian, are you all right? Yellowowowow. I think him sick. Tra la la la la.

# 57

THE heavy-set speaker was embedded in, almost encrusted by, middle age. He paused and looked toward Brian. Brian continued to stare at the map. ". . . but then they developed a better plan. They started using Dakota C-47's to drop opium into Northern Laos. Then they reshipped it— also by air, to the Central Highlands of South Vietnam—where a few American advisors and a platoon of ARVN were on their payroll. 'They' being a corrupt American general and the others I mentioned. When your brother was transferred from Thailand to the Highlands, the group needed him to participate in the operation or at least to look the other way."

The man's lazy mid-Western accent was as casual as his dress. He held the pointer beside the map as a patient but slightly bored professor might await questions from his students. The words describing the events that led to Paul's death were more matter-of-fact than the introduction of the next season's titles to salesmen at a publishing house's sales meeting. Through the window beside the map Brian could see a young Marine guard walk across the embassy lawn, his attention drawn toward the front gate. Brian spoke softly but with force: "My brother would never have gotten involved in drugs."

For several seconds no one spoke. Beside an American flag, the numerals of a digital clock clicked over to read 9:00. The glare of the morning light and his own lack of sleep caused Brian to briefly place his index finger and thumb on his eyelids. He spoke more in resignation than in anger. "My brother wasn't the type. Don't you think I knew him well enough to know that?"

Roger Webb looked toward the man at the front of the room, then to the immaculately dressed thin man, then toward Brian. He leaned forward in his leather chair and carefully slid his

glasses out of a case and put them on. "Brian, our source—
Stanley—says that your brother was promised that if he cooper-
ated, he would have been transferred back to Bangkok. He loved
. . . as you know, he loved his wife very much. Stanley tells us
Paul agreed and then had a change of heart. He went to Army
Intelligence and told what he knew. Unfortunately, an American
general stopped the investigation."

"Who killed him?"

"The son of a Chinese warlord headed the operation. And
there were several South Vietnamese soldiers on the warlord's
payroll. And Stanley and Jackson. They all went after him. Stanley
claims Jackson got him. Probably they both did."

"Who killed Jackson?"

Roger shrugged. "Whoever didn't want him talking to you.
Of course, there's an outside chance his death had nothing to do
with you. He had plenty of enemies. Anyway, Stanley was
wounded in the firefight with your brother. We can't trace the
South Vietnamese, but Stanley says two of them were killed.
Seems your brother put up quite a fight. And now we've got Stanley."

"Why hasn't he been tried?"

The man with the pointer stubbed out his cigar and spoke quietly but with as much conviction as he could muster. "We want the
American general. Retired now. And we want General Li. And another American officer Stanley claims was involved. With Stanley's
help—and with your cooperation—we might just get them."

"What's the general's name?"

"I can't tell you that."

"What's the officer's name?"

"We don't know yet. Stanley's keeping it as something to swap
in trade."

"In trade for what?"

"In trade for a lighter sentence. Stanley was caught trying to
smuggle a boatload of cocaine into a cove near Key West. He
says he'll name names in his current operation *and* in the Vietnam operation if he can get a deal. Some lawyers in Washington
are figurin' out if there's a way, even now, that we might be able
to legally get some of the bastards who killed your brother. We're
waiting for word to see if Washington OK's Stanley's request."

Roger spoke up. "Course by the time the bureaucrats in Washington make up their minds if we can deal or not we could all be

daid of old age. But if you'll give us—"

Brian continued speaking to Barney. "And Stanley goes free early for testifying against the officer and the general?"

"Most likely."

"And you don't know this officer's name?"

"Not yet."

Roger spoke soothingly. "Brian, we're also after the people who set up the deal. The American general is old and sick, he hasn't got much time left. Even if it's too late to convict him, don't let this son-of-a-bitch die with honor. In any case, the order to kill your brother didn't come from him. It came from the people who set up the smuggling arrangement. And they're still operating. A self-styled General Li Tieh-sheng and his son, Li Chin Pao. We believe the general was wounded in the Golden Triangle just the day before yesterday. His son may be dead. We're tryin' to confirm it."

Brian spoke angrily as he rose. "General and his son? What bullshit! My brother's dead and Stanley is probably lying through his teeth to get a lighter sentence."

Roger spoke quickly. "Brian, we think General Li ordered your brother's death. We think we know where General Li is heading and Barney thinks you can help us nail him. If you'll hear us out—"

Brian stared at Roger and thought of his deceptive comradery the first time he had met him in the Horny Tiger. He knew now it had been no accident: Roger Webb had been waiting for him to arrive.

Brian walked past the grey filing cabinets and shelves of hardbound manuals to the door and opened it. "I don't want to listen to anymore of this nonsense. My brother lived honorably and his death was honorable. And you people aren't about to change that with your goddamned fairytale."

As the door slammed, Barney looked toward Roger with an expression of pained resignation; the face of a professor whose favorite and most promising student has just failed an examination.

# 58

THE abbot stood motionlessly beside a shallow, sun-dappled pond covered with morning glories and lotus leaves. A young boy trudged through the pond's muddy water and transferred another fish from his glistening net into the basket on the shore.

"Would you blame that fish because it isn't as attractive as those already in the boy's basket?" The abbot twitched his left shoulder to secure his reddish brown robe and looked up at the sky. "Would you blame that cloud because it is not as well formed as the rest? Or level an accusation at that streak of sky because it is less blue than the area above our heads?"

The two men walked slowly across the open field toward the temple before Brian replied. "But that is not the same. Man has awareness. If man has free will he has to accept the responsibility for his decisions."

The abbot's voice was full of good-natured reproach. Like all Thai monks who have chosen to spend a lifetime in Buddhist temples learning and meditating, he held out little hope that Western logic—to him only slightly more fruitful than frivolous word play—could ever lead to the truth; rather his own garrulous and playful nature seemed to revel in such banter. His dark brown eyes, well sunken into his thin wrinkled face, were bright and full of vigor. His body beneath his robe was frail but his mind was alert. "Responsibility, yes. But judging the actions of others is never the path to joy. It is the path to anxiety and anger."

Despite himself, Brian could feel the anger rising inside him. "I think evil deeds must be judged. If these men are right, then my brother—"

"Who, Vijanandho, is it that judges?"

Brian avoided the abbot's steady gaze. For three months

twenty years before, with head and eyebrows shaved, and wearing a golden-orange saffron robe, Brian had been given the name of Vijanandho—'Pleasure through Learning.' The present abbot, at that time, had been one of over twenty monks and his small living quarters, or *kuti*, had been next to Brian's.

He had guided Brian through the intricacies of Buddhist philosophy and the rigors of meditation, and their discussions of life and philosophy had often lasted for several hours a day.

Two days after Brian had stormed out of the American embassy, he and Nalin had shopped for lotus, candles and joss-sticks and a large packet of tea—all tribute for the abbot. Brian had driven Roger's dust-covered and well corroded Hyundai to the temple and meditation center not far from Ayudhya and had been pleasantly surprised to find that, not only was his patient but amiable teacher of two decades ago still at the temple, but that he had now become the temple's abbot as well. Twenty years before, Paul's death had brought Brian to the temple to enter the monastic life for three months. Now Paul's possible involvement in drugs and his alleged murder had brought him back again; this time for a few hours of peace and the need for a clear vision.

They walked across the temple's spacious grounds, past nuns with shaved heads and white robes burning leaves and past young novices sweeping meandering paths. A slight breeze rang the temple bells and reduced the effect of the afternoon's bright sunlight. They approached the main temple building and sat in the shade of several Palmyra Palms. The abbot sat perfectly still as he spoke. "Do you still wear an image of the Lord Buddha?"

Brian felt the silver amulet case on his neck chain beneath his shirt. It made a jingling sound. "I always wear the one you gave me."

"Do you think the image of a Buddha has intrinsic power as many Thais believe?"

Brian felt the conversation edging almost imperceptively into a test. "The image of the Buddha may or may not have intrinsic power but by wearing it it may serve to remind one of the Buddha's path and to prevent one from committing a wrong act."

The abbot turned from watching nuns cutting and arranging flowers and stared at Brian with a smile both good-natured and enigmatic. Brian could feel in that gaze the profound sense of spiritual well-being that a lifetime of spiritual quest and selfless acts had given him. It was a force that seemed to transcend the abbot's individual personality and ego to emanate from a genuine life of spirituality.

He turned away from Brian and watched a temple boy fill water jars. "People desire so many things in life, Vijanandho. If only they could see that so much of what they think they want is simply a part of the World of Illusion."

Before Brian could formulate an answer, the monk chuckled softly, rose and entered the main chapel, or *bot*. Inside the chapel—where Brian had been ordained—it seemed to him that nothing had changed. He recognized everything: The tall clock, the faded books, antique wooden cabinets, and huge candles in front of an altar supporting several large Buddha images. The only sound was that of another temple boy, clad only in shorts, on his hands and knees polishing the floor.

At the sound of the temple's brass bell being struck, both men turned toward the doorway. Outside, a temple boy was striking the bell with a wooden club summoning the monks to evening meditation.

"Nearly four o'clock," Brian said. "I'd better go."

The abbot glanced at Brian's wrist. "You wear no watch."

Brian smiled. "It wasn't allowed when I stayed here as a monk and I never got back into the habit of wearing one."

They walked slowly down a dirt path toward the small one-story building behind the chapel. Brian stopped and *waiied* the abbot. "I had better leave you here."

The abbot gazed at Brian without smiling. "You will do what you must about your brother's death. I cannot offer you specific advice. Whatever you have learned of value here was learned long ago. I can only remind you to examine your goals very carefully. Justice is a worthy cause but revenge springs from within our own egotistical natures. Without exception, whenever we let our emotions rule us, Mara's evil army sees an opportunity to twist our motives and pervert our goals."

"I don't know what I'll do yet," Brian said. "But just being with you and being here has helped me a great deal. I will come again before I leave Thailand to say goodbye."

For several minutes Brian stood watching through the windows. On the raised wooden floor all the monks stood facing the abbot and at the sunken rear and sides of the room, devout novices and nuns stood as motionlessly as the monks. The late afternoon light poured through yellow curtains bathing the room in a golden yellow glow.

BODHESI YOSUJANATAM KAMALAM VA SURO
(The Buddha, like the sun with lotuses, awakens wise people)

VANDAMAHAM TAMARANAM SIRASA JINENDAM
(I revere with my head the Conqueror Supreme,
the Peaceful One)

BUDDHO YO SABBAPANINAM SARANAM
KHEMAMUTTAMAM
(The Buddha who for all beings is the highest refuge, most
secure)

The deep drone of the Pali chanting floated monotonously and comfortingly out to anyone within reach. In the plangent, rhythmic incantations of the monks, novices and nuns, Brian could feel a growing tranquility but also a growing longing for something he had lost long ago—a brother, a woman, a serenity, a life that might have been. He turned and walked toward the car and the soothing sounds of the chanting washed over him.

# 59

BRIAN lay on Nalin's rumpled bed watching her painstakingly apply the last touches of eye shadow. He reached for the glass of Scotch and took a long gulp, then reached for the bottle for a refill.

Nalin watched him in the mirror of her vanity table. "You drink all day long."

Brian raised the glass and bottle in salute. "You're very observant."

"What?"

"Observant, deservant, subservant. You are the prize in the Crackerjack box. The song in my heart. The apple in my eye. The pin in my grenade. Ninety-two in the shade. The Home of the Brave. Home on the range, strange, it only rains on the plains in Spains but it pores on the whores in barroom doors."

Nalin turned to look at him. He lay back in his undershorts, his head propped against the bedboard, a bottle in one hand, a glass in the other. "Karen is on her way over. You aren't even getting ready. What is the matter with you?"

"Oh, nothing too exciting my love. Just Roger Webb's recent confession—*dear* old Roger Webb—informing me that he actually works for—or rather with—the DEA. Give me a 'D'; give me an 'E'; give me an 'A.' Yea, team! As we used to shout in the Sixties. Oh, sorry, I meant Fifties."

Nalin turned again to face the mirror. "So that's why you've been so moody lately; you finally found out that Roger does things for the DEA."

Brian stared at her. "You knew? You knew Roger was a Narc?"

"Everybody on Patpong knows Roger helps the Drug Enforcement Administration sometimes. Except you. Why do you think some girls in other bars try to avoid him?"

Brian relaxed into his drunken stupor. "Roger a narc. Panic

in Lumpini Park! Poor Roger. Can't get laid because he's paid to be Bangkok's Sam Spade. Oh, say can you see if there's any opium on me?"

"Why do you need to get drunk just because Roger is with the DEA?" Nalin laughed in a childlike manner. "You do something and him catch you?"

"Please, my dear, refrain from mixing up bargirl English with the King's English. It gives me a headache and it sounds like a cheap Tequila and a Grand Cru taste when mixed together. But, yes, he did indeed catch me. He said my brother—you remember himly, perhaps, dimly, but he married your mother. My brother, your mother, the truth grimly, though I speak primly. Well, they say he was killed not by any little men in black pajamas but by the Good Guys in American olive green fatigues and their Shan State companions because he went in and out of an opium deal. In and out the window. How much is that poppy in the window?"

Nalin sat perfectly still and stared at him in the mirror with repressed anger and unwavering attention. She closed her cosmetics case, put it into her purse and stood up.

"You look ravishing, my dear. The prim white blouse, Sak's Fifth Avenue? The brown-and-yellow skirt—Bloomingdale's? It never fails—just watch for future sales! The cute pimps, oh, sorry, lovely, I mean pumps. That beautiful face. A pinup Extraordinaire. You could be—"

Nalin stood without moving and continued to stare intently at Brian. "What else did Roger tell you?"

"What else? I didn't stay to listen. If it is true I don't want to know.... My God, what pain my foolish brother gave your mother. How could he have been so stupid? The goddamn fool. She loved him so much and he threw it all away by—"

Nalin's voice hardened. "You don't know anything. My father was a good man."

"You're *step*father was a fool. You understand? A fool who got himself killed and left you and your mother to—"

Nalin moved closer to him. "My mother! You think she's so pure and good, don't you?"

Brian sat up on the bed now, shouting. "That's right! I do! And that's what she is! And she's had enough pain in her life without her only daughter leaving home to become a dancer; a *whore* on Patpong Road."

Nalin lashed out with her purse. The arc of her swing caught Brian full on the side of the face. He dropped the glass and bottle onto the floor. He knew a cut had opened on his face. Now it was Nalin who was shouting: "I may be a whore but my mother is worse than that, you understand? I hate her!"

Brian jumped up and slapped Nalin's face with his open hand. Her mouth opened in surprise and shock. "Goddamn you!" She flew at him trying to scratch his face. He held her arms but felt the effects of the Scotch in the pit of his stomach. His legs seemed unable to support him. He let her go and sat down on the bed. She slapped him once, twice and again he grabbed her wrists. Her face was wet with tears and smudged streaks of makeup. She struggled to get out of his grasp and fell backwards against her vanity table, collapsing the wooden folding stand and shattering its mirror.

Brian's head began pounding and he could feel the layer of sweat on his skin. He started to fall backwards slowly as if floating. but he heard clearly the sound of the glass shattering. His mind fought to distinguish dream from memory from present reality, and the shattered glass seemed to have been caused by Nalin's exploding anger. "Damn you! Don't you understand? Who do you think got your brother involved in drugs? My mother, that's who! And Bob Donnelly. Your brother died because of them! Damn you! Can't you understand anything?"

Brian forcibly shook his head and sat up. Nalin had disappeared and reappeared and was throwing paper at him. She stood before him screaming and crying. "Why do you think I worked in that bar? You think I wanted to? I tried to learn about Bob Donnelly and if I had to go to bed with him to learn something then I did it! How do you think I found out Bob had lent so much money to my mother? Why do you think I went with you the first night? Roger said you were Bob's 'close friend.'"

For several seconds, she stood staring at him, her breathing finally slowing. "You think I'm a whore? All right. I'll go to Ayudhya and see the real whore. I'll tell her she's won—she's the one you love—but I'll tell her what I know and how much I hate her to her face." Nalin turned and ran into the hallway, slamming the door behind her.

Brian reached over and picked a letter off the floor and another off the foot of the bed. As he read, drops of blood fell steadily, streaking the blue ink on the white-lined paper.

*August 4th, 1968*

*My Darling,*

*How much I miss you! For me each day we are apart is not a day at all but rather an endless period of mourning. . . .*

*I search the papers every day and pray that there is no battle going on in the Central Highlands of Vietnam. I know you are only supposed to be advising the Montagnards but I also know advisors have a way of getting into a battle.*

Brian skipped over Suntharee's declarations of love and description of the school's progress and flooded ricefields until his eyes spotted Bob's name.

*Bob Donnelly was here the other day and, of course, Brian visits us often. Nalin looks forward to his visits so much. She gets very upset when he can't make it. She says to send you a ricefield full of love.*

*My darling, there is something I must tell you. I can only hope you will understand. There is a way we can be together again and soon. But, it means I must speak of things I had hoped never to tell you. I know I should have but I was always afraid to lose your love.*

*You see, my father—Nalin's grandfather—did not die in an automobile accident as I told you. It was true that my mother and husband died in the car accident on the highway when Nalin was two years old. But my father is still alive. He is General Li Tieh-sheng. Yes, my darling, the opium warlord. You even mentioned his name one night when you were discussing a warlord battle in the Golden Triangle with Brian. And you mentioned that, "Li is the worst of the lot." Yes, I can't deny it, he is. But how I cried that night in the Buddha room after you had gone to sleep. Brian had left his room and happened to hear me. I told him I was just being silly because I knew you were leaving for Vietnam and begged him never to tell you that he had found me crying. I'm sure he kept his word.*

*I tell you this now because Bob visited me the other night and made me an offer. It will shock you as much as it shocked me. To put it simply, my love, my father has bought him and the others with you—as he has so many others before. I'm not sure how Bob is involved in all this, but according to him, my father has been moving opium from his base in Burma into Saigon. They move the opium into Northern Laos and then use planes to drop the opium into the area of Vietnam where you are based. He said my father has an arrangement with the other officers of your unit. The Montagnards and South Vietnamese take care of receiving the opium and shipping it to Saigon, and the few Americans there are paid to look the other way.*

*Bob said my father has friends even higher up in the American military who could ensure that you are transferred back to Bangkok long before the end of the year. If you will do as the man you replaced did before he was killed: Look the other way when the opium drops are made.*

*My darling, I know how you and Brian feel about drugs. I have tried for years not to think about them at all—because of who my father is. Please forgive my lie. I loved you so much and it seemed easier and simpler to say that my father was a merchant who died in a car accident than to admit that he was still alive—and still a drug smuggler.*

*Paul, whatever he is, I think my father is in a position to keep his promises. I think he can get you transferred back to me. If you agree. If you don't agree, you'll be reassigned to some even more remote area of Vietnam. I love you, my darling. You know what I want—I want you here! As soon as possible! And I don't care what either of us has to do to achieve that!!*

*Bob is flying up to see you with his offer and I've asked him to take this letter to you and ask you to read it before he speaks to you about it.*

*Please write to me and tell me you still love me. And tell me you will come to me soon!*

*All my love,*
*Suntharee*

*P.S. Brian and one of our gardeners took the enclosed*

*pictures. Nalin is growing so fast. I predict she is going to be a real beauty!*

The first page of the second letter was missing but Brian recognized his brother's handwriting across the unlined, wrinkled and yellowed page.

*. . . when I made it clear to Bob that I wouldn't get involved after all. I think they were just making idle threats so please don't worry. Stanley and Jackson always talk a lot; both are alcoholics and I think Jackson's on drugs as well. But I'll keep my eye on them because I think Bob has them under his thumb; and he took my refusal badly.*

*Someone in Saigon, an American, I mean, someone very high up, has managed to transfer all authority for this operation to Bangkok and have it classified, Top Secret, Cryptographic. Ever since Captain Murray was killed, the Bangkok office has been in charge. And Bob's in charge of processing the paperwork on this mission. He admitted your father has been paying him well to look the other way. Captain Murray—the man I replaced—there was something strange about his death; but I don't want to say more now.*

*I know how disappointed you will be because of this. It means instead of holding you in my arms soon it will be over a year from now but when we are together at least it will be with a clear conscience.*

*Please give my love to Nalin—how I miss her! Tell Brian I appreciate the pictures but his photography is out of focus. Maybe he needs glasses?*

> *Love you forever,*
> *Paul*

*P.S. Oh ever beauteous, ever friendly! Tell*
*Is it, in heav'n, a crime to love too well?*

*(Ask Brian who wrote that. I remembered it from somewhere.)*

Brian got up and slid the letters carefully under a large shard of broken glass on the vanity table. He stared at them for several seconds and then spoke to himself. "Alexander Pope. *Elegy to the Memory of an Unfortunate Lady.* They killed you before I had a chance to tell you."

He went into the bathroom and threw water on his face. He waited until the tears stopped and the flow of blood was slowed but not stanched, then dried his face. He walked back into the bedroom and began dressing with the determined yet languid motions of a man straining to emerge from a trance.

A small porcelain lamp had fallen across a bedside table, its bulb and shade lying askew. The unnaturally focused light now shone sideways through the shade against a nearby Buddha statue, projecting a nearly lifesize shadow of the Buddha against a wall. The statue's broad shoulders, elongated earlobes and sharply tapering finial conjured up an eerie and menacing figure of a visitation from another world.

He was just putting on his shoes when Karen knocked and entered. She walked into the bedroom and looked at the broken glass and then at the cut on Brian's cheek. "My God, what happened to you? You want me to take you to a doctor?"

Brian shook his head. "Did you see Nalin?"

"She wouldn't speak to me. Just ran by the car and got into a taxi. She was crying."

"You got a car?"

"Yes. It's not mine though, it's Boonsom's. He—"

"I need to borrow it."

Karen went into the bathroom and returned with a wet towel. "Keep this on your face. I'll drive."

"I've got to go alone."

"Not in the shape you're in. I'm driving or it's no deal."

"You always were a hard woman."

"Not hard enough."

# 60

BRIAN watched dozens of fruit stands whiz by on both sides of the highway. Eerily lit by paraffin lamps, young girls sat under straw roofs of tiny roadside huts with shelves stacked with watermelon. With less than thirty miles left before they reached the outskirts of Ayudhya, all of Bangkok's urban landmarks had long since given way to warmly lit countryside houses, dark ricefields and unevenly lit scenes of water buffalo treading monotonously on rice sheaves, patiently detaching grain from straw.

Brian turned to Karen and handed her a lit cigarette. As they sped to Ayudhya, he had told her enough so that she understood not to ask anymore. He was glad someone else was driving; he wanted to completely withdraw into himself and use the time to think.

He felt he at last understood his anger toward Nalin. He had accused her of being unreasonable. In fact, he'd known all along that someone as clearheaded as Nalin could never hate her mother without reason. He'd somehow sensed that when he learned the reason it would alter his perspective of people close to him—people he had known in Thailand for years—and he'd felt that any new insights would lead to unpleasant revelations; would in fact transfigure what had once seemed so pure and unsoiled into something sordid and piacular. He'd been angry at Nalin not for refusing to speak but for refusing to compromise. No matter what the cost to his cherished fictions.

He stared at Karen's hair. "Is your hair really red?"

She glanced at him with her forehead lined in a mock frown. "What?"

"Your hair. Is it really red?"

"Of course it's red, dummy. Wouldn't you know by now if I dyed my hair?"

Brian sat back and stared into the darkness. "You're right. No offense. I just wanted to know that *something* is real; since I arrived in Thailand nothing has been what it seems. Roger turns out to be not just a leftover drunk from the war, but a DEA man. Suntharee wasn't the woman I had idealized all these years; she was involved with Bob, and her misguided advice to Paul on drugs was partly responsible for my brother's death as well. Her father didn't die in any accident; he's alive and involved in murder and opium. A few of the bargirls on Patpong are actually men. Suntharee's letter—the letter that brought me back to Thailand—was actually written by Nalin. Oh, yes, I almost forgot about the gardeners."

"Gardeners?"

"Right. At the house in Ayudhya. Except that they don't know a damn thing about gardening which most likely means they're somebody's undercover men keeping watch. And Bob turned out to be involved in drugs. And in my brother's death." Brian sighed. "I just wanted to know that something is what it seems."

They had passed the first ancient brick tower before Karen spoke again. "What do you hope to accomplish in Ayudhya, if I may ask?"

"To separate the grain from the straw."

# 61

IN the early morning stillness, Roger Webb backed his much abused Hyundai Excel into a driveway on Wireless Road. Across the deserted road, his headlights illuminated an American Eagle on its post in front of the American Embassy. For a moment, he stared at the symbol, at the high wall topped with barbed wire, and at the delicate shapes of a flame tree's tiny leaves against the lighter sky. Then he shut off the motor, got out and crossed the street.

He entered Barney Richard's office, glanced quickly at the four men in the room and moved immediately to make his coffee. While they waited, Barney put his feet on his desk and gave the two Thais a shrug of his shoulders. He looked toward Roger with obvious distaste. "Anytime you're ready."

Roger gulped his coffee and immediately spat some back into the cup. "Christ! It's flaming hot. You tricked me!"

"Roger, this is Mr. Somchai, one of the men we've had at the house. And this is one of the men we're working with on this operation, Colonel Somnuck." Roger held his coffee cup in his left hand and shook hands with the two men. He studied their shirts briefly, looking for the inevitable bulge of a .38, found none, and decided they must have checked them in at the metal detector door.

"Colonel Somnuck is—"

Roger pulled up a metal office chair and sat down. "I know who he is. He's head of a hand-picked squad of Thai policemen who have busted more drug pushers than your agencies combined. And he's done it despite the huge bribes he's been offered and despite the constant threats on his life." Roger saluted the Colonel with his coffee cup and drank.

Both Thais were thin, middle-aged and dark, but the Colonel was nearly black. "You seem to know a great deal about me."

"I run a bar on Patpong, Colonel. Such a man hears a few things."

Barney cleared his throat. "Mr. Somchai has just come from Ayudhya. It seems General Li and a few of his top lieutenants have just arrived at the house."

Somchai said something in Thai. Colonel Somnuck translated: "And General Li seems to be wounded. Badly."

Roger threw a fist in the air. "Yaahoo! So the sly fox has finally been lured out of the Golden Triangle. Now it's the ants turn."

"Ants?"

"Yeah, Barney. Ants. It's an old Laotian saying: 'When the river is high, the fish eat the ants; when the river is low, the ants eat the fish.' What we got up in Ayudhya now is a fish out of water, stranded and vulnerable. Let's get goin'!"

Barney held his hand out like a traffic cop. "Just a minute, bartender. I'd like to take Li alive. And I don't want the woman hurt. I thought it might be a good idea to take your friend Brian with us. He might come in handy."

"You mean he might help you persuade the woman to turn in General Li. A fat lot you care about her or anybody else except how they can help you make an arrest to rescue your sputtering debacle of a career."

"Whatever the case—and I don't give a goddamned what you think—he might be of some help."

"So call him yourself."

"We did. There's no answer. We thought you might—"

The phone rang. Barney answered. "Richards here . . . what? Goddamn it! . . . Red hair? . . All right. We're leaving now." He placed the phone down carefully while weighing the implications of the message.

Roger spoke intently, his cigarette ignored. "Red hair?"

"That was one of Colonel Somnuck's men stationed near the house. The daughter just arrived back at the house about twenty minutes ago."

"Nalin? Jesus Christ!" Roger dropped his cigarette into his cup, placed the cup on the floor and stood up.

"And just now a white man and a white woman with red hair arrived. He recognized the man. He had stayed at the house for a few days a few months ago."

"Brian."

"And he's got a redhead with him."

Flip took a swig of diet coke from a can and chortled. "This is becoming a real party."

Roger leapt to Flip's chair and tilted the chair over backwards. He held on to Flip's tie and stood over him. "Look, asshole. I know you're a Yuppie with the I.Q. of a geranium but these people could be dead in ten minutes. And if anything *has* happened to them, I'm going to shove all your pretty pens right up your Preppy ass." Roger released his tie. "Now let's get up there!"

Barney stood up and grabbed Roger's arm. "Not 'we,' Roger. We don't need you anymore. You can go back to bed."

The two men eyed each other for several seconds while Barney blocked Roger's path. "Try to stop me. I'd like that."

Colonel Somnuck spoke as he held the door open. "No need to fight over this. I have three cars and several men outside. I've got room in my car for this gentleman. If you have no objection, Mr. Richards, we have room for all of you. And my drivers can have us in Ayudhya in just over an hour."

Barney turned to Flip. "You all right?"

Flip pressed his back, winced, and spoke as he righted the chair. "Yeah, yeah, I'm all right. Let's go. I'll get even with this son-of-a-bitch another time."

Barney stepped aside to allow Roger to pass. "All right, bartender, just make goddamn sure you stay in line up there. I want General Li alive."

Roger glared at him. "If you want a long and happy life, you better start giving some thought to keeping my friends alive."

# 62

THE gate of wood and corrugated iron had been pulled across the driveway entrance and wired shut. Karen stopped the car and turned off the engine. The distant straw fires lighting up a village's threshing activities glimmered far to the West. Boisterous shouts, raucous laughter and spirited sounds of village music intermingled and drifted across the fields of dry stubble.

In the fields, compact, straw-tied rice sheaves were heavy with their lackluster yellow kernels. Hundreds of these triangular-shaped bundles were lined in shadowed windrows, and the occasional distant flare of brightly burning straw lent them the appearance of both movement and malevolence. From far across the darkest field a dog's incessant barking reached the car.

Brian sat motionlessly staring at ink-black school buildings, palm fronds and tree limbs all silhouetted by light from the house. A scant amount of light spilled from beneath three Ayudhya-style hats affixed as lampshades over bulbs hung along the front of the house. The window curtains had been tightly closed and the few lights on in the house illuminated only the thick shrubbery directly below the windows creating a more intense darkness beyond. Widely spaced white fluorescent tubes demarcated the perimeter of the school grounds from nearby ricefields and vacant land. The moon had camouflaged itself as a milky white patch of an indigo blue sky. Karen lit a cigarette and opened a window. "I'll wait here."

"No way. You're coming in. You're not a chauffeur."

"What am I then?"

". . . a friend."

She stared at Brian for several seconds then took a long drag and put out her cigarette. She picked up the red-stained towel from the seat and began wiping his face. "Well, 'friend,' if you're going to confront someone, at least don't do it with a bloody face."

They crossed the checkerboard shadow cast by the small bamboo gate at the sidewalk entrance and walked in silence down the narrow path. Faint streaks of light from the fluorescent tubes passed through interstices of the school buildings' brick foundations and fell in jagged patterns across the walk.

Brian heard the sound just as they passed by the first of the school buildings: a man or animal scurrying behind the foundation wall. They stopped walking. Brian moved cautiously closer and stooped to peer into one of the dark crevices in the brick. By the time he could make out the profile of a man and the glint of a revolver, he realized the revolver was pointed at his chest.

The profile began waving furiously. Light coruscated off the rapidly moving weapon. A heavily accented voice reached Brian in excited whispers. "Here! Here! Get down and come here! Bring the woman. Quickly!" As his eyes became more accustomed to the darkness, Brian recognized the cherubic brown face of the ruggedly built man with unfriendly eyes and the bulge under his shirt. He took Karen's arm and they crawled under the building and sat in crouched positions. Brian looked at the revolver and at the man. "What's going on here?"

The man shifted position slightly and pointed through an opening toward the house. The light bathed one side of his face in a pale yellow and gave his features a grotesque, almost depraved, impression. "General Li and his men. There. In the house." He looked at Karen and back to Brian. "You know General Li?"

Brian heard movement in the shadows near the house. "I know him, all right. You are the police?"

"Narcotics Division." He pointed to the other school buildings. "We have one man in each building. Not enough. Li has twelve men with him. Maybe more. And many, many weapons. Even some men around the house. Can't do anything yet."

Karen sat on the dirt, hugged her knees and rocked slowly back and forth. "And to think I asked to come."

"Karen, I'm sorry. I didn't know there was any danger here."

She waved her hand around her stopping at the revolver. "What, you call *this* danger? I was at San Francisco State, remember? It's just that I'm not dressed properly for a shootout with a warlord; I would have worn something in khaki or denim."

Brian detected the waver in her voice and gently squeezed her shoulder. He sat facing the man whose gaze was fixed on the house. The man grunted and spoke softly. "They know we're here and we know they're there. I already called—"

"Have you seen a young girl about 25; a Thai?"

"You mean the daughter? She come maybe half hour before. I say 'stay here!' but she won't hear. She went in."

"Inside the house?"

"Yes." At the sound of movement beneath the breadfruit tree, the man crouched lower. "You listen. Around the house. In the shadows. Too many men. Too many weapons."

"Maybe so. But I've got to talk with Nalin. And with Suntharee."

"You wait."

"No. I've got to go in." Brian turned to Karen. "You'll be all right here?"

"Why don't you wait?"

"I've waited long enough already. I'll be back as soon as I can. You OK?"

"Sure, sure. Your faithful friend is doing great. Just tell the warlord we could use some coffee and donuts out here. Even day-old bagels would do."

"You're all right, you know that?"

"The next person to tell me that is going to be sorry."

Brian crawled through a side opening, stood up, and walked slowly across the lawn, between the two remaining school buildings, directly for the left side of the house.

He had no illusions that he could reach the house without being seen. He walked openly but cautiously around shrubs with heart-shaped leaves and bushes with hundreds of tiny flowers. He stepped carefully over the serpentine coils of a garden hose and passed beside a watering can, its long spout pointing in accusation or betrayal toward the still more sequestered form of a lawn rake. The susurrus of agitated leaves sounded warnings with each step. He stopped at the far corner of the diamond-shaped garden, wondering, with each step, how many weapons were pointed at him.

As a sudden movement violently shook nearby bushes, Brian braced himself for an attack. He breathed a sigh of relief as he recognized the excited honking of aroused geese.

As their cries subsided, Brian stared into the darkness beneath the house. He detected a slight movement and a faint metallic sound reached his ears. His gaze traveled up the stairs to the verandah and to the curtained windows beyond. He cupped his hands to his mouth, took a deep breath, and called out loudly. "Nalin! Suntharee!"

For several seconds there was no response. Then the door flew open and he could see Suntharee silhouetted against the light, one hand holding the door and the other holding her cheek as if she had just been slapped.

The open door threw light across dark patches of the breadfruit tree's broad leaves, and spotlighted the ground beneath where an armed figure moved back into the shadows. A man's argumentative and gravelly voice sounded inside the house. Suntharee made no reply and continued to stare out into the darkness.

Brian called to her. "Over here. In the garden." She turned in his direction and released the door. Brian watched her as she quickly crossed the verandah and descended the stairs, the color of her blouse and sarong swallowed in the darkness. He could not see her face, but he detected her emotional state by her rigid posture, quick, precise yet constrained steps and, above all, as she tread each familiar stair, the unnatural manner in which she held her hand out inches above the rail, as if she were being guided by the warm glow of something much too hot to touch.

Once she had reached the ground she passed through shadows for several seconds. When she reemerged at the opposite side of the garden he could see the outlines of two men with long hair, fatigue uniforms and automatic weapons walking slowly, several yards behind her. Light from the house streamed in most concentrated form through the centrally located arbor and through the pergola as if attempting to dislodge the carefully hung baskets and climbing plants winding about the trellises.

The strange light fell across the path's kidney-shaped flagstones in sharply divided and constantly widening streaks of light and shadow and as Nalin approached him, backlighted by the light, Brian watched a penumbral nimbus appear and disappear about her head with each step.

She moved toward him with uneasy steps, passed beneath

the arbor, and stood at the center of the garden beside the fish pond. Brian walked to her and stood facing her from several feet away. The men, and the corona about her head, had vanished.

He could hear the rustle of branches, the sounds of insects and could smell the musky odor of the garden's plants. An abandoned tree pruner lay silhouetted in the soft, uneven light like a fallen exotic bird hoping to avoid detection.

The few bamboo stalks which remained lit wavered uncertainly as she approached. While still in shadow, she spoke his name in a mixture of hesitation and fear. The fronds of the traveler's palm shifted slightly, briefly diffusing light across her eyes and hair. She was wearing no makeup and her long hair had been left down and unattended. Lines of character had deepened to reveal themselves as lines of age and anxiety, and in her eyes Brian could see that confidence had given way to terror; the terror of a woman who knows she is about to be despised by those she loves.

"Nalin told you about Paul's death. And about . . . Brian, Paul and I—"

Brian glanced toward the house. "Is Nalin all right?"

"Yes. Yes, she's fine."

"I want to see her."

"Yes. I just want to tell you that Paul and I loved each other very much. When he was sent to Vietnam, for each of us each day was as if we had died."

Her voice quavered as she began each sentence but her tone remained constant. It was the subdued recitation of someone who had given up hope of attempting persuasion, or of offering apologies, or of seeking forgiveness; rather the carefully delivered speech of someone almost paralyzed by fear trying to place each thought and each word properly and logically after the other before she was unable to function altogether.

Brian fought to retain his own composure nearly torn asunder by conflicting emotions. Only when her eyes were again in the light did he reply. "Is it true? About the drugs? About Bob?"

She held her hands tightly together in front of her waist, her arms in an unnatural and nearly rigid position; only the restless, continuous and uncontrollable fidgeting of her hands revealing the nearly unbearable intensity of her overwrought and emotionally charged agitation. The bracelet he had given her glittered at her wrist. "I don't know what she told you. I—"

"I saw the letters."

"Yes, I knew you would eventually. You see, when Bob Donnelly came with his offer, he said if I thought Paul would refuse, to let him know then and he would tell Paul nothing. Paul would simply be transferred somewhere else inside Vietnam. He said it could be dangerous for Paul if he knew too much but refused to join."

"But you decided Bob should go ahead. *You* involved Paul."

"Yes. It was my decision. I wrote to Paul and told him about Bob bringing my father's offer. He wrote back immediately. He said he would personally plant poppy seeds all over Vietnam if it meant he could see me again. You don't know what . . . what incredible joy I . . . to know he was coming. I didn't care what he had to do to come back."

Brian saw the front door open and close and watched as Nalin walked slowly across the verandah to stand at the rail. She stared in their direction but Brian couldn't tell for certain if she could see them. At the sudden brief streak of light, Suntharee paused in her increasingly dolorous explanation but never turned her head. Brian was about to call out to Nalin when Suntharee began again.

"Then I received his last letter—the one Nalin found. He said he had thought it over very carefully and as much as he loved me he couldn't be involved in smuggling hard drugs. He knew what heroin could do, he said. He didn't want us to begin our lives together with this behind us. He said he told Bob he was going to try to stop the whole . . . operation. . . ."

The slight breeze shifted and the lights of the bamboo stalks flickered, illuminating sections of a sacred white cord strung near the garden's hibiscus and frangipani bushes. Brian watched the tears streak slowly down Suntharee's cheeks and he felt the stirrings first of pity and then of a growing sense of betrayal. "And then?"

"Then I heard nothing. Two weeks later I received a visit from an American officer and sergeant telling me Paul had been killed in action. But I knew. A week later, Bob Donnelly came to the house. He said my father had ordered Paul's death, and he told me how sorry he was. I don't know who really killed Paul but for several years, I hated Bob, and, of course, myself. Then, as the years passed. . . . He showed up one day at the house. The school was failing. I was . . . alone." She wiped tears away and attempted to regain her composure. "Now my last brother has just been killed in a battle and my father lies dying inside my house."

Light from the house streaked again and Brian knew Nalin had gone in. His disappointment in Suntharee began to be overshadowed by his feelings of guilt toward Nalin.

"Brian . . . I know what you must think of me now. The lies, the foolish offer I passed on to Paul that . . . got him killed. But, Brian, please believe me—I loved Paul."

When Brian finally managed to speak he was surprised at how calm, almost detached, his voice sounded. "I'm sure you did. But in time you managed to sleep with someone involved in his murder."

She suddenly ran to him and held his face tightly in her hands. Brian stepped back just out of her reach. Her eyes widened and her attempted smile only increased the pathetic quality of her plea. "Brian, remember, this is the Kingdom of Make Believe. We can act out anything here. We could . . . we could pretend . . . Brian, please don't hate me." She threw her arms around him and buried her face in his chest.

Brian disengaged himself from her and gently held her wrists. Beneath the deceptive calm of his quiet attentiveness, he felt pity and anger and compassion and revulsion—everything but attraction. He spoke over her loud sobs. "I don't hate you. But. . . ."

She gradually stopped sobbing and looked up into his eyes. "But you could never love me. Not now."

"It's over now. I love Nalin. And I'd like to see her. Now."

The sounds of car engines reached them just before the car lights swept the compound. Several bursts of automatic weapons were fired and the lights outside the house and the fluorescent tubes along the perimeter were shot out by one side or the other. Two armed men dashed from the shadows and herded the two of them across the garden and up the stairs. As Brian crossed the verandah, he could see the outlines of now darkened vehicles alongside Roger's own.

The lights inside the house had been turned off or shaded with cloth. Curtains had been slightly parted and shards of glass from several windows lay on the floor. Soldiers in mud-stained green fatigues knelt beside open windows with rifles at the ready or else sat wearily on the floor against the walls with their weapons across their laps. All wore sweat-stained caps and mud-covered boots and all looked exhausted. The one nearest the door had a bandage wound around his head and the bill of his cap had the reddish tinge of dried blood.

Despite the occasional bursts of gunfire, the atmosphere in the house was one of resignation and fatigue—veterans reconciled to the possibility of yet another firefight—rather than the excitement of battle.

The men turned to glance briefly and indifferently at Brian and Suntharee, then, as if at a silent signal, looked away. Nalin appeared in the bedroom doorway. Her eyes were red and swollen but her blouse and slacks appeared both clean and neat and her hair had been swept back into a bun. She stood straight and still with her arms folded across her chest, and a blanket draped over them.

Something about her poise and expression gave her an air of maturity and confidence and self-control and suggested that she was more than capable of dealing with her family's crisis. It was as if, when the worst of times had finally arrived, it was she who now rightfully inherited her mother's lost composure and strength. She stared at Brian with neither rancor nor familiarity, and her voice was almost matter-of-fact. "Have you come to give my mother a new life or to watch my grandfather die?"

As Brian approached her, she turned and re-entered the dimly lit bedroom. Brian followed her in.

A man in fatigues—a teenager with a dirt-streaked face, shoulder-length hair and the eyes of an adult—crouched beside a window and rocked slowly back and forth cradling an automatic rifle. A thin man in his late forties in civilian short-sleeve shirt and trousers was taking the pulse of an elderly man who lay heavily in the bed. The stethoscope draped about the thin man's neck clashed incongruously with the colorful geometric patterns bordering his blue cotton shirt.

Photographs, celadon elephants and a vase of white orchids with crimson spots had been hastily piled on the floor against a wall and the side table which they had ornamented had been lined with a blue towel and pushed beside the bed. It now served as an instrument table with vials, syringes, forceps, scalpels, scissors, wads of absorbent cotton, rolls of adhesive tapes and elastic support bandages. A dark brown doctor's case lay on the floor beneath the table like an undetonated explosive.

Military equipment—belts, empty magazines, bandoliers, canteens and ammunition pouches—were strewn about the room. Cigarette smoke mingled with the fetid smell of injured flesh, ethyl alcohol and peroxide.

Nalin sat beside the bed and squeezed water from a washcloth into a bowl and lay the cloth gently across the elderly man's forehead. The man stirred fitfully, murmured softly, then remained still. His eyelids flickered but remained closed.

Brian walked to the foot of the bed and stood beside Nalin. He took one of her hands and held it in his. "Are you all right?"

She looked into her grandfather's face and sighed. And then nodded slowly.

"You should have shown me the letters long ago," Brian said.

She looked up at him, stared angrily into his eyes and took her hand away. "You should have shown me that I could have."

One of the men who had escorted Brian into the house walked into the room with a chair and placed it behind Brian.

The man was of medium height, ruggedly built and in need of a haircut. He stood before Brian and pointed imperiously to the chair. Brian sat down. The man's AK-47 hung horizontally at his waist from its sling across his right shoulder, its muzzle pointing slightly downward, at the level of Brian's throat.

A tattered, black-and-orange scarf had been wrapped around his neck and draped over his left shoulder. He held a cigarette in his left hand and stared at Brian as a scientist might express mild curiosity at an unusual specimen found far from its natural habitat.

Although completely at home in the presence of firearms and firefights, he seemed unable to decide how to deal with the foreigner, as if carefully considering his best approach to the unexpected. Brian watched his facial features cross from polite hospitality to those of menacing authority. He tipped his cap slightly forward and stood before Brian with his hands on his hips. He had decided to adopt a matter-of-fact tone laced with a modicum of hostility. "What you want here? Why you come?"

"I came to see General Li."

The man looked toward the bed and then back at Brian suspiciously. "General Li see no one." He leaned slightly forward and in the dim light the shadow of his cap covered his eyes like a mask. "You know General Li?"

"Yes."

The man moved one step closer. Brian could smell the Tiger Balm Ointment glistening on a bilious bruise on his hand. "He your friend?"

"He killed my brother."

The man shifted slightly backward as if he had been dealt a physical blow. His hand slid backward along the barrel and held the pistol grip. He narrowed his eyes. "What you say?"

From the corner of his eye, Brian saw the man with the stethoscope give him a brief curious glance.

Suntharee had come silently into the room and stood in the doorway. The boy at the window motioned for her to leave the lighted area but she ignored him and spoke in Thai to Brian's interrogator. Brian could follow only parts of her monologue but could hear the word for 'friend' spoken several times.

When she had finished there was an awkward silence and into the silence blared the metallic voice of someone speaking in Thai through a megaphone. The speaker was interrupted by several volleys of shots and, in return fire, by the sound of shattering glass in the next room. The man abruptly abandoned his interrogation and strode quickly into the living room, obviously relieved to withdraw from a troublesome distraction to deal with the expected, unmistakable and familiar possibility of battle.

The boy at the window tensed and peered outside. To soothe his nerves, he chanted in Mandarin in a barely audible voice snatches of a warlord marching song General Li had taught his soldiers.

Brian got up and walked slowly around the bed and stood beside Nalin. He listened to the military cadences of the boy's song and then followed Nalin's gaze down into the thin, hawk-like face of his brother's murderer.

A sickly yellow tinge had suffused the dark brown coloration of his face. A violescent bruise had formed high on his forehead and minor scratches had cut across his nose and cheeks. His breathing was heavy and labored.

A military haircut framed what had once been an intelligent, alert face. Lines had etched themselves into the rough parchment of his skin and over the years had stretched and deepened, crossed and joined and sculpted a nexus of parched river beds, rifts and ridges. It was not the face of a dying man at the end of a long life at peace with himself, but the frustrated and impatient semi-consciousness of a military man no longer able to command events.

Brian spoke to Nalin. "What happened to him?" After several seconds of silence the man across the bed spoke even as he busied himself with his task of using a small flashlight to examine General Li's eyes. His English was almost perfect. "He was lifted by an explosion and apparently hit his head on a rock. Besides a chest puncture and shoulder wound, I believe he has internal bleeding in the covering of his brain. Probably from a torn cortical vein. When he was last conscious he complained of headaches, nausea and a stiff neck. He also had mental confusion and double vision. He moved in and out of consciousness all the way here."

"You are General Li's doctor?"

The man glanced at Brian and allowed himself a smile. "I am a doctor. I practice in Chiang Mai. I was . . . 'invited' to come with them." He looked again at his patient. "They never should have moved him this far."

"Why did they?"

"Apparently, he wanted to see his family."

"Will he live?"

"I can't be sure without an exploratory operation, but this kind of serious result from a rather trivial head injury follows the pattern of chronic subdural hematoma. He has a remarkably tough will to live. If he did not, he would have been gone already. But now his pulse is slowing. With his symptoms and at his age, I don't believe he will last the night."

Several bullets suddenly crashed through the only remaining pane of glass in the window beside the boy and thudded into the wall just a few feet above Brian's head. Everyone, including the boy at the window, dropped to the floor. In the sudden stillness, Brian called to Nalin to make certain she was all right, then to the doctor. Both replied. When he called to the boy there was no answer. When Brian moved closer, he saw the fear in the boy's eyes and the boy knew his fear was visible.

In his embarrassment at his own caution, he pushed to his knees, thrust the AK-47 through the window and fired indiscriminately. When he had finished, he jammed another magazine into his weapon and sat with his back pressed to the wall, avoiding the eyes of those in the room.

The three of them stood up. While Nalin stood beside the bed with her hand on her grandfather's pulse, the doctor gave Brian a weak smile. "Of course, *none* of us may last through the night."

Brian looked down at the man who had given the order to kill his brother. He wondered why he could not feel more hatred than he did. "Will he regain consciousness?"

The doctor shook his head. "I don't know. It would surprise me if he did. But the symptoms of this kind of injury can fluctuate a great deal. You see, his eyelids are flickering again. He's fighting to wake up."

*General Li could remember confused activity, an urgent warning, a crashing explosion, an onrush of pain and the feeling of being lifted, almost thrown, into the air, and then—nothing. His instinct told him that he was in the most crucial battle of his life and General Li exerted all his strength to concentrate on the face that was forming before him. At last, he recognized the familiar face of the young woman from the city with yet again the same intense expression in her wide eyes. The woman he had loved.*

*He knew he had not lived according to her ideals and teachings, but rather than facing a justifiable disappointment or harsh reprimand, he could feel himself bathed, almost cleansed, by her infinite forgiveness and supernal empathy. He slowly, unsteadily, reached out his hand to her and she held it tightly in both of hers. Her large eyes filling with tears made her seem all the more angelic to him, and on her long, sensitive face her lips were even now lengthening into a slightly embarrassed smile.*

*His eyes were open now but the mist had thickened and the figure smiled at him through a brumous film, growing greyer and more opaque with each faltering beat of his heart. He could discern through the enclosing darkness the message she had for him: the need to struggle was over; the battle had been won. He understood the lesson and recognized the beautiful simplicity of it: "Poor men do not fight poor men." Not a lesson. Rather, a droning chant, a familiar psalm, a beloved litany, a whispered prayer. He smiled at the girl and stared into her eyes. He could feel the joy surging from his last few heartbeats into his trembling hand as he squeezed hers with his last remaining strength. And the mist grew still thicker and darkened and finally obscured all that was before him.*

Brian watched Nalin carefully, almost reverently, place her grandfather's hand back on the bed as a collector might handle his most precious antique porcelain. She bundled a wad of cotton and wiped the tears from her eyes and sat quietly observing the physician's bedside rituals.

The warlord's eyes remained open and the pupil closest to Nalin and Brian had dilated unnaturally wider than the other. The doctor felt his patient's neck and then held his wrist for several seconds. He folded the blanket down and placed the stethoscope just above the bandage on his patient's chest. Finally, he lowered the stethoscope from his ears to his neck and pulled up the blanket as before. Then he reached over and closed General Li's eyelids. He looked across the bed to Nalin. "I'm sorry."

Even as the doctor checked for signs of life, Brian could hear shouted negotiations from somewhere on or near the verandah. Proposals and counterproposals were interspersed with sporadic gunfire.

Suddenly, Brian's interrogator and the man with the blood-stained cap rushed into the room and ran to the window. The startled boy quickly moved aside for them. The interrogator peered cautiously out the window, sighting along his weapon for a target.

Suntharee reappeared and walked to the foot of the bed. She took no notice of the men at the window and stared at her father. She spoke to Brian without looking up. "Did he say anything before he died?"

"No. Nothing."

Suntharee moved to stand beside her father, opposite Nalin and close to Brian. The doctor moved away from the bed. She placed her hand on her father's cheek and left it there. As she did so, the interrogator fired several shots from his AK-47. Suntharee suddenly rushed to him and pulled him away from the window. "Stop it! He's dead, can't you see that? What are you fighting for now? It's over!"

She paused for a moment to regain control of her emotions,

then spoke to the man in Thai. Both men turned toward the bed. They walked closer and stared at General Li. Suntharee spoke to them again in Thai and they followed her out of the room. The boy resumed his post at the window.

A few moments later Brian heard Suntharee's voice outside the house and then a man's voice responding in Thai through a megaphone. Nalin continued to stare only at her grandfather.

As the shouting continued, the sounds of gunfire ceased. Suntharee returned alone and again walked to the foot of the bed. She glanced at Nalin and then stared at her father while she spoke to Brian in a monotone. "These men came here because my father wanted to see us one more time before he died. They did not really want to come and now all they want is to return to their home inside the Golden Triangle."

The doctor offered her a chair which she ignored. He then placed his stethoscope in his bag and began cleaning up the bedside table. Suntharee finally shifted her gaze to Brian. With her father's death, the emotional storm had left her drained and exhausted. She spoke matter-of-factly, almost indifferently. "The police want them to leave their weapons. They refused. But they offered the compromise that they'll take their weapons but leave their ammunition including the grenades."

The two men reappeared in the doorway, their weapons now slung across their shoulders. The boy at the window rose and limped awkwardly across the room to join his friends. As he walked, he continued to stare at the deceased warlord in the manner of a child's unconcealed awe for a hero he believed could never die.

"No one has been hurt by the gunfire so the police have accepted and have guaranteed the men a safe passage back to the Burmese border providing that you and the doctor and anyone else who wishes to leave is released unharmed." She paused and stared first at Brian and then at Nalin. "You are free to go. You are both free now." With one last long glance at her father, she left the room.

Brian sensed that Nalin's tumultuous relationship with her mother and desperate flight from his apartment had left her feeling abandoned and totally alone. All the emotional intensity which would have surfaced as hatred in an unexpected confrontation with her stepfather's murderer, had been released as grief and sorrow at the bedside of an unconscious and dying grandfather. In her abandonment, her childhood feelings for an idealized grandfather had resurfaced as an earlier and more powerful emotional layer, displacing the recent overlay of a mere several months' duration; a pentimento of poignant stirrings purposely oblivious to the real nature of the dying warlord.

Brian stood beside her. Nalin allowed herself to be embraced in his arms but she was too emotionally drained to respond. As Brian held her he felt a strong desire to comfort her, not as a lover, but as someone she could trust; someone she could turn to. Somehow, the combination of recent events leading to his return to Ayudhya had given him new insight into his own emotions. As if a bolt of lightning had suddenly revealed a hidden guidepost, he knew at last what he had to do.

# 63

BRIAN placed the palm of his hand against the large white letters of the door plaque and pushed the door open. Bob Donnelly looked up from his desk in surprise. He quickly mastered the flicker of apprehension which crossed his face and attempted a smile. "Brian! Well, come on in."

Brian shut the door and stood in front of it.

Bob started to stand, then thought better of it. His attempt to maintain his smile forced his lips to move at strange angles. "What's wrong? You look like you haven't slept for three days. Sit down."

Brian remained standing. "General Li is dead, Bob. Killed in battle."

Bob's smile faded. "General Li? I don't think I understand."

"Sure you do, Bob. You were on General Li's payroll, remember? Maybe you still are. You tried to get Paul to go along with your smuggling operation. He wouldn't. So you and General Li decided to have him killed."

Bob shook his head in amazed disbelief. "Look, Brian, I don't know where you got this—"

"Don't bother denying it, Bob. I just came from Ayudhya. I know everything."

Bob stared at Brian for several seconds then closed a folder on his desk and leaned back in his chair. "All right. I did some business in the past with General Li. I was approached soon after I got to Bangkok. It was my job to check the records of any operation in Vietnam that involved the loan of our people. You know that. I could see at once something was wrong. I couldn't figure out how the people in Saigon had missed all the obvious signs of doctored reports: People, planes, shipments; it didn't make sense."

"Unless they were on the take."

Bob hesitated for just a second then nodded. "Unless they were on the take." He looked toward his phone and then continued. "So I reported my discovery to Major White. You remember him? Had two years left in the Army. Well, he took the file and that night he and a Thai general I never saw before took me to dinner. Then we had drinks at the old Balcony Club on New Road. Remember it?"

"Keep going."

"Well, they explained that the Central Highlands site was involved in a private operation. And they handed me an envelope."

"Your first payment."

"Brian, there was ten thousand American dollars in that envelope! All in hundreds." Bob leaned forward again and waved his hand for emphasis. "Brian, *everybody* was on General Li's payroll. I mean everybody based up there. And everybody in charge of keeping the records. Saigon *and* Bangkok. Everybody joined in the gravy train."

"Except Paul."

Brian watched as Bob grew more wary and more nervous. He sank deeper into his leather chair and looked down at the desk. "Brian, Paul wouldn't just say 'no.' That would have been one thing. But he told me he wanted to stop the operation."

"Like Captain Murray tried to do before him. So when Paul turned you down, you turned him in."

"I didn't know they were going to *kill* him." Bob's hands hit the chair's arms for emphasis. "I thought he might get transferred or—"

"You're a lying son-of-a-bitch."

"Brian, wake up! A lot of people involved in Vietnam did a lot of things they'd rather forget about. The graft and corruption wasn't endemic to the Vietnamese. Americans made black market fortunes in Saigon. Civilians *and* military. The highest ranking enlisted man in the army—a Sergeant Major!—headed a syndicate that systematically ripped off millions from military clubs. And he did just what I did—he manipulated personnel transfers to serve his own ends. He even did it from the Pentagon, for Christ's sake!"

Brian suddenly remembered the fat man in the embassy. The man with the pointer. What were his words exactly? Something about a corrupt American general 'and another American officer

Stanley claims was involved.'

Bob lowered his voice and allowed himself a sigh. The sigh of exasperation of a reasonable man attempting to enlighten someone too obstinate to understand simple facts. "I wasn't an exception in this war, Brian. I was the rule! Everybody who could take, took."

"Save it for your trial, Bob. But whatever you say, you're going to rot in a Thai prison for a long time."

A new confidence, almost smugness, entered Bob's tone. "Brian, you're talking about something that happened twenty years ago. There's a statute of limitations on this kind of thing."

"Probably. But in Thailand some statutes get enforced and some get forgotten."

Bob waved his hand to dismiss the threat. He looked with obvious pride at the photographs of Thai VIPs on the walls of the room. "I've got friends in Thailand, Brian. I've made it my business to have the right friends in the right places in this country."

"I doubt that you've ever had a genuine friend in your life. If you think these people are going to dirty their hands in public on your behalf, you really don't know Thailand."

Bob considered this for several moments then spoke with an affected nonchalance. "Anyway, what proof do you have?"

"Paul's letters."

Bob's lips curved into an indulgent smile. "You're not going to tell me Paul wrote that I was about to murder him."

"No. I mean that Paul's letters are what you paid Jackson to remove from Nalin's apartment. The letters that got Oy killed."

"That is absurd. I had nothing—"

"You wanted the letters Nalin had taken from Ayudhya. So you sent Jackson. But he hadn't figured on any murder; just a simple theft. But then he found Oy at Nalin's apartment. And Oy knew who he was. So he had to kill her. But the police nabbed the Thai gangster who killed Jackson. And he named you as the man who sent him. You're going to prison for murder in the second degree."

"I doubt it, Brian. I didn't kill anybody."

"Your kind never does. You just whisper things to other people—people as rotten as you but with more guts—and they do your dirty work for you. People like Jackson and like those you paid to shut him up so he wouldn't lead me to you. What was he, extorting money from you? Doing your dirty work for you? He lived on your money and he kept you from getting your hands dirty; but when you had too much to lose, you had him taken care of. That about right?"

"I think I'm going to have to ask you to leave."

"I think you should know there are some police waiting in your outer office to take you to their office for questioning. Some very incorruptible Thai police from Homicide Division."

Bob hesitated then reached for the phone.

"They've already closed your office for you. Sent your employees home."

Bob slowly took his hand from the phone. "Well, it appears that I should get myself a lawyer."

"You do that. A felony murder should be good for at least 15 years to life. You can have a lot of prison dinner parties. Interesting guests."

Bob began toying nervously with a letter opener. "Aren't you forgetting I only . . . I mean I'm being charged with only arranging for someone to steal letters, not to kill some bargirl."

"I'm told it doesn't matter much. You'll be charged with criminal solicitation, criminal facilitation, criminal conspiracy, criminal—well, you get the idea." Brian made a fist and rubbed it back and forth along his unshaven jaw. "Tell me one thing before I go. How far back does your relationship with Suntharee go?"

Bob glanced at the family portrait on his desk, then briefly puffed out his cheeks—the globefish under attack.

"I'd just like to hear it from you."

Bob looked at him and spoke in a matter-of-fact, slightly subdued manner. "About three years after Paul's death I heard the school might go under. I knew Suntharee hated me because of Paul's death but she wasn't about to let the school close. So I began lending her money."

"And then you made yourself available to fill in her lonely hours." Brian began walking slowly toward the desk. "And then, when the opportunity arose, you took her daughter to bed too." Brian stopped beside the chair.

Bob spoke smoothly but with lack of conviction. "Come on, Brian, you're not the type given to gratuitous physical violence."

Brian stared at him without speaking, as if weighing something in his mind, then seemed to make a decision. He turned and walked back to the door. "Unfortunately, you're right. I don't have it in me to rough you up. I only fight in self-defense. And I don't want to soil my hands." Brian opened the door. "But the police have agreed to let an old friend of yours in to have a word with you before you leave."

Bob gripped the sides of his chair. "Old friend?"

Brian stepped aside as the door flew open. Roger stepped into the doorway, nearly filling it, his arms hanging loosely at his sides, his hands tightened into fists.

Bob gripped his desk and pushed his chair toward the far wall. "Brian, wait a minute. This isn't like you."

"I know. I feel real bad. Anyway, you two have a nice chat."

Brian closed the door and walked through the short hallway. He nodded to the three police officers who sat patiently smoking foreign cigarettes and speaking quietly to one another. As he crossed the office toward the exit, he could hear unmistakable sounds of a disturbance coming from Bob's inner office.

# 64

BRIAN watched the melting wax flow over the drip pan and slowly drop onto the splotched silver base of the candlestick. The waiter appeared and moved the candle to the far side of the table and refilled their wine glasses.

Brian stared at Nalin's face now, due to the positioning of the candle, sidelighted in a soft glow, and wondered if she felt as he did; as if a threatening storm had finally broken and passed, but rather than leaving behind a cleansed landscape and a sense of regeneration, it had forever uprooted and transformed all they had shared together.

Brian spoke after the waiter left. "So, if I'm not making my feelings clear, I'm sorry. This is not easy for me."

"I think I understand, Uncle Brian. And you don't have to apologize. Though you always denied it, I think I knew all along that you saw a young Suntharee in me; the woman you never won when you were young and in love. I think women are more sensitive; they sometimes see what a man really feels before he does."

Brian nodded. He detected no flirtatiousness of any kind when Nalin called him 'Uncle Brian'. "And," Brian asked, "isn't it possible that some of your feelings toward me were mixed with a desire to keep me away from your mother?"

"I think so, Uncle Brian. But I thought I really loved you."

"Yes. I thought I was in love with you, too. But neither of us stopped long enough to question our real feelings. I don't know how to express it except to say that the love I feel for you now feels right. A different kind of love."

Nalin sipped her wine and looked at him. Tears welled up in her eyes. Brian looked at her long hair framing her beautiful face as it cascaded over her blue evening dress and wondered if it all could have ended differently.

Brian continued. "You were incredibly confused, hurt and angry. You needed a friend. And my idolizing attitude toward your mother didn't make it any easier for you. I'm sorry."

Brian watched a tear course steadily down her cheek. "It wasn't your fault. I wasn't so pure in my motives either."

Brian thought of Hose Ferrar as Cyrano de Bergerac reassuring a young cadet after unwisely boasting of the glory of past battles that it was he, Cyrano, who was most at fault as he was the older of the two.

Brian glanced around the restaurant. They were the only ones left. Two waiters were clearing a corner table. He turned back to Nalin. The center of her chocker—a stylized orchid—glittered in the candlelight. "And what will you do now?"

"I'll go back to school. I want to continue studying Drama. How about you, Uncle Brian?"

"I'm going back to New York. I've been fired, remember? Why do you smile?"

"It seems both of us are starting over or, at least. . . ."

"Picking up where we left off? You're right about that, Little Tadpole." Brian called for the bill. "I just want you to remember that you're a very resourceful, intelligent and beautiful young woman. I don't want you to think *all* of my feelings were confused. Finish your education and you'll find a young man who'll love you very much."

"And when I do will you come to the wedding, Uncle Brian?"

"You know I will."

# 65

A S Roger maneuvered his Hyundai back into line narrowly avoiding an oncoming, horn-blaring, pick-up truck, Brian glanced again above his head at the three gold leaf squares and white Sanskrit lettering, which he remembered with nervous gratitude, were symbols affixed by Buddhist monks for protection of drivers and, Brian hoped, for passengers as well.

It was almost noon and they sped along the highway toward Ayudhya at a speed which Brian found excessive to the point of suicidal. Late morning sunlight wove bright golden patches across untended fields and among isolated compounds. For awhile Brian concentrated on simply watching the rural scenes fly by. He had gotten very little sleep the night before, drinking and talking with Roger until early in the morning. Despite his best efforts his eyes began to close and Roger's voice slipped farther and farther away.

In an attempt to stay awake, he shifted his gaze from the scenery to the interior of the car. But there too the surroundings seemed to have been arranged to induce sleep. A garland of jasmine with a dying rose attached hung from the car's mirror and, beside it, a large Buddha amulet hung from a strap. Both moved slightly back and forth in unison, as captivating as a hypnotist's metronome. A sudden blast of car horns brought him out of a light sleep.

Roger was working on a bottle of Singha beer and obviously not worried about whether his listener was fully awake or not: ". . . and I'll put up with Spanish-style townhouses and Greek-style townhouses and Bavarian-style townhouses and Mr. Donut and Pizza Hut and Video hut and all the rest of the imported, franchised, sanitized, westernized bullshit that's come to Bangkok over the years, but the first 'singles bar' opens in this city—I'm gone!. . . Of course, where I would go *to*, that I don't rightly know."

"Karen might have some suggestions on where you might go."

Roger chuckled and passed the bottle to Brian. "Now, hold on a minute, ole' buddy, we may have stopped arguing but we ain't *that* close. Anyway, she's hard at work back in Hong Kong with a genuine exclusive on the death of General Li and the arrest of Bob Donnelly and all the other related nefarious activities this lovely country is known for."

Brian felt the cold beer waking him as it ran down his throat. "When I spoke to her on the phone last night, she said she'd be back in Bangkok over the weekend. She mentioned your name."

Brian noticed a blush spread across Roger's cheeks. "Well, what the hell, she is some woman."

Brian handed the bottle back. "That she is."

Roger noticed Brian staring at him. "What's the smile for *amigo?*"

"Just remembering something. Nothing personal, you understand, but the last time I was on my way to Ayudhya, I toyed with the idea that maybe you had been involved in Paul's death."

Roger raised his eyebrows and bulged out his eyes. "*That's* nothing personal?"

"Not really. Once I realized that nothing in Thailand is what it seems I started thinking about who else might have been involved. You were flying around Vietnam at the time. Could have flown anywhere. Even to the Highlands. Years later, you and Bob own a bar together in Bangkok. If you were involved, *you* might have sent someone to Nalin's apartment looking for letters that might have had *your* name in them. When Jackson said the Horny Tiger was the 'perfect' place to meet, I thought the ironic reference might be to you; I didn't think of Bob then. So *you* might have tried to have Jackson killed. You see, if I redesigned the puzzle, some of the pieces began to fit."

Roger gulped some beer, wiped his mustache, and stared at him. 'So do I call a lawyer or did you change your mind?"

Brian stared hard at him and then smiled. "Something about exotic Asia can make a fellow paranoid. Anyway, you drink too much beer to be a drug dealer, let alone a murderer."

"I'm glad you changed your mind. I hear the beer in Silom

Prison ain't very cold."

"Well, I do apologize, Roger. Something about this country affects me so I can't see the forest for the trees."

"Not many forests left in this country. Cain't see the whorehouse for the hookers is more like it."

Brian reflected on the changes to the city he had first known as a young man and wondered when Bangkok had finally surrended its soul not, like Ayudhya, to Burmese warriors on elephant-back, but to the spirit-killing demands of modern commercialism. Perhaps that moment when the first luxurious, five-star hotel raised its roof above the city's skyline, higher than any temple's tall, tapering chedi containing royal ashes. Or that moment when a building's location—decided by a board of directors—soared higher than any whose location had been determined by the route of a white elephant, the edict of a king, the advice of a fortune teller or the dream of a venerable monk.

Roger interrupted his thoughts. "How's Nalin doin' now? I mean, she got over the shocks yet?"

"I think so. Nalin's a pretty level-headed girl. She learned some shocking facts about those she loved very much in a very short time. But she'll be all right. . . . I'm still not sure about Suntharee, though."

Roger threw the empty beer bottle to the floor. "Don't worry about her. She's well liked by a lot of high-ranking Thais. There won't be any repercussions for her. Well, not legal ones, anyway."

Brian opened another bottle and drank nearly half the contents in one long gulp.

"You tryin' to get drunk in a hurry, *amigo*?"

"I keep remembering that *I* was the one who told Bob about the letters Nalin had found. . . . My God, I—"

Roger held up his hand. "You had no way of knowin', so don't go blamin' yourself."

"So what will happen to him?"

Roger took a long swallow of beer and gave forth with a belch which Sid Vicious would have admired. "Well, generally speaking, Bob should be living in new surroundings for about 15 years minimum. Of course, I said *generally*, and this ain't *generally*, this is Thailand and, this bein' Thailand, anything can happen. But if Uncle Bob tries to beat the rap, that takes money, lots of it, and I figure I might soon have an opportunity to buy out his shares in the Horny Tiger real cheap."

"You think he can buy his way out of this one?"

Roger's voice became dead-serious. "I hope he does. God knows I hope he does. Then I can get at him."

"I think you already did."

"Nah, that was just season's greetings."

"I feel sorry for his wife."

"Fay might just be better off. She's too smart to stay as somebody's trophy wife in a dead marriage." Roger finished off another bottle and threw it to the side of the road. "Anyway, should you change your mind about leavin' you can be a partner in a bar in Bangkok's notorious red light district. What say to that?"

"Thanks. But I've got some great manuscripts and I'll get a good price for my shares in Barron Books. I've made up my mind to go back to the Big Apple and set up my own publishing company. It's time to put my own money where my mouth is. Besides, I miss the change of seasons." Brian opened their last bottle and handed it to Roger. "And Thai beer is beginning to taste better to me. That's a sure sign that it's time to leave."

"Well, there'll always be a cold one waiting for you at the Horny Tiger."

"Much obliged. But I've got one thing to do before I can go. One very special thing."

Roger nodded and raised the bottle as a toast. "Whatever."

"Take me about a month. And no beer allowed."

Roger's arm stopped suddenly and he lowered the bottle from his lips without drinking. A long, slow smile spread from his lips and invested his eyes with equal amounts of suspicion, delight and surprise. "Hell, you ain't goin' up to Ayudhya to say goodbye to some abbot at all."

"No. I'm not."

"But you ain't saying you gonna' up and do what I think you're sayin' you gonna' up and do. . . . Are you?"

# 66

BRIAN watched the faint rays of the setting sun pierce the fronds of distant palm trees and tinge slowly drifting clouds with shades of pale pink and delicate gold.

At the sound of the first 'click' he stiffened. Then, slowly, with a deep breath, he relaxed. He smiled up at the temple boy assigned as his novice and at the smiling abbot standing beside him. The first lock of hair fell onto the towel around his neck like a discarded and slightly dishonored insect.

The bespectacled monk acting as temple barber stood quietly behind him and Brian felt him grab another lock of hair. Another 'click.' Brian picked up the first lock of hair from the towel and stared at it in his open palm.

In just over one month from now he would be working 12-hour days as a struggling New York publisher and trying to find time to read the Sunday *New York Times*, let alone attend any of the events it chronicled. But, now, as a candidate for monkhood, he felt all his cares and disappointments, past fears and future hopes drop away with his hair and he knew he was already beginning to feel as he had twenty years before—the peace of one who dissolves his individual ego and personal identity to seek the truth of the Buddha's teaching.

He thought of the abbot's words on the porch of the *kuti*: how Christians believe, once this life is over, they will be punished for their sins by a just, wise, anthropomorphic God; but how Buddhists believe they will be punished not *for* their sins, but *by* their sins, as their acts in this life determine how they will be reborn in the next. Brian thought of how strongly Buddhists believed this and he wondered, if it was true, just how he would be reborn.

Then he allowed himself another few seconds to reflect on the events of the past ninety days, and then he let go. His quest was now a spiritual one. Now, he was home. But it had been a long journey.

# The Author

Dean Barrett first arrived in Thailand as a Chinese linguist with the Army Security Agency during the Vietnam War and was stationed with the 83rd Radio Research and Special Operations Unit. He later returned to Asia and lived for 17 years in Hong Kong and Bangkok. His writings and photography on Thailand have won several awards. His other novels set in Asia are *Memoirs of a Bangkok Warrior - A Novel* and *Hangman's Point - A Novel of Hong Kong*.